BARTIMAEUS, THE BLIND BEGGAR OF JERICHO

GEORGE V. SABOL

ISBN 979-8-88644-246-5 (Paperback)
ISBN 979-8-88644-248-9 (Hardcover)
ISBN 979-8-88644-247-2 (Digital)

Copyright © 2023 George V. Sabol
All rights reserved
First Edition

All rights reserved. No part of this publication may be reproduced, distributed, or transmitted in any form or by any means, including photocopying, recording, or other electronic or mechanical methods without the prior written permission of the publisher. For permission requests, solicit the publisher via the address below.

Covenant Books
11661 Hwy 707
Murrells Inlet, SC 29576
www.covenantbooks.com

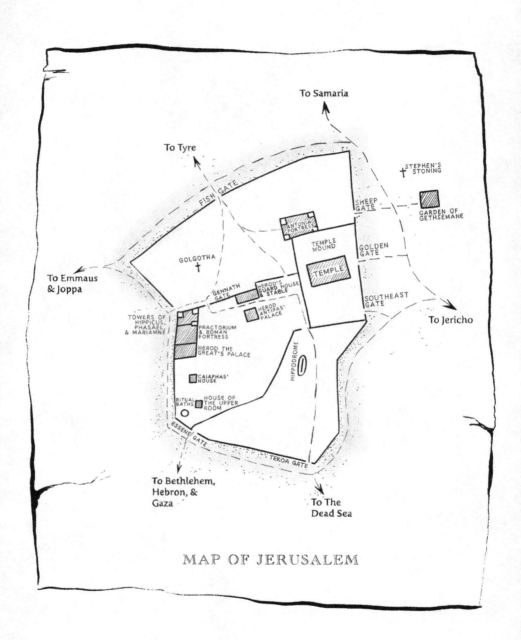

MAP OF JERUSALEM

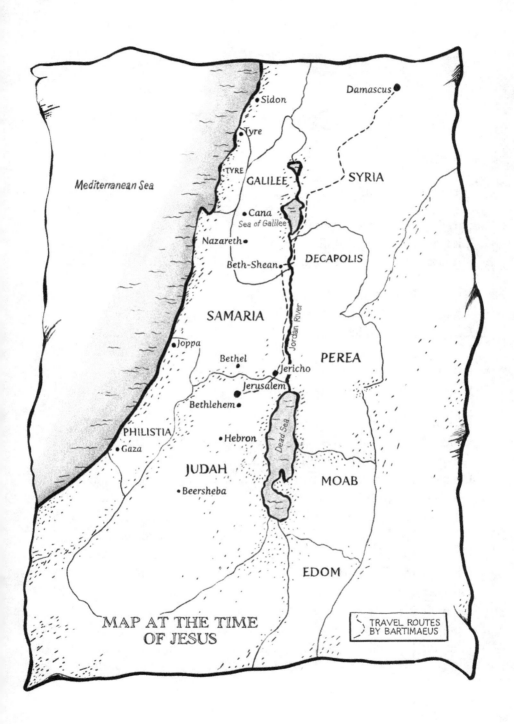

Contents

Introduction viii

Part 1: Jerusalem and Bethlehem
Chapter 1: In Herod's Palace in Jerusalem 3
Chapter 2: Bethlehem 9

Part 2: Thirty-Three Years Later in Jericho
Chapter 3: The Gate of Jericho 21
Chapter 4: Monica 35
Chapter 5: Gamela 45
Chapter 6: Susanna 56
Chapter 7: Passover 64

Part 3: Jerusalem
Chapter 8: Jerusalem 75
Chapter 9: Saul of Tarsus 84
Chapter 10: Thomas Didymus 91
Chapter 11: Joshua 102
Chapter 12: Thomas and Matthew 105
Chapter 13: Bartimaeus and Joshua Return to Jericho ... 108
Chapter 14: The Apostles Return to Jerusalem 120
Chapter 15: To See Again 124
Chapter 16: Peter and John 130
Chapter 17: The Apostles Are Arrested 135
Chapter 18: Chuza's Story 141
Chapter 19: Going Home 149

Part 4: Damascus
Chapter 20: Stephen and Saul 161
Chapter 21: Paul of Tarsus 164
Chapter 22: Messengers Arrive in Jerusalem 171
Chapter 23: Paul's Escape from Damascus 177
Chapter 24: Bartimaeus Leaves Damascus 199
Chapter 25: The Way of Blood 206
Chapter 26: Three Years Later—Paul Returns to Jerusalem 222

Epilogue 237

INTRODUCTION

The story of Jesus curing the blind beggar at the gate of Jericho is told in the Gospels of Matthew (20:29–34), Mark (10:46–52), and Luke (18:35–43). Mark names the beggar Bartimaeus, the son of Timaeus. There are many miracles and cures by Jesus related in the gospels, but seldom are such occurrences told by two of the gospel writers, much less by three of them. Furthermore, the person that was cured or the recipient of the miracle is not named unless there is greater relevance, such as the miracle of Lazarus being raised from the dead. These two facts led me to ponder the questions, why did the three gospel writers present essentially the same story, and why did one of them not only name the man but also his father? This caused me to wonder if there is more to the story of Bartimaeus. Was Bartimaeus well known in the early Christian community? Had he, and possibly his father, performed or been party to some historic event that was meaningful and known to that community?

This story of Bartimaeus and his relation to the apostle Paul is fictional. However, I have attempted to maintain the facts and spiritual essence of the accounts of the apostles in Jerusalem after the death and resurrection of Jesus, and of the conversion of Paul in Damascus as contained in the Acts of the Apostles. In some cases, the narratives in this book, such as the killing of the innocent baby boys in Bethlehem ordered by Herod the Great and of Paul's escape from Damascus by being taken over the city wall in a basket, are biblically founded but are embellished with story-line details that are fictional. Some readers may find fault with this story in the characterization of Saul prior to his conversion, but I attempted to capture the proper image of the renamed apostle Paul after his conversion that is correct to historical fact and the letters of Paul.

BARTIMAEUS, THE BLIND BEGGAR OF JERICHO

The author is a water resources engineer and horseman. I could not resist weaving irrigated agriculture into the setting near Jericho, and I found pleasure in incorporating the role of horses throughout the story.

Part 1

Jerusalem and Bethlehem

1

IN HEROD'S PALACE IN JERUSALEM

Chuza watched the small brown mouse hug the wall as it crept along the polished marble floor. It stopped occasionally to inspect an interesting item that could be a morsel of food. Then it continued its way in his direction. Chuza tensed hoping that the mouse would not come to where he stood beside a table covered with sweet breads, fruit, and wine. He remained motionless, barely breathing and pressed against the same wall wishing that he could be as inconspicuous as the mouse. Cautiously, looking out of the corner of his eye toward the two men in the room, he carefully turned his head back to focus on the older man. He did not want his gaze at the mouse to direct that man's attention to fall upon him and the mouse. Worse, if that were to happen, he feared the venom that would spew forth from the older man in such an event. The room was filled with an abundance of anger as it was. More importantly, he did not want any of that wrath vented in his direction.

He knew well the older man; he was King Herod the Great. The other man was much younger but clearly of importance, and his uniform told Chuza that he was a member of Herod's palace guard. Chuza had seen him talking to Herod several times recently. Neither of the men were concerned with him or his presence. He was there only to serve the needs of King Herod. Herod was seated listening to the other man relate an account to him. The younger man stood some distance away with his head bowed with hands outstretched and turned upward as if seeking forgiveness for an offense. That man was the head of Herod's palace guard, and although clearly of physical presence as a soldier, he had garnered his position mainly due to the wealth and influence of his family among the people of Judea. Herod had wisely directed the composition of his more than two-thousand-man palace guard not only for security but also to appease two diverse groups: the Romans that he served at their pleasure and the Jewish people that he governed. His guard had to be regarded equally by both the Jewish leaders, especially the priestly high council, and the authorities in Judea and in Rome. For that purpose, the guard was composed of men from influential Jewish families and men from the Roman Empire, especially from Egypt and Gaul that had earned the confidence of Rome. Herod had personally selected the man now before him, Hezekiah, to lead the palace guard, and Herod expected that favor to be returned in unquestioning loyalty. Herod's orders were to be carried out without compromise or failure whether given directly or, more often, with a wink and a nod. Hezekiah understood all this and performed accordingly.

Chuza was also of an influential Jewish family. His father, Nicodemus, was a priest in the temple that Herod had recently constructed to replace the temple that Solomon had built. The new temple was grander and more glorious than the temple of Solomon, a point that Herod always pressed when he met with the religious leaders, something that Herod, clearly, was not.

Nicodemus was not simply a temple priest. He was also a member of the Sanhedrin. Every city in Judea had a Sanhedrin, which was the ruling body for Jewish Law and religious matters. The Sanhedrin were comprised of twenty-one judges. The Great Sanhedrin in Jerusalem was the supreme court for Jewish Law, and it had seventy-one judges. Nicodemus had distinguished himself in the temple for his knowledge of the Torah, the five books of Moses, and the entire Jewish tradition in all its sacred writings. More importantly, Nicodemus, early in his ministry, had distinguished himself not only for his wisdom but also for his quest for what he believed was the eternal presence of a compassionate God in the lives of the Jewish people. Nicodemus was the youngest member of the Great Sanhedrin, the youngest ever to hold that position.

The Romans allowed the Sanhedrin to continue to serve the role of self-governing to the Jewish people with limited authority, but they no longer had the authority to execute a death sentence for violations of the Law. However, fanatical Pharisees still carried out stoning of transgressors of Jewish Law without regard for the hated Roman rule.

It had been a difficult decision for Chuza's family to allow him to serve in Herod's palace. Although Herod outwardly presented himself as a Jew, it was understood that this was more a concession to the people of Judea than a fervent religious belief, and it was convenient for Rome to have its locally appointed ruler be Jewish. There were many in Judea that rejected Herod, and he was especially condemned by the Sanhedrin because of his brutality. Nicodemus had relented to Herod's request for servants of the palace to come from the families of temple priests more out of gratitude for Herod's return of a temple for the Jewish people, and also to possibly have some, although minor, influence on life in the palace. Regardless, Chuza would rather have been with his young friends in the streets of Jerusalem than with Herod in his palace.

Chuza's mind drifted to the schooling that he received from his father and in the temple. He recalled the stories of the patriarchs: Abraham, his son Isaac, and his grandson Jacob. Among Herod's other construction projects, he had built the Tomb of the Patriarchs in Hebron where Abraham, Isaac, and Jacob and their wives were buried. From Jacob and his twelve sons had come the twelve tribes of Israel. Those tribes had been relocated to Egypt during a famine and then been enslaved by the Pharaoh. Finally, they had been set free and brought to the promised land by Moses with the exodus after wandering forty years in the desert of Sinai.

The Jewish people were to trust in their God, and He would provide for their needs, but the people had wanted a king. Saul was the first of many kings. After Saul came King David, and Chuza smiled at the memory of the boy shepherd killing the Philistine giant, Goliath. Then came David's son, Solomon, who built the first temple and had given the Jewish people words of wisdom. But there had been more kings that were not true to their God, and the people were punished. The Babylonians conquered them and sent many into exile and destroyed Solomon's temple. Even then, God blessed them with great prophets and examples of faithfulness such as Daniel and Elijah and Isaiah. Israel had been defeated by invading armies many times. After Babylon, there were the Persians then the Hellenistic Greeks. Finally, they were defeated by the Romans not long ago. Chuza knew of old men in Jerusalem that were boys when the conquering Romans arrived. Foreign armies had come and had gone, but the people of Israel, the chosen people, would always remain faithful to their God. He believed that the Roman army would leave this land as the others had, and the Jewish people would return to living as God had promised.

The territories to the east of the Mediterranean Sea had been vanquished by the Roman army under Pompey. With that conquest, the vast Roman Empire had been joined to the lands of Egypt under the rule of Cleopatra and Mark Antony. Herod was from Edom, a territory to the south of Judea, and the Edomites were converts to Judaism. Herod's father had curried favor with Mark Antony and had become a Roman citizen. Herod, as a young man, had joined the Roman army and, with his father's influential contacts, had quickly risen in the ranks. Herod's success with military victories over regional uprisings had further attracted the attention and regard of the Romans. With the patronage of his friend, Mark Antony, the Roman Senate appointed Herod the king of the area including Judea and Galilee at the age of thirty-six.

As the regional king, Herod undertook major construction projects which enhanced his personal prestige and brought economic benefit to much of the population. Among those accomplishments were the Fortress of Antonia in Jerusalem, the port of Caesarea, and the embellishment of numerous cities including Damascus and Antioch. But Herod's greatest accomplishment for the Jewish people was the complete reconstruction of the temple which was grander than the temple built by Solomon.

Chuza was startled back to the event in the room. Herod had risen out of his chair and was now standing in front of Hezekiah and shouting at him. "Why did you let those Parthian dogs go without following them? You should never have trusted them to return. You are a fool, Hezekiah. I expect better out of those that have my favor and my silver. Those dogs! Acting as if they are so wise! So they have seen a sign in the sky, and they have been led here to see the messiah of the Jews! Another of the Jews' redeemer kings! I am the king of the Jews, and one of my sons will be the next king of these wretched people. That is, if any of those spineless, idiot sons of mine can quit sucking their mother's milk and become a man. The Jews' king will not be some unknown goat herder born in that flea-infested Bethlehem."

Herod snatched his goblet and drank, his pox-marked face was red with rage, and his eyes protruded with the pent-up emotion. His gut burned and twisted, and no amount of wine or treatment from his many doctors could stop his constant agony. He moved to regain his seat on the edge of his throne, clutching his side. He heaved heavily; his head was bent to the floor. "They came to me wanting to know where the messiah is to be born. As if I care or believe in this dream of a messiah. The Jews have had many so-called messiahs, and today they are slaves of Rome as they have been the slave to many others. They are a miserable lot. But they dream of a return of a David or a Solomon. Ha! More saviors from Bethlehem. Well, the Roman army is not the Philistine army, and I am not as foolish as Goliath. I will not allow some weakling to sling a rock at me."

Herod stopped and wondered at his own words. He stared into his goblet and rubbed it with his thumb nervously. He recalled that the Jews had managed to find surprising leaders and had often defeated its enemies in the past. The greatest of those leaders had risen from obscurity, often as children. Besides David, there was Joseph, who had been sold off by his brothers to Egypt, and Daniel in Babylon. But he, Herod the Great, would not allow some peasant child to be a threat to him. With a jerk, he raised his head and glared menacingly at the other man. "Hezekiah, the Jewish priests told those three that the messiah is to come from Bethlehem. I will not be bothered by this again. Do you understand? Do not disappoint me again. Take care of this. I will not hear of it after this day. Leave me now."

Alone in the room, Herod thought. *These Jews are a troublesome lot.* He had built them a temple grander than Solomon's and a seaport to rival Alexandria. He had brought the favor of the Caesars and protection of Rome to this stubborn and insolent people. The chosen people of God! *Ha, no god would choose them.*

He brought the goblet to his mouth and emptied it. Grimacing, he muttered through a clenched jaw, "I will not let this talk of a messiah cause me trouble. There will be no messiah or a false king with dung on his feet for the people to cling to. They are not a great nation. They never will be." He turned his head toward Chuza and, thrusting his fist clenched to the goblet, shouted, "Wine!" Barely had the word been said, and Herod's goblet was filled.

Herod looked at his servant. He was still a boy and handsome. He had dark, curly hair down to his shoulders, and although he was inside the palace much of the day, he was well-muscled and had suntanned arms and legs. He preferred boys rather than men for servants. They could be trusted. Herod returned to his chair and, leaning back, waved the back of his hand in Chuza's direction. "Now, leave me," and he scowled as Chuza hurried out of the room and closed the door behind him. Once out of the chamber, Chuza, with his arms hanging limply at his side, exhausted as if he, rather than Hezekiah, had borne the brunt of that verbal lashing, watched the mouse scurry quickly away down the hall, and he wished that he, too, could run and hide, for he sensed impending evil.

2

BETHLEHEM

Timaeus's horse made a right turn and an uphill climb on the road from Jerusalem to Bethlehem. As he made the turn, the horse changed from a left to a right lead. With that change, Timaeus felt the momentary suspension in the saddle, and now his right leg felt the downward thrust with each stride as his left leg brushed lightly against the horse's wet side. Through the change of lead, the horse kept the same steady pace which the rider had expected. He reached down and patted the horse's sticky, wet neck. "So you are getting a little tired, my friend. It is not much further, and you will get a rest."

His hand came away with sticky sweat which he wiped on the horse's mane. Timaeus could hear the heavy breathing of the other horses behind him. The riders had left the stable of Herod's palace guards in Jerusalem on a mission to Bethlehem. Timaeus was a member of Herod's guard where he had served for more than ten years. He was an officer, well trusted by his friend, Hezekiah, and personally known by Herod.

He knew the usual missions, each having its own regularity. Delivering a message only took a man or two and could usually be trusted to a junior member of the guard. An escort required more men, the number depending on the importance of the person to be guarded and the route. Tonight's mission was not to deliver a message nor to accompany a dignitary nor to bring someone safely back to Jerusalem. But clearly, this mission had great importance, maybe even something for Herod himself. This mission had an unusual feel. Why else would Hezekiah have selected the men and delivered the order himself. Although Hezekiah was only a few years older than Timaeus, he was Timaeus's senior officer and the leader of the guard. Hezekiah's father had been in the service of Herod for many years, and Hezekiah had taken over the palace guard responsibilities upon his father's death. Hezekiah was viewed by some to inherit that position, but his strong leadership and dedicated service was well known. He was someone who could be trusted with any undertaking and had earned Herod's confidence, as much as Herod could trust anyone. Knowing that, Hezekiah was not about to lose the trust, and more importantly the rewards from Herod, and he saw to it that Herod's every wish was met with success.

Earlier that evening, Timaeus had seen Hezekiah outside the barracks. He was talking to a man that Timaeus did not know. Being a member of the guard, Timaeus had learned to judge men, and this man had the look of one that Timaeus did not like. Timaeus saw Hezekiah put money into the man's hand and then had watched the man ride off in a hurry on a fresh horse.

That night, it was cold. The full moon was up, and it would be many hours before the sun brought its warmth. According to Hezekiah's instructions, this was not to be a lengthy mission, and they would be back in Jerusalem later that night. He was to report to Hezekiah as soon as he got back. But what was he to report? Timaeus once more replayed the orders from Hezekiah in his mind. This assignment was strangely different. Typically, a senior officer was selected, and his unit of soldiers then made up the contingent to carry out the order. In this case, Hezekiah had not only selected Timaeus as the leader but also the ten other men. Also, most units were a mix of men that were Jewish and some that came from elsewhere in the Roman Empire. This was for the purpose of stimulating a sense of camaraderie among the soldiers without bias toward either Jew or non-Jew. However, in this case, Hezekiah had not selected any Jewish soldier other than Timaeus, and no two of those selected were from the same unit.

BARTIMAEUS, THE BLIND BEGGAR OF JERICHO

When Timaeus and the ten selected soldiers met with Hezekiah, he had an anxious look about him. They were cautioned to carry out the order exactly as given; there could be no deviations. They were to depart immediately for Bethlehem. No one else was to be told about the mission, and they were not to stop along the way. If there was a problem or an accident involving any of the men, the rest were to go on. Nothing was to keep them from completing the mission. They were to make haste to Bethlehem and to go directly to the gate at the north wall. That wall would be in the shadow of the moonlight. A man would meet them there, and they were to take final instructions from him. All must be accomplished that night, and they were to return to Jerusalem immediately and not stay in Bethlehem. They were soldiers, the most reliable in the guard, they knew well how to carry out orders, even when the mission was unclear. But this was different. There was more than the usual secrecy. After talking to the men, Hezekiah had taken Timaeus aside and, when out of sight of the others, had taken him by the arm and told him that although he could not tell him any more about the mission, he must trust those that he would meet in Bethlehem. Squeezing Timaeus's arm, he stressed the importance and concern that this be done without incident or mishap.

Bethlehem came into sight, and Timaeus signaled to bring the horses back to a walk. They let the reins slip through their fingers as the horses dropped their heads. The horses, being well used, walked easily on a loose rein. They took the road to the north gate. As they approached the gate, a man with his cloak pulled over his head came out of the shadow of the gate buttress. He walked nervously toward them, looking over his shoulder through the open gate. He met them some distance before they reached the gate, and standing in the road in front of them, he spoke in a hushed voice. "Tie your horses here and come with me." They walked through the gate. They were used to spending long days in the saddle. Even so, it was good to be walking and letting their legs stretch. "Over here, quickly, and do not speak. You must do exactly as I say. You are not to ask any questions, nor can you speak to anyone except with the words that I tell you."

The man stepped away from them and looked back again through the gate before speaking. When the man turned back, Timaeus had stepped forward to better see the man's face. He immediately recognized the man as the one that he had seen talking to Hezekiah and had received money from him. Timaeus looked him in the eye. As a soldier, he had looked many men in the eye. In some, he found honor and was drawn to them, even in conflict. In others, he saw the low stature of a man without honor; men that had lost any dignity, those with only the smell of self-interest. This was such a man, and Timaeus immediately disliked him. How was he to take orders from such as this? This was not a man that easily gave orders but rather a man that when he spoke, he judged whether the listener believed what he was saying because often it was a lie. The cloaked man caught Timaeus's stare and immediately stepped back a few steps.

With Timaeus watching him intently, the man spoke in a low, uneasy voice. "These are times when some forget that we are a people under the rule of others. Rome sets on the throne those that keep Rome satisfied so that we can live without fear of reprisal. There are those in Bethlehem that must be taught that obeying the king is the best for them. Tonight, we will give a little lesson to those of this city that do not appreciate the benefits of an orderly way of behaving and of respecting the king's wishes." He stopped talking and, with a quick glance, once more looked over his shoulder. "We are here to remind the people of Bethlehem that they are under Roman rule, and Rome has given them a king. King Herod has done great things for these people. You especially know that. Herod is our king. After Herod, Rome will give us the next king. This dream of a messiah to free them from Rome is dangerous. We are here to help the people to understand that. Oh, they will object, but do not listen to them. They lie most eloquently. All their pleading and cries will be lies. You must do exactly as I say. We are only teaching them a lesson. No one will be harmed. Herod is a good man and a compassionate ruler. He just wants to give these unrealistic zealots a message. In a day or two, all will be forgotten, and they will have learned not to return to their foolish dreams and fantasies of a messiah. We will do this not by beating them or sending them to prison. They will learn the wisdom of our ways. No harm will come to anyone. Your presence is to keep the peace and to assure them that no harm will come to them"—he paused—"or their families."

He stopped, and his eyes went quickly from one to another of them as he spoke, carefully weighing each word. "Two of you will accompany another man as he visits a family. Each of these families have a small child, a boy. The man that you accompany will do all the talking. You are there only to keep order. They will recognize your uniform and will not resist you. The children will be brought to me in the house near this gate. The families will be told that their child will be returned to them shortly. If they are quiet and stay in the house, no harm will come to the child. They will be told that their child has been chosen for a special honor and that they will be informed of this in the morning. They are not to worry. Others will take care of these matters in the morning. There are only a few houses to go to. This will not take long. You will be on your way back to Jerusalem tonight. That is all that will be needed of you." He smiled, but Timaeus found no comfort in what he said. "You are to do exactly as I told you. Do not say anything else to them or listen to anything that they say to you. Do you have any questions?"

One of the soldiers asked, "Are we to use force?"

With an unassuring smile and a shrug of his shoulders, the man answered, "If needed, yes, you are to do all that is necessary. The important thing for them to understand is that if they are quiet and cause no trouble, the boys will be returned safely in a little while. We will take care of the rest. Come now, let us get started. This will not take long. I am sure that each of you have much more important matters to attend to for Herod than this little annoyance."

With that, the cloaked man turned and opened the door to the house immediately behind him which appeared to be unused. Five other men came out. He said, "Two of you are to go with each of these men and do as I have told you. Timaeus, you are to remain here by the gate. You can render help as might be needed by any of your men. I will tell you if there is anything else that is needed."

With that, the five groups departed, and Timaeus walked a short distance back to the gate. He walked through the gate to check on the horses. He knew the mounts well since his main responsibility with the guard was the training of the horses and the selected soldiers that rode them. That is what he enjoyed most, and that is what had attracted him to join the palace guard. His family in Jericho were breeders and trainers of horses for many generations, and they had been selected to provide horses for Herod's palace guards. It had been rather easy to accept a position with the guard because he could spend most of his time in Jericho with his wife, Ariel, and his three young children. He had a daughter, Susanna, who was barely two years old, and Ariel had just given birth to twin sons, one named Bartimaeus after him and the other named Barariel after his mother. He was anxious to get back to Jerusalem where he was on a temporary training assignment, and he intended to return to Jericho and his family the next day. He was anxious to hold those two newborn boys in his arms. He laughed aloud as he dreamed of riding with his sons and teaching them all that he knew.

His thoughts went to sweet Susanna and how she would run out to meet him when he was riding in the training arena next to their house. He would swing her up on the horse with him, and she would laugh and hug him. Then his thoughts went to Ariel. Oh, how wonderful to be back in her loving arms again. The life of a soldier was difficult, and in that regard, he regretted his lot. But overall, he had a good life and enjoyed what he did.

He finished checking the horses and went back through the gate. It was late, and the houses of Bethlehem were, for the most part, dark. Light could be seen coming from only a few homes. He watched as one of the men carrying a baby accompanied by two soldiers walked toward the house that the cloaked man had entered. When they got near the house, the man holding the baby stopped and spoke briefly to the two soldiers. The two soldiers stayed where they were, and the other man entered the house with the baby and soon returned. Then the three went back down the street and disappeared into the darkness. This was repeated several times by each group of three.

As Timaeus stood by the gate and as more babies were delivered to the house, he heard the nighttime cries from within. With more babies delivered, there was soon a chorus of sounds coming from the house. After a few deliveries by each group, the soldiers stayed outside the house joining Timaeus by the gate. One by one this was repeated until the last of the five men stood together outside the house and the ten soldiers had joined Timaeus.

Now there were the sounds of many babies coming from the house. No longer could the cries of individual babies be heard. The sounds all melted together indistinguishable one from another. Timaeus listened to the men relate their stories from each house. In all cases, the fathers had protested and wanted an explanation, and the mothers had pleaded and cried. Only in a few cases had the soldiers been needed to restrain the fathers or even in some cases, the mothers. In all cases, the parents were eventually assured that the babies would be safe and would be returned to them shortly. They were even promised to be recognized for a special award but never how or by whom that would come.

Timaeus's attention was drawn back to the sounds from the house. That had changed. Now he could only hear the sounds of individual babies, no longer the clamor of all the babies that had entered the house. Then there were only sounds from a few babies, then two, then one, then none. All was quiet inside. Timaeus could not comprehend how those babies could be asleep and quieted so quickly and effectively. Were there others in the house? He took a few steps away from his men and stopped to listen again. With that, the soldiers themselves quit talking. All was quiet. The soldiers had also turned their attention toward the house when they noticed Timaeus's reaction. Timaeus turned and looked back at his men. Their expression offered the same question that he had. What was happening in that house? Timaeus returned his questioning gaze back to the house then to the five men standing outside. They offered no explanation, and Timaeus stepped forward toward the door. One of the men stepped into Timaeus's path. Timaeus never broke stride and let his hand go down to his sword. Looking into Timaeus's eyes, the man stepped aside as Timaeus brushed past him and pushed the door open. He stepped inside.

The windows were draped shut, and there was no moonlight in the room. He let his eyes adjust for the dark. There was no one else in the room except the man that had talked to them outside. The man turned to face him but stood motionless. His arms hung at his side, and he tried to conceal a bloody knife in the folds of his cloak. Timaeus looked from the man's hand to the floor behind him. There, along the wall, were the still bodies of the babies. It was as if each was asleep. Still wrapped in their blankets, eyes closed, head laying to the side. Only the garish stain of blood on the blankets close to the heart gave truth to the horrible scene. Timaeus was in shock. He felt blood pounding in his head. There was buzzing in his ears. He swayed back on his feet. He stood frozen, not breathing but with pounding heart. His eyes went back to the cloaked man who he looked to for an answer. But what sane answer could be given? There was only one possible answer. Only a mad man could have done this.

Timaeus stepped further into the room as the cloaked man tossed the knife behind him in an effort to hide it. The man looked toward the open door, then his eyes darted toward Timaeus where they locked as if by some power other than his own. But the eyes of the cloaked man were of desperation caught in the inescapable act of evil. Timaeus's eyes conveyed only indignation that such evil could be allowed to exist. The cloaked man rushed toward the open door. He knew that he had no recourse but to escape into the night. Just as quickly, and with righteous resolve, Timaeus stepped into his path. He drew and held the point of the sword at the man's ribs nearest the heart. The man froze in his steps as he felt the sharp point against his flesh. For only a second, the two men stood face-to-face each gauging the other through the window of their eyes. The silence was broken when the man said, "Please, I only do what others tell me to do. This is not my doing. It is others that do this. Have mercy on me."

Although a soldier, Timaeus had never killed a man, never wanted to. But this was an evil that could not be tolerated, an evil that must be destroyed. His thought went to his twin boys at home with their mother. He shook his head as he saw in his mind his own boys laying on the cold ground with the others. He once more focused on the face of the disgusting beast before him.

"Mercy," he said through a clenched jaw. "Mercy, what mercy did you show to those children or to their families?"

In an uncontrollable spasm, his arm crammed the sword upward into the man's chest and into his heart. This was not an act of murder; it was an act of ridding an evil pestilence from all that is good and to be cherished. The cloaked man collapsed to the floor. Timaeus left his sword in the body. He stood there stunned, shocked, and unaware of any thought or impulse. His eyes drifted to the bodies of the babies, and he looked down at each of them. How could they look at such peace when he was bereft of anything but hollow emptiness? Why was this done? How could this happen? How could he be made a part of this?

In place of emptiness, suddenly anger erupted in him. There was no room for tears or sorrow at this tragedy. Only the animal instinct to strike out remained in him. He needed to defend not only those that he loved and cherished but all that is good and pure from such monstrosity. He turned and ran from the house, past the five men that stood looking in the door, past the soldiers. He threw himself on his horse and spurred it back to Jerusalem.

Part 2

Thirty-Three Years Later in Jericho

3

THE GATE OF JERICHO

The people of Jericho were proud of their heritage and the protection that the ancient walls and tower had provided to the residents for thousands of years. Jericho was important to the Jewish religious culture and the peoples that came to the promised land. Monica knew the story of her people. Moses had freed the people from the pharaoh and had led them out of Egypt. After forty years of wandering in the desert of Sinai, Moses did not enter the promised land; rather, Joshua had taken the people across the Jordan River only a few miles east of Jericho and into the land that their God had given them. At that time, those ancient stone walls of Jericho could not hold back God's people. At Joshua's command, the people marched around the walls of Jericho for seven days carrying the Ark of the Covenant with the stone tablets of commandments given by God to Moses on Mount Sinai inside the Ark. Then, on the seventh day, the day of God's rest, Joshua had the people blow trumpets made of ram horns, and the people shouted until those walls of stone tumbled down. Jericho was the first of God's victories for His chosen people in the land that He promised them.

    Jericho was a prized jewel among all the cities of Judea. It sat in the Jordan River Valley more than eight hundred feet below sea level. The Jordan River itself was only a few miles to the east from the city. Not far to the southeast was the Dead Sea. And to the west were hills, rising more than two thousand feet above sea level to Jerusalem at the summit. From Jericho to Jerusalem was only eighteen miles, barely a day's walk, but uphill and a dangerous road with many bandits preying on travelers. The road was known as "The Way of Blood" for its evil reputation. Only well-armed men or groups of travelers with armed escorts were advised to travel that road.

Monica's family had lived within the walled city of Jericho for many generations. In fact, there was no known history of her family living elsewhere. She had been born there less than twenty years ago. Her father was a simple cobbler, and her mother worked beside him in the shop suppling the leather and cutting it to make sandals and other items. She had an older brother that lived in Joppa, several days' journey from Jericho, and he rarely visited the family. She did not know him well. Her parents were old when Monica was born. They live in a modest house and worked at their shop in the center of Jericho. Monica visited them often and made sure that they were well cared for. She had learned early to be a gentle and compassionate caregiver.

Monica had left Jericho only twice in her life, and she had traveled the road to Jerusalem both times, once as a child with her family for a celebration at the temple. She could still remember the long walk up the winding road and the narrow passages where she imagined that bandits would ambush them. She remembered seeing the majesty of the temple that Herod the Great had built. The other time that she traveled to Jerusalem had been easier for she rode with her husband, Barariel, in a horse-drawn chariot. Barariel was a soldier in Herod's palace guard, and they had traveled to Jerusalem with a contingent of soldiers including his brother, Bartimaeus. There was no danger in that travel. That was a beautiful, dreamy memory. She and Barariel had just wed, and she traveled with him to Jerusalem where he was stationed at Herod's palace. She was able to stay with him in Jerusalem for several weeks before she returned to their new home to Jericho. Those were marvelous days. She and Barariel alone together. No worries, no responsibilities. It was just the two of them enjoying the start of their new life together with no thought of what the future would bring. Monica's husband, Barariel, was also from Jericho, but he had not been raised within the walls of the city. He had lived in the country where his family raised horses and trained them for Herod's palace guard.

While Jericho within the walls was filled with homes and shops and businesses, outside of the walls was green with planted crops and palm date trees and pastures for animals. The land itself at the base of the hills was rich soil. The soil was decomposed rock from the surrounding hills, soil particles that had broken free from the hillslopes over hundreds of millions of years due to rain and wind. Rock that had been heated by the sun and then cracked by freezing nights. Soil that was filled with nutrients from primordial floods gushing out of the hills far to the north. This was good farmland, and the men and women working the fields brought their bounty to Jerusalem where it was sold, and the people of Jericho lived a good life.

Although Jericho was hot and humid in the summer, the winters were pleasant. Being in a rain shadow of the hills, the sky was typically clear, and cool westerly afternoon winds refreshed the valley below. That temperate climate allowed food goods to be produced year-round. Fresh fruit and vegetables were always available. But it was not just the weather and the good soil that made Jericho a garden spot in the desert; it was also the availability of water. The hills to the west cooled the moist air blowing in from the Mediterranean Sea causing the moisture in the clouds to condense and fall as rain in the hills. From there, the rainwater seeped into the fractured rock and made its long, tortuous path through streams and underground toward the Jordan River. At the base of those hills were springs that irrigated the crops. There was even a spring named after the prophet Elisha. An aqueduct, Wadi Qelt, furnished fresh, reliable water to the city of Jericho.

Bartimaeus and Barariel, as their father, Timaeus, and generations before, had used that rich land not to grow crops but to breed and raise and train the finest horses in the land. So fine that their reputation had gone as far as the palace of Cleopatra. Not long ago, Mark Antony had made a gift of a matched team of those horses to Cleopatra. That reputation was not lost on Herod, and he made Timaeus's family the source of the horses for his mounted palace guard. Barariel and his brother, Bartimaeus, oversaw the breeding and training of those horses, just as their father, Timaeus, had before them. Timaeus's brother, Ezra, along with his sons, worked the land and managed the many mares and prized stallions. It had been a good business arrangement for Timaeus and his brother, Ezra, as it was for Bartimaeus and Barariel before tragedy struck the family.

The abundance and alluring ambiance of Jericho also caught the attention of the wealthy families of Judea, and there were many beautiful villas built in the city and outside the walls as luxury homes away from the crowded and clamorous cities such as Jerusalem. Herod the Great, through his influential friends in Rome, had acquired the country palace outside of the walls of Jericho that had been built for Cleopatra not many years ago. Herod used that as his winter palace where he could escape the confines of Jerusalem and live in luxury with fresh food and fruits and wine. It was also a good place to entertain guests from Rome and from throughout the empire. As such, this dignified his role as king, even if not born to it, through his distant association with the likes of Cleopatra and Mark Antony and even Julius Caesar. That palace, set against the surrounding cliffs, was a reminder that Jericho, Judea, and much of the land were under the control of Rome through its senate-appointed kings. Herod the Great had died at the winter palace. Now, his son, Herod Antipas, was the puppet king for the Emperor Tiberius in Rome.

It was late afternoon when Bartimaeus arrived at Monica's home in Jericho. He had departed Jerusalem that morning and had traveled on foot with a troop of palace guards that were sent on duty to Jericho. Since his blindness, he normally stayed at the barracks in Jerusalem, but he had decided to return to Jericho for a visit to his family during the feast of Pesach, the Jewish celebration of God delivering his people, the Hebrew nation, from slavery in Egypt. His sister, Susanna, lived in Jericho with her husband and children, and he planned to stay with her. He did not know if he would return to his home to visit his family at the horse farm outside of Jericho. He knew that he should spend time with his children; his son, Saul David, and his daughter, Mariam, and that his mother, Ariel, needed to see him more often. But he knew how such a visit would end with his wife, Gamela, and the pain that it would bring to both of them.

BARTIMAEUS, THE BLIND BEGGAR OF JERICHO

When the troop had arrived at the barracks outside Jericho, one of the soldiers had walked with him into Jericho. He told the guardsman to take him to Monica's house. It had been some time since his last visit with Monica, and she was not expecting him. He had stayed with her more frequently in the past, especially after her husband's death, and after he was blinded. More recently, he had become concerned for her that people may notice him staying the night in her house even though he was the brother of her husband. His twin brother, Barariel, had been married to Monica only a short while before he was killed in a battle with zealot Jewish Pharisees protesting Herod. Shortly after Barariel's death, Bartimaeus had been struck blind in a fall from a horse. That was three years ago. For both Bartimaeus and Monica, those were difficult times, and they found great comfort in the company of the other.

Bartimaeus had stepped to the side when the guard knocked on Monica's door. Monica was startled when she opened the door and saw a guardsman standing there. That instantly brought back painful memories. Her shocked expression turned to a joyous smile when she saw Bartimaeus next to him. She hardly listened to the guard's greeting as she reached out to take Bartimaeus's hand to guide him into her house. As Bartimaeus stepped in, he turned to the guard and thanked him and told him that Monica would take him to his sister's that evening and that the guard could return to the barracks in Jericho. As the guard walked away, he added that he will have a family member take him to the barracks when he is ready to return to Jerusalem and not to be concerned about him.

Monica led him into her house and sat him on a bench at the table. She poured him a cup of water from a clay pitcher then she sat on a bench opposite him. After the usual greeting of two dear friends, she asked his plans. He told her that he came to Jericho to be with Susanna for the Pesach and to once more be with family for the Passover meal. He did not say anything about possibly visiting family other than Susanna, and Monica, noting that silence, did not ask. He told her that he was on his way to Susanna's but knew if he did not stop at her house that he may not get another chance. He quickly added that he wanted to check on how she was doing. He told her that after their visit, she should take him to Susanna's house. She protested and told him that she would take him there, but first he must allow her to prepare a meal for them so that they could have time for a proper visit. He attempted to resist, but she stood and told him that she must go out to buy food for them and that he must rest. She took him to a padded bench along the wall and told him to lie down until she returned. She grabbed a bowl and scurried toward the door. As she walked past him, he reached out his hand which she accepted. He handed her a small pouch of coins and said, "Hezekiah continues to pay me even though I can no longer serve the guard. I have more coins than I need. I send most of it to Gamela, but I want you to have some too." He gently placed the pouch into her hand and closed her fingers. She raised the pouch to her breast, and the smile left her face for the first time since he walked in. The smile did not return as she walked to the door and closed it behind her.

Bartimaeus was curled up on the bench when she returned with a bowl of lamb meat and a skein of wine. He did not awake until she touched his shoulder. He opened his eyes and pushed himself into a sitting position. As he started to rise, he said, "I need to leave and go to Susanna's."

She placed her hand on his cheek and, turning his head toward her, said, "Bartimaeus, it is late. You are tired. You need to eat and get a good night's rest. You can go to Susanna's tomorrow."

His hand slid to hers. "Yes, I would like that."

The next morning, Monica's thoughts were not on the previous day's surprise visit by Bartimaeus or of her past life with Barariel. Rather, she was focused on her discussion with Bartimaeus that morning about his desire not to go immediately to Susanna's but to go to the gate of Jericho to sit with the beggars. He had done this before. He did not need the money, and he did not beg. She had argued against that, but he had insisted. Now, against her better judgment and desire, she was leading him to one of the city gates where he would sit and listen to the people and horses and carts of commerce coming and going. When he had done this in the past, it helped calm his mind as he focused on the myriad sounds surrounding him. Usually there were others at the wall, especially beggars, sometimes blind beggars that he enjoyed talking to.

It was early morning, and the streets were mostly empty. He and Monica each had on common, unbleached wool cloaks, and they moved in the shade of the buildings with the sun still low on the horizon. Monica walked a half step ahead while he followed with his right arm outstretched with his hand on her shoulder. Although they did not move quickly, they also did not linger along the way. The night before he had told her that they were to leave early in the morning when it was unlikely that they would meet people that they might know on the way.

He was thirty-three years old, clean-shaven but with the stubble of a few days. He was taller than average, lean, and well-muscled from his duties as a soldier and horse trainer. In no way did he look like the blind man that he was, but then he had only been blind for three years. She was much shorter than him with long, dark hair tucked under the hood of her cloak. Although considerably younger than him, she was every bit a woman honed of gentle strength and quiet confidence. There was no question of her resolve that morning as she walked ahead of him with head up and eyes focused before her. She had the presence of someone that had seen the hardship of life but without being defeated or languishing in self-pity.

After a short walk from her house, she stopped and turned to him. Taking his hand in hers, she looked up and focused on his eyes although she knew too well that he could not see her. Her forehead was wrinkled as painful memories pounded away at her. He stood motionless, waiting for her to speak. Finally, she said, "Bartimaeus, we are here at the north gate."

Although he could not see, he was familiar with the gate, the street where they stood, and the road leading from the gate northward toward Galilee and Syria. He had ridden that road and passed through that gate many times. His head instinctively turned toward the gate. He knew that he could not leave her without a word of comfort for her. Keeping his head turned toward the gate, he said, "We did not talk much last night. I fell asleep sitting at the table with you."

"I know that you were tired. You do not need to say anything to me. I know you and what is on your mind."

"Monica, Barariel was your husband, and he was my brother, my twin brother. He and I were together in my mother's womb. We grew up together. We learned to ride and to take care of horses. We became soldiers together. We were hardly ever separated except after he married you. There is no one that was closer to him than you and me. Yes, my mother and my sister still grieve him deeply, but they have others to cling to in that grief, but for you and me"—he turned toward her with a smile and shrugged his shoulders—"we only have each other."

Neither was able to speak for the searing ache in their hearts and the tears welling up in their eyes. Finally, Bartimaeus broke the silence. "Monica, I love you as my sister. Better than if you were only my sister. Where Barariel was my best friend, now you are. I am sorry that I cannot come to Jericho as often as I used to. A blind man on foot cannot travel as easily as when I rode a horse to visit you."

"Bartimaeus, you know what your friendship means to me. My best memories are of you and Barariel doing those foolish things together. I would laugh at the two of you. And I know Barariel was always trying to impress me. I think that you would often let him beat you at whatever foolishness the two of you were about. I never needed that. I just wanted to be with him. He was good to me. He loved me, and I loved him. In those early days of our marriage, you had Gamela. The four of us had many good times together." She paused then, with a forced lilt to her voice, quickly added, "How are the children?"

"They are well. I do not visit them very often. They are with Gamela and my mother at the farm. Saul David helps with the horses, and Mariam helps her mother and grandmother in the house and with meals." There was silence, both knowing what the other was thinking. He could feel her eyes on him, and she gave his hand a squeeze. He wanted to say more but could not find the right words. Stumbling for speech, he said, "You need to leave me now. You have your work to do. I will have someone help me to your home at the end of the day. Then you can take me to Susanna's, although I think that I could find it myself."

She quickly added, "No, you must come to me when you are done here. I will see that you get to Susanna's. I would like to visit her myself."

With a feigned laugh, he added, "Oh, I will be ready to have a good visit with you and Susanna after my rest here at the wall. You know, I am not much of a beggar!"

Playfully tugging on his arm, she said, "I see a good place next to another man that is blind." Then with a chuckle, she added, "Maybe he can give you some advice about begging. At least he probably will not get up and leave when you bore him with your stories! Yes, I know, all of your stories are true as you insist on telling everyone!" With that, she led him over to the wall next to an elderly, blind beggar.

Squeezing her hand, he said, "Thank you, Monica. This is good. I will join you this evening. And I want to talk to you some more. We have not done that much. Shalom."

"Shalom, Bartimaeus," and with that, she turned and walked away.

After a pause, he whispered, "I will miss you."

He was startled back to the present. "Bartimaeus, son of Timaeus. Shalom to you," his blind companion for the day greeted him. "I too am named as a son, for me the son of God, Bar-El. God must not have loved this son very much since I was born blind. How could I have sinned in my mother's belly that I was cursed to be born blind? Or was it my mother's sin, or my father's? What father or mother would do that to their son? Was it Bar-El's sin? I do not know! We all sin, do we not? But not all are blind. Those good Jews, those Pharisees, looking down their pious noses at us. I do not go to the synagogue anymore. Even the kind people there do not offer help to me for fear of the Pharisees. But to sit along the main roads, there are good people here that will drop a copper in my basket and give me a kind word. Please join me."

Taking a knee next to him, Bartimaeus said, "Shalom, Bar-El. You were born blind, and I was struck blind. Which is worse? I have seen the sun and moon, flowers and animals running free, and a woman's face and bare body but never to see those again! Sometimes the thought, the fear is too much. I want to escape, but no matter where I go, there is no escape." He stopped talking and whispered to himself, "There is no escape in my mind. It will not let go of me. Only my eyes are blind, not my mind."

"The woman that brought you here, is that your wife?" he asked.

"No," he replied. "She is my brother's wife. Her name is Monica."

Bar-El reached out a hand to feel for Bartimaeus and touched his cloak. Bartimaeus took his hand. "Sit, my friend. Did you bring a basket for the alms?"

"No. I am not much of a beggar. I told Monica this morning that I wanted to come here where I could just sit. I have much to think about and plan for the next few days visiting my family. But I do not want it to be alone or where it is quiet. I want to feel activity around me."

Bar-El shrugged and added, "You are welcome here. There are always many people coming and going. Spread your cloak on your lap. Maybe someone will throw a silver coin your way."

"Anything that I receive, I will give to you."

"Then, I hope that a plump woman falls on you!"

"I hope not too plump!" and they both laughed.

Bartimaeus sat with Bar-El. At times, Bartimaeus's being would calm, and he would doze then wake with a start. There were a few coins on his cloak which he moved to Bar-El's basket. Bartimaeus did not need money. He was well cared for. He could stay at Herod's guard houses either in Jerusalem or near the winter palace in Jericho. There, he helped with the horses as much as a blind man can, and the guards were his friends. Hezekiah, the guard commander, had made it clear that Bartimaeus was to be treated like he was still a soldier and that included his pay. Hezekiah had always looked after Bartimaeus and had encouraged him to join Herod's guard as his father, Timaeus, had. In fact, Hezekiah had fostered him and his brother as if they were his own sons. Hezekiah had often told him and his brother stories of their father, but no one knew what had happened to his father. All that was known was that Timaeus had left Jerusalem to return home to Jericho but had vanished along the way. He was never found, and it was presumed that he was killed by bandits along the road. Bartimaeus did not know his father since Timaeus had disappeared within weeks of his birth.

The horse farm and training stable for Herod's guard was outside the walls of Jericho. Bartimaeus's father, Timaeus, had been responsible for that farm and training stable. When Timaeus disappeared, his uncle, Ezra, had taken over the farm, and Bartimaeus had grown up there. After he married Gamela, they had lived there except when he was on duty in Jerusalem. Since Bartimaeus's accident and blindness, others had taken over the managing and horse training responsibilities.

Soon after Bartimaeus was seated, Bar-El started his begging. "People of Jericho, have mercy on me. People of Israel, have mercy on me. People of Abraham, have mercy on me..." There was, seemingly, no end to his litany of Jewish patriarchs and prophets to cry out to for mercy. Bartimaeus learned that once Bar-El called out, "People of God, have mercy on me," that he had depleted the names of those that God had sent into the world for the chosen people, and it was time to start over again. "People of Jericho, have mercy on me..."

Bartimaeus found Bar-El's cry soothing since it quieted the voices in his mind, and he was able to rest; to be at peace with the cry for mercy filling the air. He prayed that he could have that calm every night, every day. Bartimaeus thought, *Yes, God, have mercy on me.* With the rhythmic cry of Bar-El beside him, the drowning hubbub of the crowd, the warm sun and cool breeze, Bartimaeus fell asleep.

When he awoke, the crowd was louder, but it was not the cacophony of the dissonant sounds of the crowd. Rather, there was a recurring pattern. Something was happening! Someone was coming; someone from Nazareth, a descendant of David, a man named Jesus. There was excitement. Jesus was coming to Jericho. He had heard of this Jesus. Many in Jerusalem talked of him. He was a miracle worker, maybe the Messiah. Even those in the guard house talked about him. He had cured many, the cripple, the blind. He even raised a man named Lazarus in Bethany from the dead. Maybe this Jesus would cure him, would give him his sight back. He thought, *What do I do? I cannot let this opportunity pass. I must yell out. I must get his attention. What do I say? What? What?*

In desperation he shouted, "Jesus of Nazareth, son of David, have mercy on me!" Again, he shouted. He could not stop. He had to be heard above the crowd. "Jesus of Nazareth, son of David, have mercy on me. Jesus of Nazareth, son of David, have mercy on me." He kept shouting his plea.

Voices were now directed his way. People were talking near him. He heard someone talking in front of him. "Be quiet. Jesus is on his way to Jerusalem. This is an important journey. We have great things to do there. The people will see Jesus as the Messiah."

The crowd became quiet. Now, only a few people were talking. Bartimaeus could hear them say that Jesus had stopped. Jesus beckoned the man that was trying to quiet Bartimaeus. When the man returned to Jesus, Jesus spoke to him and then pointed at Bartimaeus. The man then hurried back to Bartimaeus.

"Come, the Master calls you."

Bartimaeus sat in shock! He thought, *What is this? He is calling me to him! I cannot delay. I need to get up. Leave my cloak. Leave everything. Hurry!*

The man reached down and took Bartimaeus's hand. "Come with me. This way."

The man's voice sounded excited. He led Bartimaeus to Jesus. The crowd was now very quiet. Everyone strained to hear what Jesus was to say, to see what he was to do.

Jesus spoke, "You were calling for me to have pity on you. What do you want?"

Bartimaeus was puzzled by the question! What else could a blind man want? Then he spurted out, "I want my sight back."

Jesus responded, "Oh yes, you will see again."

Jesus stretched out both arms and put his hands over Bartimaeus's eyes. Bartimaeus's eyes were open, but he saw only blackness. Then, with Jesus's hands on his eyes, the black started to fade into red. Soon it was bloodred, then Jesus removed his hands. The red penetrated his mind. It felt as if his head would explode. He no longer saw red, but it had turned brighter and brighter and finally as if he was looking directly into the sun. He blinked and shaded his eyes with his hands. He saw faces looking at him. He held his hands up and looked at them. He turned his hands over and rubbed them together. People reached out and took his hands. Hands were now all over him. They touched his shoulders, his back, his head. People were laughing and clapping. They were talking to him.

"You can see!"

"He can see!"

"He has been cured!"

"Jesus cured him!"

Now all were shouting. Then they all rushed off down the road. The crowd followed where Jesus had gone.

Bartimaeus was still standing as he was when Jesus had placed his hands on his eyes. He wondered, *"how long have I been here?"* He looked around. The street was nearly empty. A man that he did not know was standing in front of him. Bartimaeus said, "Are you Jesus?"

The man answered, "No, I am not."

Bartimaeus said, "Where is he? Is he gone?"

"Yes, he is on his way to Jerusalem, and all left to follow him through the city. I wanted to stay and see you. To see what Jesus had done."

Bartimaeus looked at him. "Who are you?"

"My name is Thomas. I am one of his followers. When we entered the gate and you started crying out, Jesus stopped and looked your way. He had a troubled look on his face. A look of great sadness. His face was shaken as if in pain. I felt sorry for him, and I wanted his pain to stop. That is when I came to you and told you to be quiet. But you shouted out all the louder. I looked back at Jesus where I had left him. He had not moved. He was looking right at you. He never took his eyes from you. With his hand he beckoned me. I went to him, and he had me bring you to him."

Bartimaeus looked at the crowd disappearing down the street.

He said, "I need to thank him. I do not know what to do. Do I run after him?"

Still looking down the road at the disappearing crowd, Thomas said to him, "Jesus does not do this for thanks from anyone. He knows what is in your heart. I have heard him say to others, 'Your sins are forgiven.' Thank him in your heart."

They both looked toward the wall. Only Bar-El remained where Bartimaeus had left him.

Thomas said, "I must leave. We are going to Jerusalem. Follow us when you can. I want you to meet Jesus. When you are there, ask his followers to take you to me. They call me Didymus. Shalom, my friend."

Thomas turned and hurried after the crowd.

Bartimaeus watched him go. He spoke in wonder to himself, *"Didymus, the twin! Who are you the twin of? I will see you in Jerusalem, Didymus. You, and Jesus, and I hope your twin also."*

He stood there, as if he had lost his way. He looked at silent Bar-El. He turned and slowly walked toward him. What would he say to him? He stopped in front of the blind man. Bar-El sat motionless, his face straight ahead, his eyes open but still blind. He said, "Have they all gone?"

"Yes, they are gone."

Quietly and slowly, he said, "And the man… Jesus?"

"Yes, they all followed him."

There was no sound, only stillness. Bartimaeus stood there looking at Bar-El with his basket and a few coins on his lap. His face expressionless, a vast emptiness of all emotion, all understanding. Without the least movement, Bar-El almost whispered, "You said that anything that you received I could have."

Bartimaeus knelt. "I will follow after Jesus. I must see him. I must thank him. When I do, I will ask him to cure you too. I must do that." He collapsed into Bar-El's arms, and they both wept.

4

MONICA

Bartimaeus and Bar-El clung to each other huddled against the wall until it was dark. The people that followed Jesus had come back a few at a time. Some stopped and studied the two men as they sat clutching each other. They talked softly and occasionally nodded their head in the direction of the men. Others approached, and they could be heard talking among themselves as if the two men could not hear. "Did not Jesus cure one of them? What of the other? Is he still blind?"

"Why did Jesus not cure both?"

"Does anyone know them?"

"I do not recall seeing the one that was cured. Maybe he was not really blind."

"It would not be fair to cure one and not the other. What kind of man would do that?"

"Now, what will he do? Where did he come from? Who is he?"

The cold of evening was coming on before the two men moved. They were both emotionally spent. Bar-El broke the silence. "You can see, can't you?"

"Yes, I can see." Bartimaeus knelt up. He held Bar-El's hands and looked into his face. "I should have asked him to cure you too. I did not think of that. It all happened so fast. He just asked me what I wanted. Of course, I wanted to see. To see again is all that I wanted." Peering intently at Bar-El, he spoke almost in a whisper as if the other man would not hear. "And you, my friend, have never seen. I am sorry."

Tears came to both men's eyes. Bartimaeus spoke with a breaking voice. "When I lost my sight, the only thing that I wanted was to see again. But there was nothing that I could do. I went to the best doctors, to the priests in the temple. Oh, how I prayed. Please, God, let me see again. But I was damned. I heard others talk. I must have sinned. I was being punished. It was wrong for me to be a soldier for Herod, to be friends with Romans. I was unfaithful to God, unfaithful to my family, unfaithful to my wife. But I was not. I was not."

Bartimaeus sat and wiped away his tears. Bar-El spoke. "I know, my friend, I know. It is not fair. People are not fair. But not all. Some are good people. They take care of me. But for others, I am worse than dead. The living dead. Sometimes I pray to die. But I go on. I know that there are others worse than me. Those poor lepers. I am told that there are blind lepers. God have mercy! Now, my friend, Bartimaeus, it is time for me to go home. I still have family that cares for me."

Bartimaeus rose and helped Bar-El up. He stooped and gathered Bal-El's basket and the cloak that he had cast aside. He left his walking stick on the ground. "Let us go, my friend."

Bartimaeus and Bar-El followed the street toward the center of Jericho. The houses and the shops there were the oldest in the city, some had been built hundreds of years earlier. The homes were generally small and very simple. Some with only one room, usually with shaded sleeping quarters on the roof. Bar-El knew his way and could have returned to his home without help, but Bartimaeus could not leave the man that he felt he had, somehow, abandoned that day. More importantly, Bartimaeus was struggling with what he should do. Deep inside he wanted to strike out immediately for Jerusalem, to catch up with this man, Jesus. He needed to thank him. More so, he needed to learn who he is and why he cured him. There was also his family outside the walls of Jericho: his wife, Gamela, and his son and daughter. Should he not go immediately to them? And his mother, Ariel, it would bring blessed relief to her to know that her son had recovered his sight. She already had too much grief in her life. Oh, to walk back down the road to join his family. To see the homes and his uncle Ezra and his family. To see the horses running free in the pastures and then to be on a horse again. That was a dream come true! Then, he would have his life back. He could return to his work, return to his family.

He weighed each of those in his mind repeatedly as he walked with Bar-El. But there was one more thought that he could not escape—Monica! She had left him at the gate that morning, and she expected him to return to her. It was now late. What if she went to the wall where she left him and discovered him gone? What would she do? She might think that he went to Susanna's house, but he would have told her that morning if that was his plan. It would not be fair for her not to know what happened. She is the only one who knows what he is doing and where he is. He thought to himself, *I must go to Monica first. After talking to her, I will make plans for what to do next.*

After a last embrace and leaving Bar-El at his home, Bartimaeus hurried to Monica's house. When he turned the corner and could see the house, he stopped. A dim light was on inside. She was home. Maybe she would be making bread and a meal for him before she took him to Susanna's. He wondered, *How will I tell her? She will have so many questions, and I have few answers. How did this happen? Who is this Jesus? Yes, who is Jesus?*

Bartimaeus opened the door quietly and stopped in the doorway with the door left open behind him. He spoke, "Monica."

She was across the room placing bowls on a table. She turned her head to look at him. "Bartimaeus, it is late. I was worried about you." She turned toward him while wiping her hands on a towel. "Bartimaeus, what is it? Why are you standing there? What happened? You are scaring me."

"Monica, I can see." Neither moved. Her hands went to her mouth. "I have been cured."

She dropped the towel and rushed across the room to him. Standing on her toes, she threw her arms around him and hugged him. She stepped back, and putting her hands on his face, she looked directly into his eyes. "How? When did this happen? How did you do this? How do you feel? What can I do?" Dropping her hands to his, she brought him into the house. "Sit. Tell me all about it. I want to know everything. Bartimaeus, this is amazing. Thanks be to God." She ran over and looked out the door before closing it. Then she hurried back to the table and pulled a stool close to him and sat looking at him. "Well, tell me!"

"Monica, it happened so fast I am not sure that I know. I was sitting where you left me next to the blind man, Bar-El. We talked a little, then I fell asleep. When I woke, there was much commotion about Jesus of Nazareth entering through the gate. Have you heard of Jesus?" She nodded but did not reply. Bartimaeus continued, "Something came over me. I do not know what it was. But I knew that I had to do something. I am not a beggar, but I cried out like a drowning man. I kept crying out to Jesus to have mercy on me. A man came to me and told me to be quiet, then he returned and said that the Master wanted me. I jumped up and left my cloak on the ground. He took me to him. Then, Jesus asked me what I wanted! Can you imagine? What does a blind man want? I told him that I wanted to see again. He put his hands over my eyes. I do not know how long. I do not know if he did anything else. I stayed still, then there was light, bright light, and I could see. People were looking at me. When they knew that I could see, they started screaming and shouting and jumping up and down. They almost knocked me over. Then they ran down the street following this Jesus, I suppose. I did not know what to do. I was left alone." He paused, but she did not say anything as if she knew that there was more, and she did not want to interrupt. "Well, not really alone. There was another man standing right in front of me, looking at me. He said that his name was Thomas. He said that he was a follower of Jesus. I think that he was the one that brought me to Jesus. We did not talk much. I think that he stayed to see if I was really cured. I suppose that one is never sure about mysterious events such as this. There must always be doubts even among friends"—his voice broke—"even among family. We can never be certain of anything, can we?"

A tear came to her eye which she brushed away. They sat there quietly for a few minutes, each trying to read the other's thoughts.

Thoughts that neither wanted to pursue. A tear once more came to her eyes, one that she did not brush away. He reached over and wiped it away. He smiled at her, and she returned the smile. They squeezed each other's hands and in the same instant, withdrew them.

Bartimaeus continued, "The man that stayed, the one named Thomas, he said that they call him Didymus, the twin! Do you think that he, like me, is also a twin? I want to see him again, talk to him, to get to know him. I felt something between us. Something that I have not felt between myself and another man for some time. Then he too left." She smiled and nodded before he continued, "The other blind man, Bar-El, was still there. He was not cured, Monica. He is still blind. I did not know what to do. I sat with him. We just sat. I cried. We cried. I could not stop. For him? For me? I do not know. I do not know."

They both sat there in silence not knowing what more to say or to ask. Monica looked deep into his eyes. Was this real? She did not want to stop looking, as if he might be blind again if she was not there with him. He could not take his eyes from her beautiful face, brown eyes, and dark hair. She had on a well-worn, soft woolen tunic that was light brown with white threads interspersed. He had seen such material many times, but never so glorious. The lamp flickered and sent shadows dancing on the walls and floor. Every tone, every texture, every object played before his eyes. Nothing that he had seen had ever been this beautiful before. They sat in stillness, nothing more to be said, and nothing more to attempt to understand.

Monica leaned over and kissed him lightly on the cheek. She said, "Now, what will you do? Are you returning to Jerusalem? What of your home and family here? What of Jesus? How will you find him? You must thank him, talk to him. Who is he?"

He had the same questions and more, and no answers to either hers or his. "I need to go to Jerusalem. I need to find this Jesus. If he can cure me that easily, I could also lose my sight again. I cannot let that happen. Does he want something of me? What can I do for him? I must thank him. He does not even know me. Yes, I must go back to Jerusalem."

"But you cannot go back tonight," she protested. "It has been a long day. You just arrived from Jerusalem and now this."

"I need to go back," he insisted.

"But it is dangerous, especially at night. There are robbers along that road. You have no horse or sword, nothing to protect you."

"I have traveled that road many times. And there are guard houses along the way. I can stay there if needed. The guards know me. Even many of the Roman guards are my friends. They are not all bad, even though there are some people that would have us believe that. There is a lot of good that some refuse to see." He stopped, but Monica knew what he was thinking. There were those, even in his family, that could not admit to good if it did not conform to their Jewish Laws and beliefs.

"Please stay and eat with me," she pleaded. "I made fresh bread and a piece of lamb. Then you can go to Susanna."

Monica got up and brought the warm bread and the pot of lamb to the table. She ladled the lamb into a bowl and broke off a large piece of bread for Bartimaeus. They ate in silence. He broke off another piece of bread. "This is very good. My brother was a fortunate man to have you for a wife. Very lucky indeed. He loved you very much. He would brag about you."

She did not respond and, looking away, changed the subject. "How is your mother?"

"It is best for my mother to be where she is. I talked to her about that when I left our home to live in Jerusalem. It is good for the children to have her close. She is a great grandmother. They need her."

She reached out and touched his hand. "And what of you? Your children need you too! And you need them."

"They are doing well. Gamela takes good care of them without me. I think that they understand. It is Saul that worries me. I do not want him to have any influence on them. What he has told his sister about me is bad enough. I hope that Gamela does not let him talk to the children. He may be the brother of my wife, and because of that a member of my family, but he and I have become bitter enemies. He used this blindness of mine to turn Gamela against me. He has become fanatical in his beliefs. He never cared for the fact that I was a soldier for Herod, but then when I was struck blind, he used that to convince her that I was a sinner and unfaithful to her. I am glad that Saul is in Jerusalem studying in the temple with that Pharisee, Gamaliel. He will certainly master all 613 Jewish Laws and how to punish sinners that break any of them. Even punish those that do not break them. But let us not talk of that."

They finished eating, and Monica cleared the table. Bartimaeus watched her. She was good at what she did, and what a pleasure to be with. He began to doze while sitting at the table.

She said, "Bartimaeus, I know that you want to rush off to Jerusalem tonight, but it is late, and you are tired. So much has happened today. And you cannot return to Jerusalem before you tell Gamela and your family that you can see again. And what of your plans to visit Susanna and to be with your family to celebrate the Passover meal? Do you want to go to Susanna's now?"

He looked toward the door. "Monica, I know that I should go to Susanna's, but I am so very tired. I do not have the energy to tell this tale to her right now. I am not going to Jerusalem now. I must tell my family what has happened to me. Could I sleep a little here and then leave early in the morning for Susanna? I always feel such peace here with you. You and this house are good memories for me. But you know that I worry about others knowing that I stay here sometimes. You know what trouble that could be for you."

Angrily and with her arms crossed, she said, "Yes, I know what others could say or do, but there is nothing. Nothing for me to fear. Certainly not from our God. Now please lie down on the cushions here and rest. I will get ready for bed."

Bartimaeus laid down, and Monica put out the lamp. She went to her bed and started to undress. She stopped and looked back at him. "In the past, when you visited me, I could undress in the room with you. Now you must turn your back."

He rolled over and closed his eyes. He was asleep before long, but not until he stopped hearing the rustle of clothing and Monica climbing into her bed.

Bartimaeus woke and looked at the sun's rays playing on the adobe block wall across from him. Monica had her back to him preparing food. He watched her with her long, dark hair tied behind her and hanging down her back to her waist. He thought how young she looked, even childlike. She was small with olive skin. Her eyes were almost black and seemed to be always smiling. She would not be called beautiful compared to his wife, but she had that warm, feminine being that was attractive, maybe very much so, for many men. When he first met her, she was serving food to the soldiers at the barracks in Jericho. She was young, she seemed only a little more than a child, but she did her job with confidence and grace. Bartimaeus was impressed by her and asked the steward about her and where she lived. Bartimaeus was already married and had two children with Gamela, but Barariel had not found the woman for him. Bartimaeus told his brother about her, and Barariel was soon having all of his meals at the barracks and sitting at the table that Monica served. It was not long before he and Monica were married. He and Barariel, with their wives, were good friends, and they shared all their free time together.

Monica turned and saw Bartimaeus watching her. At first, she was startled. Then she saw that he was smiling, not a big smile, more of the smile of a man at peace, and she smiled back. "Good morning. I was trying to be quiet so as not to disturb you. You were sleeping so well."

"Yes, I did not awake until now. Then, I immediately opened my eyes. You know, a test. Was yesterday real or a dream? I could see. I saw you. My God, how I had prayed for this. It is still a mystery to me. There is so much that I need to learn about this."

She walked over to him, and he stood up. She stopped, not wanting to get any closer. They stood looking at each other in silence. He turned his head toward the door. She said, "I know. You must leave. Are you going to Susanna's now?"

He turned back to her. "No, I decided last night before I fell asleep that I am going to go immediately to see Gamela. I want her to be the first to know that I have been cured, that I can see again. My blindness is what separated us. It was not her fault. It was her brother

Saul that used my blindness to drive us apart. Now that I have been cured, we can return to the life that we had before. I need to go straight to her. I am sure that she will want to know all about it. And I need to tell the children and my mother. I can see again. This is a miracle, isn't it?" She lowered her head so that he could not look into her eyes. He noticed her hesitancy and, needing reassurance from her, repeated in a questioning tone, "It is a miracle, isn't it?"

She raised her head and returned eye contact. With a reassuring smile, she responded, "Yes, Bartimaeus, it is a miracle."

Knowing that there was nothing more that she could say, she returned to the table. As she walked away, she could not shake the feeling that Gamela may not see this as a miracle or even as a blessing. She bit her lower lip and was glad that her back was to him. "Come, let us eat before you leave."

It was strangely quiet as they sat together eating. In the quiet, he looked about the room, and he was filled with memories. Barariel and Monica had built this small house shortly after they were wed with the plan to add on to the house as they needed and could manage. They had not shared it for long before Barariel was killed. In the silence, he stole a glance at her. His hands came to rest on the table as he watched her. In that moment, he suddenly understood that this house and all that it contained were her most precious memories. This was all that she had. He lowered his head and closed his eyes. For the first time, he realized how much she had given him in his need but that he had not likewise given to her in hers. He unconsciously rocked in his chair with the sudden realization that the return of his sight, although certainly recognized as a blessing by her for which she was truly grateful, but it also posed a threat to her losing the last solace that she had left. He had failed Bar-El yesterday with his needs; he vowed to himself not to fail Monica in hers.

Bartimaeus and Monica finished eating in silence, each lost in their thoughts. When Monica rose to clear the table, Bartimaeus stood and moved to her. He put his hands on her shoulders and, with gentleness, pulled her to him. She moved to him but did not raise her head. He bent over and kissed her forehead then, dropping his hands, walked toward the door. He opened the door and looked back. She had turned her back to him. "I will stop to see you before I return to Jerusalem."

She nodded and replied, "Give my love to Gamela and the children and your mother. Tell them that I miss them."

"I will."

He walked away troubled in his heart by the realization that the marvel and joy of his restored sight was also a threat to the bonds that his blindness had nurtured between him and Monica. Bonds that could neither be allowed to exist and flourish, nor that either would want broken or to abandon.

5

GAMELA

As he walked the streets of Jericho, maybe for the first time he noted the houses within the city walls had no space, no openness, and no freedom. He thought how much different Monica's house was from his and Gamela's outside of the city walls. His house had been built many generations ago and then enlarged by subsequent generations including his father. There were two houses: one that he had grown up in and where Gamela and the children lived, and the other where his uncle, Ezra, and family lived. The two houses were separate but enclosed within a common wall.

Ariel stayed in her house after Timaeus disappeared where she raised Bartimaeus and Barariel, and Susanna. Gamela had moved into the house after she and Bartimaeus married. They had their first child, a son, Saul David, within a year after marriage. He was named after Gamela's brother, Saul, a learned Pharisee in Jerusalem. Bartimaeus added David to his son's name so that he would proudly bear the name of the first two kings of Judea. It was several years later that they had their second child, a daughter, Mariam. Ariel had moved to the adjacent house with Ezra and his family after Mariam was born. By then, Ezra's children were grown, and she felt it best for Gamela to know that it was now her house. Saul David was twelve years old and already very good with the horses. Mariam was five years old and very much her father's delight.

Gamela, although Jewish, was not from Jericho or even a native of Judea. She had come to Jerusalem with her older brother, Saul, from Tarsus in Cilicia. Their mother was Jewish and had married a successful merchant in Tarsus where they had two children. Saul was older than his sister, and he had mastered his trade as a tent maker in support of the family business. Both parents died during an outbreak of a disease when Gamela was still a child. From there, Saul and Gamela were taken in by the brother of their mother who was of strong Jewish belief. Saul, early on, had embraced his mother's religion. His father, a Roman citizen, had followed the culture of the Roman gods more from the perspective of a business interest rather than any spiritual inclination. The uncle, not necessarily wanting to be responsible for two more in his household, did not object when Saul suggested that he move to Jerusalem to better learn of his religious heritage. Further, and importantly to the uncle, he was willing to take his young sister with him and to support her. With that easily decided, Saul and Gamela left Tarsus and journeyed to Jerusalem.

Once there, Saul, being both a Jew and a Roman citizen, was able to find good employment as a tent maker and lovingly cared for Gamela. She grew into a beautiful young woman of marrying age, and Saul, being the head of the family, soon had offers of marriage from eligible men of Jerusalem. Gamela, being equally strong in her aspirations, was not willing to accept any of the offers of marriage that Saul brought her. On a Sabbath, she saw the young, handsome soldier, Bartimaeus, at the temple, and in her heart, she made the decision that her brother had not been able to achieve. With her insistent prompting, Saul introduced himself to Bartimaeus and invited him to meet his sister. Bartimaeus, on meeting Gamela, was immediately spellbound by this graceful, golden-haired beauty from another world. However, Bartimaeus, being a soldier of Herod, did not possess all the necessary credentials for the future brother-in-law. But Saul was willing to satisfy his sister's wishes, especially where a husband was concerned. Soon after meeting, Bartimaeus and Gamela were married, and she moved to their home in Jericho. Saul became entrenched in studying the Jewish religion and became a Pharisee. With his newfound focus on the Law, he soon was seeing his soldier brother-in-law in a different light. Bartimaeus was a soldier for Herod, a Roman-appointed usurper king of the Jewish people. Bartimaeus also did not practice the Law as Saul expected, nor did he teach that practice to his wife or their children. Once struck blind, there was no need of further evidence that Bartimaeus was a sinner and was to be cast out of the family so as not to defile others with his sinful ways. Where Gamela could not see what was proper according to the Law, her brother could and did. Blind Bartimaeus was cast out of his home and separated from his family.

That morning, after leaving Monica's house, Bartimaeus retraced his previous day's path to the north gate. Once at the gate, he stopped to look for Bar-El, but he was not there, and he wondered how Bar-El had managed that night. Bartimaeus well knew the haunting feeling that would attack his troubled mind, and he hoped that Bar-El had learned to vanquish that demon better than he himself had. Maybe, having been born blind, Bar-El had well learned to manage that disability. He hoped so for Bar-El's sake.

Jericho had three main gates and a road outside of the wall that encircled the city. Jesus had passed through the center of the city and exited out the west gate which led directly to the road to Jerusalem, the road that he would soon follow on his own way back to Jerusalem. The south gate led to agricultural fields and the Dead Sea. Shaking off his thoughts of Bar-El, he exited Jericho through the north gate. Once outside of the wall, he looked at the patchwork of irrigated fields with crops that fed many people throughout Judea. This was a good place to raise horses, as his family had done, and why Herod had established stables to breed and train horses for his mounted guard there.

Walking the road that led north to Galilee and further to Damascus, Bartimaeus recalled growing up there and the adventures that he and his brother and sister had. The river valley was lined with trees that provided shade and a good place to have adventures. He and his brother had ponies, and Ezra taught them to ride at an early age. When old enough, they had been allowed to take the ponies on long rides to the river. Later, when they were older, they would take horses and be gone for several days. They learned to ride and to care for the horses and for each other.

The road to his home passed over an irrigation ditch. He remembered playing in the slow moving, cool water and his mother walking the ditch in spring harvesting the fresh asparagus that grew wild. And there was the apricot tree from which they enjoyed the sweet fruit of summer. It all was beautiful and fresh and clean and peaceful. He thought how he longed to return to that time.

His home was a short distance off the main road. He turned in and walked by the pastures with mares and foals. The houses had a walled courtyard in front with a gate. If the children were outside, they would probably be there. He did not hear any voices from within and opened the gate slowly and looked around. He did not want the children to see him until after he had talked to Gamela. Not seeing anyone, he entered the courtyard and closed the gate. He stood there and tried to remember how he would tell Gamela what had happened. It was all clear as he rehearsed it on the way there. Now it seemed so inadequate. His mind went blank, and he surrendered any thought of the right words. He opened the door and stepped into the house. The room was empty. He walked through to the next room and into the bedroom. Gamela was folding clothes. She heard someone enter the house and looked to the doorway expecting the children. Seeing him, she looked down and continued folding the clothes. "Bartimaeus, I did not expect you. Who brought you? Did the children or your mother see you? Do you want me to take you to them?"

He stood there watching her. She was slender and lovely. Hair the color of gold, blue eyes, and fair skin. She was wearing a simple white gown with bare shoulders and open at the neck. Her skin sparkled, and he remembered its smooth, warm feel.

"No one brought me. I came alone."

She looked up. "How? You should not travel by yourself."

They stood looking at each other. He took a step forward while staying locked on her. He saw the frown come to her face and realized that she noticed the eye contact.

"I can see, Gamela."

Her arms lowered, and she dropped the piece of clothing to the table. "How? When?"

He took another step into the room. "I really do not know how. A man did it, Jesus of Nazareth. He came into the city, and he cured me. Then he left. I never saw him. I never spoke to him. He was gone. I do not know why he did it. I do not know him." He spoke in an apologetic fashion although he was not intending to do so.

He had barely finished when she said, "When did this happen?"

He answered holding out his hands, palms up and tipping his head to the side shrugging his shoulders, "It happened yesterday afternoon."

There was silence. They stood trying to find the next words to say. Finally, she said, "I need to know all about this."

"Yes, I will tell you everything. Let us sit down. And I need some water. I think that you probably could use some too."

She walked past him through the doorway and into the main room. He followed her, and they sat facing each other. He started, "Where are the children?"

"At Ezra's house with your mother. She gives them lessons. She is very good at that."

"Yes. *Ima* was a good teacher to me too. That is good for all of them. For you too."

"Yes, but it is very quiet here when they are gone. It is worse now that they are older." She paused then continued, "Well, you were gone so much. In Jerusalem and on duty with the guard. You often were not here. But the children were always here with me in this house. It is different now. But I want to hear about how you were cured. Tell me."

Bartimaeus told her the story starting with sitting at the north gate with Bar-El as a beggar and how Jesus passed by and that he had called out to Jesus, pleading for mercy. He tried to explain how Jesus cured him, but there was not much that he could tell. Jesus put his hands on his eyes, and he was cured. There was no medicine or prayers that he heard. Jesus only touched him. She had several questions about how this happened, but he could not explain it any better since he did not know himself. When he could see, Jesus was gone, and he never saw him. He finished the story and waited. Then he added, "One of his followers stayed until I opened my eyes and could see. He said that they called him Didymus. I wonder if he is a twin, and of whom? Isn't that strange?"

"Yes, Bartimaeus. That is very strange. But the whole tale is strange." They sat quietly for a bit. Finally, she asked. "So where did you stay last night?"

He answered, "It was dark by the time that I walked Bar-El home, and I was very confused. I did not know if I should follow Jesus. I wanted to come to you, but it was late, and I did not want to scare you and the children showing up at night. I needed to think. So I stayed with a friend in Jericho and got up this morning and came here. It is good to see you. You look good. How are the children?"

She answered, "You should go see them and your mother. They will be shocked to see you and amazed at your cure. That is good to hear. I am so happy for you. I still cannot imagine how that happened. You must be in shock yourself. You can see!"

"Yes, I must go see the children! They will be surprised to see me! My mother too. She will cry, you know. And my uncle Ezra and his family. Let us go." He stretched out his hand. "It is good to be with you. I have missed you."

She took his hand as she stood. "I missed you too, Bartimaeus."

It was a short walk to the other house. When there, he opened the gate, and she entered first. The children were in the courtyard. When they saw their father, they quickly looked to their mother. She said, "Your father is here. He just arrived, and he has something to tell you."

She turned to him. He said, "I have been cured. I can see again."

They both rushed to him. He knelt, and they clung to him. They kept shouting, "You can see!"

Hugging and kissing them, he said, "Yes, I still cannot believe it myself."

By now, all in the house had heard the commotion and came out to join in the celebration. Ariel stayed back in the doorway with her hands to her mouth. When Bartimaeus saw her, he stood up and went to her and held her tight. "*Ima*, I am cured. I can see. All your prayers are answered. God heard you. Thank you. I love you, *Ima*."

Ezra's wife invited them in. "Come inside. Sit. Ezra, get water for everyone. I will prepare some food. We need to celebrate. And you need to tell us how this happened. Come in! Come in! This is wonderful."

He sat alongside his mother and then told the story again. Saul David stayed and listened to every word from his father. Mariam, being younger, would sit for a bit then would dash out of the room to join her mother and the other women preparing the meal.

When the food was ready, they reclined around the table, Gamela on his right and Ariel on his left. Before eating, Ezra said the blessing and thanked God for curing Bartimaeus. During the meal and after, at prompting of all, he again told details of the story and answered the questions as best he could. Eventually, all realized that there were many questions that could not be answered, and it became silent. Bartimaeus took that opportunity to ask questions of his own. The children told him stories. Mariam had many stories to tell of what her and her friends had been doing, while Saul David talked about the horses that he was helping to train and one special one that he talked about in great detail and delight. Ezra said that they could talk at another time about the horse breeding and training that was underway, and he explained, "I have had to hire men to train the horses. I cannot do that alone with all else that is needed here. They do their job well enough, but not as good as you and your brother. Barariel worked marvels with the horses." He paused, then smiling, added, "Oh, you were great with the horses too, but your brother, he had something special with a horse. It was a gift from God how he could communicate with them. I loved watching him train them. It was as if they could read each other's minds. I hope that you will be able to join us here again. We certainly could use you here. Not to mention your family and your mother needing you too."

Smiling and putting his hand on Saul David, he said, "I would like that. Especially to be back with the family. Yes, I hope to do that. But first I have a few things to take care of in Jerusalem. I need to report in and see if I can return to my duties." With that, he looked at Gamela, but she did not return the look. "And I need to find this man Jesus and thank him. I want to know more about him. I know nothing. There is much to learn." Gamela turned her head toward him and caught his eye but said nothing.

It was now night, and Gamela told the children to say good night to everyone. Bartimaeus got up and walked over to her and took her hand. He said, "I will visit a bit more here. Then, I will meet you at home."

Taking her hands from his, she said, "Yes, we have more to talk about alone."

He kissed her on the check then hugged each of the children and told them that he would see them tomorrow. Watching them, he said to himself, *"Yes, I really will see you tomorrow!"*

Ariel reached over and touched him. "Let us step outside. I need some fresh air and to talk with you." Once outside and away from the house, she asked, "Have you had a chance to see Susanna yet?"

He looked at her and laughingly said, "No, and I cannot wait to see her. You know that she will scream with delight when I tell her! I love her and have missed her! I came to Jericho to celebrate Pesach with her, but after I was healed, I decided to come home to you and Gamela first."

"It would be good for you to go to her tomorrow. Susanna and the family are coming here tomorrow afternoon for the Passover meal. Ezra has already slaughtered the lamb. Tomorrow we will roast it. Gamela and I need to stay here to prepare food and to get ready."

He thought a second then said, "I can go to her in the morning. I need to spend some time to tell her what has happened. I can have the morning with her. Then I can help her carry everything that she is bringing, and we can have a good, long talk on the way back here. Will they need to return home that night?"

"No, they will stay the night in the two houses. The children will stay with Gamela and your children. Susanna and Judah will stay in Ezra's house. I suppose that you will stay with Gamela, won't you?"

"I do not know, *Ima*. I need to talk with her, and I best do that now."

He stopped and looked at her with a big smile. "I may have to sleep in the stable tonight, you know!"

"Do not dare!" she exclaimed as she smacked him on the shoulder. He laughed.

They walked back to the house, and he hugged and kissed her. "Good night. I will see you early in the morning. It will be a busy day for all of us. I love you, *Ima*."

"Having you back here where you belong has pulled the dagger from my heart that has been there since you left your home. Losing your father when you and your brother were newborn babies, then the death of Barariel, and then shortly after that your accident was very bad, but worse was seeing the love between you and Gamela being ripped away. That has been very difficult for me to bear. If it were not for your children and those that I love here, I would not have survived. Your children are a great source of love, and I love Gamela. It has not been easy for her either. I just wish that her brother would not visit her. She has dark days after he leaves. I do not know what he tells her. He is all caught up with the high council in Jerusalem. This Roman occupation does not help. Herod is a puppet of Rome, and as you well know, you being in Herod's guard greatly troubles him. I just wish that he would leave it alone and let you and Gamela work out whatever problems that you may have yourselves."

"Yes. Saul and I have always had bad blood between us. He was against me from the start with Gamela. He reluctantly agreed to our marriage. Then my fall from the horse and being struck blind was all that he needed to convince her that I was a sinner, an unfaithful husband. He planted seeds in her mind, and that was all that was needed to turn her away from me. I am not perfect, and I have done things that I am not proud of. I am a soldier, and sometimes we must do as we are told. But I have always been faithful to her. I may not be the best Jew. I know that I do not obey all of the Laws, but I am not a bad person. I cannot believe that I was struck blind because of anything that I did. And it cannot be anything that you or my father did. Why would God punish me for that? All that I have heard of my father is that he was a good man. Hezekiah was father's best friend. He always tells me what a good man and great soldier my father was. No, I do not believe that my blindness was because of sin. I do not care what that high and mighty Saul says." He kissed her on the cheek once more. "I should not get this angry before I talk to Gamela. Good night, *Ima*. I love you, and it is good to be here with you again."

He walked her to Ezra's then turned toward Gamela's house. When he entered the house, she was waiting for him and was in her night clothes. She motioned for him to sit beside her. "This has been quite the two days for you, hasn't it?"

"Yes," he said. "It all happened so fast. I had given up hope of ever seeing again. The doctors said that if my sight did not return shortly after the fall that it never would. We both knew that. Then, suddenly I was cured. I know that you are not prepared for this, and neither am I. Now what do we do? What are you thinking?"

"Bartimaeus, I do not know what to think. I need some time. You know with this cure you need to go to the temple. There are certain rights of the Law that you need to perform to be cleansed. You need to talk to Saul. He will know what you need to do. He will help you."

He inadvertently sat back and grimaced. He did not speak, but he immediately thought, *Oh, yes, I am sure that Saul will be anxious to help me.* Leaning toward her, he smiled and, nodding his head while trying to hide his frustration at what he had just heard, said, "I will return to Jerusalem in a day or two. I will talk to Saul and find out what the Law requires, and I will do whatever is necessary. Then I will come back, and we can sort this out. I do want to come back to you. To be with you and the children here in this house again. I want my life back again. I want our life back."

She looked straight at him and, with unblinking eyes that also told of hidden hurt, said, "Bartimaeus, I want my life back too. I want to feel good again. I want to know that you love me."

He reached out his open hands toward her and, with a touch of impatience, added, "You know that I love you. I always have. I still do." He lowered his hands to his knees.

They sat there looking at each other. Finally, she slapped him in a playful manner on the back of his hand. "Speaking of being cleansed, you need to bathe. There is a jug of water out back and a towel. I put a blanket on the cushions in the spare room and some clean night cloths. Please clean yourself. Come to my bedroom in the morning. There are still some of your clothes in there. I suspect that they will be a little big for you now. You need to start eating better. Good night."

"Good night, Gamela. I love you."

"I love you too, Bartimaeus."

6

SUSANNA

Bartimaeus had a restless night. He had returned home with expectations that he would be successful in talking to Gamela and assuring her that all that she had been told by Saul about him was without basis. He believed that he could explain to her that his services with the guard and to Herod, although seen by some as violating the Jewish Law and even betraying his God, were not true. His services were mostly in providing well-schooled horses and the training of the mounted soldiers. There was little, if anything, that he did that was a direct service for Herod. Hezekiah had often assured him and his brother that they would not be sent on assignments that came from Herod, and he had often wondered why Hezekiah seemed to find it necessary to assure them of this. Bartimaeus had attempted such discussions in the past with Gamela which were not successful, and he sensed a reluctance by Gamela to be willing to listen to that argument again. He had concluded that there was little hope of reconciling with Gamela until he was successful in convincing Saul of his innocence of any sin against Gamela or against his God. That required him to return to Jerusalem.

He stayed in bed with thoughts of what he needed to do the next few days and what he would do once he returned to Jerusalem. He struggled with whether he should first seek out Jesus or whether he should immediately go to Saul. He decided that it was best for him to find Jesus first since that may provide what he needed in his meeting with Saul; besides, he felt it necessary to thank Jesus as soon as he could.

When he got out of bed, he went to Gamela's room and looked in through the open doorway. She was sleeping, and he watched her quietly breathing with her hair in twists and tangles down her side. With the cold morning chill, he wanted to slip in beside her warm body. He backed away and proceeded to the children's room where all was quiet but for the sound of their easy breathing. He remembered the many times that he had taken them to bed and told them stories and played games with them and listened to their laughter as he left them. He longed to return to those simple, joy-filled times. He smiled, nodding his head to himself filled with this moment of peace. He returned to his room where he dressed in clothes that he had left there years ago. Although it was cold enough for a cloak, he left it hanging on the wall. The days had been clear and sunny, and the walk into Jericho would keep him warm. He would return from Susanna's in the heat of the day with his arms full of supplies that she would bring for the Passover meal, and he did not want to have a cloak to either wear or to carry. The Pesach would begin that day at the setting of the sun.

There were no sounds from the bedrooms as he walked out. He saw a lamp shining at Ezra's, and he joined Ariel and others at the breakfast table. They talked about the plans for the Passover meal and what was needed to be done that day. It was good to be back with those that he loved, but he soon departed for Susanna's.

From Ezra's home, he walked past the stable and the pastures. He watched the horses and wished that he could ride to Susanna's rather than walk, but that was not possible since he and the others would be carrying the supplies for the meal which Susanna was preparing when he returned home. He would have time to ride in the days to come. He had talked to Ezra who said that there was a horse that was to be delivered to the stable in Jerusalem which he looked forward to doing in a few days. He had not been on a horse since his accident, and he longed to once more share that mutual trust between him and such a beautiful, powerful creature. He never ceased to be amazed how his intention could be conveyed to another creature without a word being spoken by a mere change in his seat or a movement of his legs or a squeeze of his fingers. He wished that he could achieve the same trust and understanding with Gamela.

At the end of the short walk to the road, he stopped and looked to the left. That road led to Galilee and further north to Damascus and Syria. Jesus had walked that road from Galilee only two days before on his way to Jerusalem. Jesus had passed right by his house and had been that close to Gamela and the children. He wondered what it would have been like for Gamela and the children if Jesus had stopped at their house. Maybe he would have worked a miracle for them. He asked himself, what would they have asked for? He wondered what had taken Jesus to Jerusalem. He thought of Thomas being with Jesus in Jerusalem that morning. Maybe they were meeting with the priests in the temple. He wondered if he had been in Jerusalem with the guard rather than blind at the gate of Jericho, that maybe he could have escorted Jesus to an audience with Herod. He once more longed to return to Jerusalem and to find Jesus. He smiled to himself that would happen soon, but not today.

He turned right on the road that would take him to Jericho and, in a few more days, further to Jerusalem. It was an hour walk to Jericho and, with the walls of the city before him, he struck off. His thoughts went to his sister and the good times that he had with her. His blindness and reliance on others had drawn him even closer to her.

She was a few years older than he and Barariel. The three had been close as children. As a young woman, Susanna had married Judah, and they had three children in their home in Jericho. She was a good mother and wife, and she easily attracted friends to the family. The death of Barariel had brought them even closer as they clung to each other and to their mother in their grief. She was also a great comfort to Monica who had only been married a short while before Barariel died. Susanna had invited Monica to join them in her home, but Monica had chosen to stay in the house that she and Barariel had built. They had grown as close as sisters, and they sought comfort from the other.

BARTIMAEUS, THE BLIND BEGGAR OF JERICHO

As Bartimaeus entered the north gate of Jericho, he stopped and recalled sitting against the wall with Bar-El only two days ago. He walked to the spot where he stood when Jesus cured him. His mind once again went to Jesus. He spoke to himself, *Where is Jesus on this day before the Pesach? What is he doing? Has he performed other miracles? What do the people think of him? What about the temple priests and the high council? Surely, a man of his power and following with the people must be attracting their attention. Maybe Jesus is a prophet or even the Messiah. He is probably in Jerusalem for an important meeting with the Jewish leaders.* His thoughts went to Saul. Maybe Saul would meet Jesus and even help him find the man that had cured him. He once more hoped that Saul would have a change of heart toward him and help him reunite with Gamela.

He shook his mind free of those thoughts and moved on. Soon, he came to the street leading to Monica's house. He stopped. His mind wandered; it would be good to see her smiling face. He could stop on his way to Susanna and visit her. It would only take a minute. Then the realization came to him that he could not do that; it would not be fair to her. He nodded his head to fortify his decision and walked on. It was not far from Monica's house to Susanna's. That was good, they could easily visit each other, and Susanna could look after Monica. He opened the door and walked in.

"Hello, Susanna. It is your brother."

Susanna and the children came running into the room shouting his name and cheering him. He was startled as the children ran up and hugged him, and the little ones tugged at his clothes. Susanna was the first to speak. "Oh my, Bartimaeus, it truly is good to see you. We have been so excited! Well, maybe I should say so excited for you to see us again!"

He gladly accepted the hug and kiss from Susanna and beamed at the children at his feet. He stumbled out, "So you know? How?"

"Yes, we know. Monica came over yesterday morning. She told us everything. Which is not much. She said that you were healed by this man named Jesus. We have heard rumors of him. You know, everyone is hoping for a great leader or even a messiah to free us from this Roman occupation. Could this Jesus be him?" She continued, taking him by the hand, "Come, come. Sit down." Turning to the children, she said, "Get your uncle some water and some of our breakfast. He will be thirsty, and he needs something to eat after walking here."

They sat and enjoyed each other's company. She said, "Well, tell us everything. When Monica came by, she said that she did not know very much, only that you had been cured. How did that happen? Have you seen Gamela and the children? They must all be so happy. This has been a terrible ordeal for all. Now tell us."

He told the tale again with as much detail that he could provide. Then he told about going to his home and seeing Gamela and the children and his mother. She asked about how they had reacted, and added that surely, they were shocked. Susanna asked a few questions, but for the most part was content to just let him talk.

Finally, after he was done, she added, "Oh, I wish that I could have been there when you saw *Ima*. This has been difficult for her. First our brother was killed, then shortly after that you had your accident." She paused, then looked him in the eye. "And then you left. That was the worst for her."

They sat for a moment, then he added, "Yes, that was bad. There were times that I could hardly go on. It did not matter where I was or what I was doing. I felt the need to go somewhere else. But it did not matter. My mind was racing. I could not turn it off. The slightest, inconsequential detail of something that I could not remember would terrorize my mind and my being. I really did think that I was losing my mind. That is just what I needed, to not only be blind but to be insane too! Thankfully, I had found a way to calm my mind. I would close my eyes. That really helped because I could almost forget that I was blind. Then I would try to empty my mind, to not think of anything. I found that it helped if I listened to my breathing. Eventually this became easier for me. I had nothing but time, so I had a lot of practice. It was very restful, and sometimes I had, I suppose they were dreams, where I saw things or learned things. I did not always remember everything in those dreams, just some parts." He stopped as if to question what he was saying, then added, "Those times were very peaceful." They sat quietly for a moment. Then he added, "So Monica came by yesterday. I am glad that the two of you are such good friends."

"We are like sisters. She said that she had planned to come by anyway. She was going to go with us to your house to celebrate the Passover meal. Then she decided to stay in Jericho to be with her parents. That is too bad for us. It would have been nice to have her with us, especially to help us celebrate your recovery."

He thought that she never said anything about how Monica knew that he had been cured, or why he did not come to her house after he was cured. Nor did she ask where he spent the night after visiting Monica. He suspected that she knew that he spent time with Monica and maybe even that he often stayed the night with her. If she knew, and she probably did, she never said anything, and she did not say anything about it now.

She stood and said that it was time to finish preparing the food that she was bringing. She was baking bread. That was her specialty, and it would be warm as they traveled back home. When the bread was baked, they packed it in baskets and covered it with cloth. They stopped along the way at the market where Susanna's husband, Judah, owned a shop. There they gathered fresh fruit for the meal, and they departed.

It was early afternoon. The sun was high in the blue cloudless sky as they walked through the gate, but shortly, he noticed off to the west that dark clouds were building. Rain clouds and storms always came from the west. The moisture from the sea would push in over the land and be cooled as it rose over the higher ground near Jerusalem. It looked like today would be one of those stormy days. The runoff would flow from the hills to the west and provide water for the fields near Jericho. He thought the rain was good, but this was not the time of year that normally had such storms. He thought of his cloak hanging on the wall at home, and he wished that he had brought it as he watched the storm clouds quickly build.

As they walked, he and Susanna drifted a little back from the others so that they could talk. Susanna again asked about Ariel and how she had reacted to the good news. They talked a bit about Ezra and the horse operations and what Bartimaeus's plans were in that regard and if he was planning to return to work in Herod's guard. She reminded him of how difficult that was for their mother since her husband had been a soldier, and although no one knew what had happened to their father, all assumed that he was on a mission for Herod during which he mysteriously disappeared. Their father had never been one to share such details of his work with his wife or family.

They eventually talked about Gamela and how she was responding to his cure. They briefly spoke of the problem that Saul had caused. Finally, they talked of Monica and how she was doing and what the family could do to support her.

It was midafternoon when they were in sight of their destination that the heavy, dark clouds over the mountains of Jerusalem seemed to explode. They were no longer gray but had turned almost black and had reached higher than any storm clouds that he had ever seen. Suddenly the cloud was filled with lightning flashes that were so massive and so frequent that the huge cloud seemed to be filled with an intense fire. Then, thunder erupted unlike any thunder that he had ever heard. It was an angry roar, like a bellowing from the sky to the earth below. The hills disappeared into the enveloping cloud out of which burst a wall of sand that rushed at them in a flurry. They were blinded as the windblown sand knocked them to their knees. Susanna, Judah and Bartimaeus let go of their baskets and grabbed the children to keep them from being blown away. They turned their backs to the wind and were slammed to the ground by an unrelenting force with the children beneath them for protection. The wind did not cease. Within seconds, they were pelted with hail that beat upon their bodies. The children cried out, and the adults tried harder to pull them under each of them. The hail bit their skin and bounced off. Soon, the ground was covered with white ice balls. As quickly as the hail started, it stopped. Immediately they were drenched with a torrential, driving, cold rain that soaked them and turned the earth to mud. If it had lasted longer, they could have drowned where they lay.

As sudden as the storm started, it stopped. All was quiet. They laid there motionless, shocked, and afraid to move. No one spoke.

BARTIMAEUS, THE BLIND BEGGAR OF JERICHO

Just as Bartimaeus was about to lift himself off the ground, he felt a quiver through his body. He fell back face down to the ground and spread his hands into the mud. He watched as the mud and the water puddles started to shake, then he felt it. The ground was moving, was shaking. All were frightened, and the children began to scream and cry. The adults clung to them and held them tightly now fearing for their own life.

The ground stopped shaking, and all was quiet. It was frighteningly quiet. No one moved. Bartimaeus slowly got to his knees then to his feet. The others likewise rose. They were soaked with water and covered with mud. They looked at each other standing wide-eyed and trembling. First the children reached out, then all clung to each other. Then cries were heard, wounded and inexplicable sobbing fear.

Bartimaeus had lived his life with nature, and as a soldier, he had experienced fear before, but that was a fear of man, never a fear of anything of the world. He looked to the west where the hills of Jerusalem were still draped in blackness like a funeral shroud. He felt completely at the mercy of an unknown power as he did when he stood before Jesus only a few days ago. A sense of overwhelming need to cry out for mercy struck him as once more he spoke with a trembling voice, *"Jesus of Nazareth, son of David, have mercy on us."*

7

PASSOVER

Bartimaeus and Susanna's family were physically and emotionally spent when they trudged up the road to Ezra's house. Bartimaeus, Susanna, and Judah each had one of the three children by their hand to comfort them. Their clothes were soaked, and mud clung to every part of them. Those that were waiting ran to them as soon as they were in sight. The children went along with their mother to Gamela's house to bathe and put on dry clothes. Bartimaeus went with them and gathered clothes for both him and Judah and then returned to Ezra's house to bathe and change.

It was night when they finally reclined for the Passover meal. All that Susanna had prepared was lost when the wind blew the baskets away. The women baked bread. It was warm out of the ovens when they finally ate. All were emotionally spent, and for the most part, they talked about the ferocity of the storm and the terror of the earthquake. There was talk among the adults as to what, if anything, those fearsome events might foretell. Ezra reminded them that on Mount Horeb, Elijah did not find God in the storm or in the earthquake; rather, he found God in a tiny whisper. The children said that they could not have heard a whisper in all that roaring wind and storm. Gamela told them that their God is very powerful and that he does not need to speak loudly to be heard. Mariam asked *ima* if she ever heard God's whisper. Ariel replied that she never heard God's whisper, but she knew that God listened and answered her prayers. She reached over and, with a loving smile, touched Bartimaeus.

Looking at his daughter, Bartimaeus said, "Mariam, I know that you prayed for me to see again—I know that all of you did. I prayed for that every day. At the end, I suppose that I had given up praying. I thought that I would always be blind, that I would never see any of you again. Worse, not only was I blind, but my heart was broken. I was scared, but I was too proud to ask for help. I never talked of this before." He looked at his children, then continued, "When I was sitting at the wall with the beggar before Jesus arrived, I had fallen asleep. I awoke, as I told you, when Jesus arrived, and everyone was calling to him. What I had not told you before was that while I was asleep, I had a dream. I did not recall that dream until after the storm yesterday when I was walking here and we were all so terribly frightened. In that dream, I was alone in a small house in a forest. A man came to the open door, and with a friendly smile, he motioned for me to go for a walk with him. On the walk in the forest, the man told me everything that I ever wanted to know and much more about everything. In my dream, I remember thinking that I must not forget anything that he told me. The man in the dream told me that I would see God's love. He told me all about that love. When I awoke, there were tears on my face, but I did not remember anything except that I was told that I would see God's love. Immediately after that I heard the crowd shouting that Jesus of Nazareth was coming. That dream is what gave me the courage to shout out to him. You know what happened after that. It is strange that I never saw the man, Jesus, who cured me. I have often thought that maybe the man in my dream was Jesus. But since I never saw Jesus, I do not know."

No one spoke until Mariam broke the silence. "Maybe when you see Jesus, he will tell you how you will see God's love, and then you can tell all of us."

"When I find Jesus, I will ask him."

Still holding on to Bartimaeus, Ariel said, "All of this has caused me to wonder. This Nazarene, Jesus, passed through Jericho where you were sitting. Without you seeing him, you shouted out to him, and he cured you. Then he traveled on to Jerusalem. Three days later, on the day before the Pesach, this terrible storm swept down from the hills, and the ground trembled. That has shaken me to the depths of my soul. That has caused me to wonder what Jesus is doing in Jerusalem. We all know that the prophets have not fared well there." Ariel stopped and glanced toward Gamela, but nothing was spoken by either of them. Bartimaeus knew that his mother was thinking of Saul. Looking at Gamela, her expression told that she too was thinking of Saul.

Judah broke the silence. "It has been a trying day. Let us rest and greet tomorrow with refreshed spirit."

Gamela and Susanna gathered the children and went to her house. The others cleaned up from the meal and departed for their beds. Bartimaeus walked his mother to her room. He said, "We know too well that Saul has been a problem between Gamela and me. We know that she was dependent on him as a child and that he was both mother and father to her. His becoming a Pharisee, and worse, a fanatic Pharisee, has turned him against me. I will be going to Jerusalem in a few days, and I will meet with him. We will get this all straightened out, and Gamela and I can return to the life that we had before. I believe that we can make things right again. Thank you for all that you do, *ima*. It is good to be here with you again."

She said, "It bothers me to see you suffering so, and the children too. Now that you have your sight back, I hope that you can put all of this behind you. I hope that Saul is willing to listen to you and to believe that you have done nothing wrong to deserve this. I hope that you can find Jesus and thank him."

"Yes, *ima*. That is my wish too."

Susanna's family could not travel on the Sabbath and had planned to stay one night with Gamela and Ezra after the Pesach. However, their ordeal during the storm required them to stay an extra day to recover. The following morning, Susanna and her family returned to Jericho. Bartimaeus worked with Ezra repairing damage to the stable and cleaning the horses. That afternoon, he saddled a horse and rode out to view the storm and earthquake damage. The road was washed out in several places, and there was some damage to the walls around Jericho.

He wondered how Monica had faired. He assumed that she was all right. Susanna would check on her when she returned to Jericho and would report if Monica needed anything. He thought of visiting her but decided against that. He took a long ride home having convinced himself that it was a good time to school the young horse and relished being on a horse again. He covered many miles on the roads around Jericho before returning home. On the way home, he decided that he would travel to Jerusalem the following day since there was little more that he could accomplish at home.

That evening, he and Gamela talked. He told her of his plan to leave for Jerusalem the next day. Once there, he would visit Hezekiah and tell him that he was ready to return to his duties. Then they talked of his need to find Jesus. To this, Gamela added that first he must speak to Saul about the incident and get his understanding. Then, he must follow the prescribed Laws to be cleansed. He agreed that he would meet with Saul, although his heart was not fully into that.

The next morning, Bartimaeus woke while it was still dark and picked up the clean tunic that Gamela had laid out for him. Before pulling it on, he held it to his face and breathed in the fresh smell and felt the softness that both his wife and his mother had put into the clothing of the family, and he felt a longing to once more share in that tender connection. He walked through the quiet house and out the door.

He saw a light in Ezra's house and knew that Ezra and his sons would soon be going to the stable to tend the horses. Wanting to be alone, he turned toward the pasture where the mares and foals were grazing. In the pasture he savored the touch of each mare and foal. The tranquility of the moment drove him to his knees with tears of thankfulness.

The sun was well above the hills to the east before he rose from the grass. He turned toward home. In the stillness, he wondered what more he could tell his wife and his children for he did not know himself. Entering the house, Saul David and Mariam were at the table finishing breakfast. Mariam ran to him and took him by the hand.

She said, "*Ima* made your favorite breakfast. We were hungry so we started to eat, but you can join us now."

As he approached the table, Saul David rose and came forward to greet him. Putting an arm around his father and looking toward the table he said, "Good morning, *aba*, we did not eat it all. *Ima* told us to save some for you."

The three sat at the table as he filled a bowl and broke a piece of bread. Before taking a bite, he looked toward his daughter then turning toward his son said, "I was in the pasture with the mares and foals. It looks like you have some fine horses that you will soon start training. Do you have a favorite that you are looking forward to?"

His son, not stopping from eating replied, "Oh, I like them all, but I suppose that the grey will be really good."

Mariam, sitting with one leg under her and the other on the floor so as to jump from the table if needed, quickly added, "Ezra lets me ride the old bay mare in the arena. He said that once I am a better rider I will be able to join Saul David when he goes out for long rides."

"That is great Mariam. You always liked to ride sitting behind me and hanging on to my tunic when I would go for rides. I suppose now you will want to ride your own horse."

With a bit of a frown she replied, "I would still like to ride with you, *aba*, like before… but not always."

Saul David had stopped eating and watched his sister and father as they talked but did not join in. He was still looking at both when Gamela entered from the bedroom. Looking at the children she said, your *sava* will need some help this morning. Finish eating and go join her at Ezra's house. You can visit with your *aba* later."

The two finished eating and Saul David was the first out the door with Mariam scrambling close behind yelling, "Wait for me!"

Gamela sat down across from Bartimaeus. She said, "The children don't understand what has happened. They know that you had an accident and that you lost your sight. I tell them that you stay in Jerusalem where you have better treatment to restore your sight. I send them out of the house when my brother, Saul, comes to talk to me." She caught the concern in Bartimaeus's face and quickly added, "He hasn't been here for some time, more than a year."

He nodded, then she continued, "Saul David has learned enough of the Law of Moses to suspect that something wrong has happened, but Mariam just thinks that you lost your sight in an accident and that someday it will come back."

"That is what happened, Gamila. I lost my sight in an accident. I know that! What I don't understand is why Saul convinced you that something else happened and that I am being punished by God for that!"

"I don't understand either Bartimaeus. You were away from me so much in Jerusalem and I must trust my brother. He knows the Law and he lives in Jerusalem. Maybe there are things... well, that he is not telling me."

"There is nothing more to tell." He stopped talking but kept his eyes on her. She was looking down at the table. With a sigh, he, too, hung his head in silence.

He rose and stepped to her side. She remained seated. Reaching down, he placed his hand on hers. "I need to leave for Jerusalem." There was silence as he turned and walked away.

When he entered Ezra's house, the children were sitting at the table with their grandmother. They watched him approach the table, then turned to their grandmother. She nodded to them, "*Sava* needs to talk to your *aba* before he leaves."

They quietly rose and left the room. He sat next to her, and she leaned over to put her hand on his.

"They don't understand. They don't know what to think. I told them that it is good that you are home and that you will be staying."

"I hope so, *ima*, but I don't know. I had hoped that Gamila would be glad that my blindness was over and that I could return home. But I don't feel that."

"This has been hard for her too. She does not know what to believe. She needs time. This cure may be more troubling to her than your blindness. With that, she had hope that she or someone else could fix what had happened. Maybe that her brother would say prayers to God to make you better. Now she doesn't understand how you could be cured when all else failed and you cannot explain it to her."

"I can't explain it to myself."

"The children are happy that you are back. They told me. Ezra's family is happy that you are here, and they are ready to return to the way things were before this terrible thing happened to you, to all of us. And I am so happy to have you with us again. I thanked God last night and again this morning. It will take time for Gamela, but she still loves you. Please believe that. She needs to know that you love her, too. Be patient with her. Show her your love. That is all that she needs."

He stood and reached for her hands to help her up. She stood and he put his arms around her, and she hugged him. He whispered, "I love you, *ima*. And I love Gamila. I will be patient with her." He could feel his mother tremble as he held her for a few moments close to him. She watched him as he turned and walked out the door.

Ezra was waiting for him at the stable. The young horse that he was to deliver to the guard in Jerusalem was saddled and it stamped the ground impatiently ready to go when Bartimaeus arrived. He embraced Ezra, "Thank you for taking care of *ima*." Ezra nodded, "And the children and Gamila." With nothing more that could be said by either man, he mounted and left the stable. He kept a close rein on the spirited horse as he walked away. At the road, he turned south toward Jericho and Jerusalem.

He came to the north gate of the city. He stopped and looked at the gate where he had met Jesus, and he thought again of Bar-El. He continued on the road outside of the wall and shortly came to the west gate where the road turned toward Jerusalem. He again stopped, and this time thought of Monica. He told himself that he must turn his attention away from Bar-El and Monica and even Gamela and his family. He knew that for the days to come, his efforts must be toward finding Jesus and to a meeting with Saul.

That day, since walking away from Gamela and the children asleep in the house, he had been haunted by the anxiety of leaving what he knew and going to what he was not sure of. Several times that morning he had wanted to turn back, but he knew that not continuing would haunt him worse then returning home. Now, with Jericho only a short distance behind him, he was once more seized by uncertainty and fear and, worse, by an empty feeling of abandonment. He neither wanted to go to Jerusalem nor to return home. His senses were blaring. He was aware of every detail that surrounded him—sights, sounds, movement of the horse—and he found comfort in none of it. His mind was buzzing with thoughts of seemingly inconsequential events of the last few days. A feeling of complete inadequacy overwhelmed him. He felt trapped within himself. He swung down from the horse and pulled off his hat and cloak and threw them across the saddle. He tried to take a drink of water, but he could hardly swallow. He stood there, looking up and down the road, and he thought, *My God, why has this feeling come back to me? I do not need this, not now. Stop! Breath! No more!*

He took the reins in his hands and continued walking up the road toward Jerusalem. He stopped and put his hat back on. He tied the cloak to the saddle and remounted. Then, he put the horse into an easy canter toward Jerusalem. He had only gone a few strides before he sat back into the saddle and spun the horse around. He squeezed, and the horse sped toward Jericho.

Entering Jericho, he went to a stable and told the boy to pull the saddle off, but that he would be back shortly and to keep the horse ready. He threw the cloak to the boy and told him to keep it with the saddle.

When he entered Monica's house, she was sewing a piece of cloth on her lap. She looked more beautiful than he had ever seen her. He remained fixed in the doorway wondering how he had never noticed such beauty in her before. She had looked up as the door opened, and on seeing Bartimaeus emerge, she was spellbound. Neither moved nor spoke. He watched her as the sunlight from the window began to sparkle in her eyes. He saw tears roll down her golden cheeks. Her lower lip and chin tightened. She stood, and the cloth dropped to the floor at her bare feet. She cried with a breaking voice of a child waking from a bad dream, her arms hung at her side with white knuckles showing in her tightly clenched fists. "Bartimaeus, what is going to happen to me? What is going to happen to us?"

He watched her as tears splattered to the floor. He felt strangely at peace, a peace that he had not felt in a long time. He stepped out of the doorway toward her. Slowly, not taking his eyes from her for fear that when he looked back she would have changed, he closed the door behind him. He went to her with her arms and fists frozen at her sides. He embraced her, and she leaned, melting softly into him, and wrapped her arms about him. She stood on her toes and stretched her head up and tenderly kissed him on the lips.

Part 3

Jerusalem

8

Jerusalem

Bartimaeus woke that morning while it was still dark. He moved slowly so as not to disturb Monica, but before his feet touched the floor, she had her hand on his bare back. He turned to look at her, but neither spoke. Their eyes said all that was necessary. After a few moments, he said, "I must leave." She nodded. He got up and began to dress.

As she pulled the blankets off, he turned his back to her. When he was finally dressed, she came around wearing a white tunic with her hair tied and hanging down her back. She said, "Can I make you something to eat before you go?"

"No, I should leave now. I want to get to Jerusalem as soon as I can."

"Let me get some food to take with you."

He started to object knowing that he could get food at the guard stations along the way but stopped when he saw the wetness in her eyes. He warmly smiled to her. "Yes, some of your bread would be wonderful."

She wiped a corner of an eye with her finger and went to the table. He watched her bare feet move quietly across the floor. She cut bread into pieces and wrapped them in a cloth. Then she cut a piece of cheese and wrapped it separately. She placed them both in a cloth pouch and tied it closed. With both hands, she carried it to him and stretched out her arms while looking into his eyes. He reached out one hand to take the package and with the other grasped both of her outstretched hands. He leaned over and lightly kissed her on the lips. She stood motionless. He turned and, without another word between them, walked to the door. Without looking back, he opened the door, walked out, and closed the door behind him. Outside, he stood for a moment but knew that he could not go back in. If he did, he knew that he would never leave.

When Bartimaeus entered the stable, a man greeted him. "You did not return to get your horse yesterday. My son pulled the saddle off and fed him. He said that you did not look well when you arrived, so he was not surprised that you did not return. He said that he has seen you before but did not know who you are." The man looked to Bartimaeus for a reaction and, finding none, said nothing more.

Bartimaeus handed him two coins. "Thank you. My plans changed unexpectedly. I am sorry if it caused any concerns."

The man saddled the horse and brought it out. He handed the cloak to Bartimaeus. "Here. You may need this. I pray to God that we never have a storm again like the other day. Even the ground shook. It terrified the horses—it terrified me!"

Bartimaeus nodded to the man then, taking the reins, led the horse out of the stable and through the gate before mounting and walked the horse toward Jerusalem on the road known as the Way of Blood. That rugged road followed a valley with an ephemeral stream cut through the surrounding rocky hills. The recent storm had damaged that important travel route, and there were numerous places where the raging water of the other day had overflown the banks and washed out the road. In other places, large boulders were left where the flood waters had deposited them. There were still remnants of running water along the way. Although the road generally followed the stream, there were places where the stream was incised into the rocky hillside where the road could not go.

Midway between Jericho and Jerusalem was an oasis enclosed within formidable rock and separated from the road by an outcrop of large boulders through which was a path wide enough for a small cart to pass. The path opened into the grassy basin with a cobble streambed passing through it. The stream had cut through narrow rock crevices at each end, and the only way to enter or exit was through the boulder-lined path. The oasis itself near the center of the basin was surrounded by old large acacia trees that provided cooling shade. Bartimaeus seldom stopped there, but on that day, he turned off the road and entered. Once inside, he dismounted and walked the horse to the oasis where the horse stuck his muzzle in the pool and lipped the water noisily then sucked in the cool water. When the horse was finished, Bartimaeus led it to some grass. Standing beside and holding the reins, he let the horse graze. This oasis was in a desolate, rock-covered region with nothing except the grass and trees that were sustained by the water within the basin. It was far removed from any area where shepherds grazed sheep, and for the most part, the oasis was only used by travelers. But then, only by the most wary travelers and never after dark. The road itself, though much used, was notorious for marauders and thieves. The oasis, being secluded, presented an even greater risk and was generally avoided except under extreme need for water or by well-armed travelers. Even with his sword at his side and with a reliable mount, Bartimaeus kept a watchful eye on the opening through the boulders for anyone that would join him. Despite the peril, he marveled at the beauty of the area and promised himself to look for other opportunities to enjoy its serenity even with its veiled dangers.

    He opened the saddle bag and removed the bread and cheese. He allowed himself to recall the peace that he had felt with Monica last night. He wondered if that peace were meant for him, a peace that he wanted, that he deserved, and whether he could find that same peace again with Gamela. But he also knew that the price of that peace with Monica would come at a cost, a cost not only to himself but to others. He did not need to make that decision now, but someday he would. He returned the bread and cheese and carefully closed and tied the bag. He held it a few seconds longer before placing it in the saddlebag.

    On the journey, his mind had been at rest as opposed to the day before when he had ridden to Jericho. On this day, his mind was clear as he went over all that had happened and what he must do. First, he needed to go to the barracks and talk to Hezekiah about resuming his duties. He assumed that that would not be a problem. Hezekiah had always taken special interest in him and his brother. Certainly, he expected to return to the guard, although, he anticipated that Hezekiah would demand that he take it easy and not rush into work too soon. He remembered that was also Gamela's warning. That was good with him because it would give him time for the second task, which was to find Jesus and talk to him. Thinking of those two tasks gave him a clear purpose and calmed his mind. Like the soldier that he was, he planned every action until he was confident of its expected outcome. But as a solider, he was also prepared for the unexpected.

Try as he might to stay focused on those two thoughts, he could not keep his mind from wandering to Gamela and to Monica. Thinking of either was troubling to him, and when he became conscious of those thoughts, he would squeeze the horse into a canter. The familiar rhythmic motion and gentle rocking would soon clear his mind.

Riding a horse was calming and comforting to him. All other thoughts would vanish; there was no pressure, no external demands, only being in tune with the amazing creature with which he was intimately joined. The only thing that mattered or existed was the present. His body would become one with the horse. Every movement of the horse was met with a corresponding, unconscious response of his body, and every change in his seat or legs or hands was to transmit an intended cue to the horse. This was indelibly programmed into the rider and the horse from countless repetitions. At the canter, his mind was at rest, and he was at peace.

Today, the young horse was responding well. Although not fully trained, he would bring the horse down from a canter to a trot and then to a walk. After calming the horse and letting it relax, he would return the horse to a trot then a canter, alternating right and left leads. He laughed to himself and stroked the horse's neck each time that the horse executed those moves correctly. Soon, the horse was picking up the left lead and the right lead on cue and without rushing. Bartimaeus relished the simplicity and tranquility of those moments. At such times, he was at peace, with nothing else on his mind than simply being in harmony with a beautiful, powerful, fellow creature.

Bartimaeus arrived in Jerusalem midafternoon and entered a gate near the barracks and stable. He did not know the stable caretaker, and without being in a soldier's uniform, he was unknown to the man. However, the man saw the quality of the horse, and with a coin pressed into his hand, he took the reins and led the horse to a clean stall. From there, Bartimaeus went to the barracks which was close to the palace of Herod Antipas. After a short walk, he stopped in the shadow of the building and recalled the many times that he had entered or exited that building and ridden through the gate. Those were good times. He was a valued member of the guard. He had responsibility, not only for training the horses but also for training the mounted soldiers—a very select and privileged group. They were not the main fighting element; that was reserved for the infantry. The mounted soldiers were the messengers of Herod, the commanders in the field, and they carried out special assignments. Bartimaeus had risen quickly in the ranks. Being the son of a distinguished mounted soldier had its advantages. Then, having the commander, Hezekiah, as an old family friend had its benefits. Bartimaeus was aware of his good fortune, and because of that, he always worked hard to avoid criticism for his favored position. Bartimaeus went to the big iron and wood door and rapped the brass knocker several times. He heard footsteps and finally a voice. "Who is there?"

He called back loudly, "It is Bartimaeus."

The window opened, and the doorman said, "What are you doing here at this hour, Bartimaeus? Do you need lodging? You should have come earlier, but I suspect that I can find something for you. Come in, come in. How have you been?"

Bartimaeus stepped in, and without pause, he reached out and grabbed the arm of the doorman. The doorman, not expecting that, was shocked and looked directly into the other's face. Bartimaeus smiled. "Hey, old friend, it is good to see you!"

"What? You can see? I cannot believe it! I saw you only a few days ago. You have been blind for what, about two years."

"Yes, for three years. And now I can see again."

The doorman was stunned, and Bartimaeus pulled him close and threw his arms around him. "This all happened only a few days ago, and honestly, I am not used to it myself. I think that I could really scare the others, couldn't I?"

"Yes, you probably could put the fear of the gods into that band of ruffians. But I do not recommend it. No telling what they might do to you!" Reaching out and squeezing Bartimaeus's shoulder, he said, "Let us go. I want to see everyone's shock."

The two men walked down a hall that opened into a courtyard that served as a meeting and training facility. Around the perimeter was a wide portico with tables and chairs interspersed between doors that opened into rooms for the officers. There were a few soldiers relaxing and talking or playing betting games.

When they entered the courtyard, the doorman shouted, "Look who is back! It is Bartimaeus! He can see again! The horse gods brought him back to save them from your iron hands and your lazy feed-sack asses! Ha-ha!" He slapped Bartimaeus on the back who joined in the laugh.

The men ran to him, grabbing him, and peering into his face and eyes to find evidence of his cure. They plied him with questions, which he answered in no coherent fashion but which satisfied their curiosity. When that had run its course, he turned to the doorman. "Do you know if Hezekiah is in?"

"Well, I do not know," he replied, "but let us go and see if we can find him." They turned down another hall and, after passing several open doors, came to the end of the hall with a large, closed door. The doorman knocked and heard answer from inside.

"Come in."

The doorman opened the door but did not enter. Pushing his head in, he said, "Look who has returned!"

Hezekiah looked up from his table covered with scrolls and a map and answered the doorman's announcement with a blank stare. Then his eyes went to Bartimaeus still standing in the hall a step behind the doorman. He said, "Bartimaeus, welcome. You have already returned from Jericho? I thought that you would stay longer this time."

BARTIMAEUS, THE BLIND BEGGAR OF JERICHO

The doorman laughed heartily and, with his hand on Bartimaeus's back, gave him a shove through the doorway. "He is back because he can see again!"

Hezekiah placed both hands on the table and sat motionless looking directly at Bartimaeus. Then he rose and hurried to him. Grabbing Bartimaeus by the shoulders, he said, "This is remarkable! Great news! I could not have wanted better! When did this happen? Did the doctors find a cure? Your eyes look normal. I do not see any marks. How did this happen?" He dropped his hands from Bartimaeus's shoulders, and he clutched both of Bartimaeus's arms above the elbows and gave him a shake. "Come inside. We need to celebrate." He pulled Bartimaeus into the room.

With that, Hezekiah and the doorman exchanged glances, and the door closed leaving the two together. Hezekiah motioned toward the chairs, and Bartimaeus immediately began to tell the tale over again. When Bartimaeus said the name Jesus, he noticed that Hezekiah pursed his lips and frowned. Bartimaeus paused on seeing the reaction, but since Hezekiah did not interject comment, he continued with the story to its end. When finished, they sat quietly for a bit, then Hezekiah leaned forward and peered directly at Bartimaeus. He spoke slowly and directly. "So Jesus of Nazareth is the man that cured you?"

Bartimaeus, being somewhat taken aback by Hezekiah's manner, responded directly with emphasized clarity, "Yes, and I need to find him and talk to him."

Hezekiah, not changing his position or eye contact, stated flatly, "He is dead."

There was silence. Neither spoke. Finally, Bartimaeus said, "How could he be dead? I just saw him. He was going to Jerusalem."

Hezekiah, with all the compassion of a father telling his son bad news, told him that Jesus was executed by crucifixion last Friday, right before the Pesach.

Bartimaeus was stunned. He sat in disbelief not knowing what to say. The inevitable words fell from his lips, "Why?"

Hezekiah stood and went to a table and poured two generous cups of deep red wine. Coming back, he handed one to Bartimaeus.

Sitting down, he proceeded to tell how Jesus had entered Jerusalem, and the people had welcomed him as a prophet or possibly even as the Messiah. But not all were pleased with his return to Jerusalem. Many of the temple priests, Pharisees, and members of the Sanhedrin spoke against him and warned the people that he had not been acclaimed by the leaders of the temple. They spoke of him as a sinner and even as a false prophet. There was much confusion by the people as to what to believe. Were they to welcome him and listen to his words, or to reject him until the Sanhedrin decided? Most agreed that Jesus was a miracle worker and a man of mystery. One certainty was that the high priest and some of the Sanhedrin were strongly opposed to Jesus and declared him a heretic and blasphemer. They plotted to have him arrested and executed. This past Thursday night, he was arrested by temple guards and brought before the Sanhedrin. He was sent to Herod and from there to Pontius Pilate. Out of fear of an ugly disturbance and possible public riot, the Romans crucified him.

Bartimaeus sat shaking his head. He stood and walked to a window. He placed his hands on the windowsill and leaned over. He pushed himself off and spun around. "How could they do this? He was a good man. No one else could heal me. Only someone that has God's favor could do what he did. Why?"

Not having an adequate answer, Hezekiah said, "I do not know. People sometimes make decisions that they regret later. Regret with a passion. At times, we can be very weak, Bartimaeus. I know. I have had to do things that I later regretted. Then we try to make amends for those bad decisions. We do things to be forgiven without ever asking forgiveness…because we believe that we cannot be forgiven."

Bartimaeus leaned forward and looked intently at the man that was like a father to him. It seemed there was more that Hezekiah wanted to say. Then Hezekiah broke eye contact, and Bartimaeus leaned back. With outstretched arms, he pleaded, "How can anyone make amends for killing a good man?"

Hezekiah shook his head. "I suppose, Bartimaeus"—he paused looking for the right words—"in that case, one does the best that he can and begs for forgiveness in his heart." With no further reaction by Bartimaeus, he continued, "I do not know if we can believe this or not, but there is word among the people that Jesus still lives. After a few days, his tomb was empty. His body was gone. There are those that say that he is alive, resurrected from the dead, they say. Others, especially those that listen to the priests, say that his followers stole his body. I do not know, Bartimaeus. I do not know what to believe."

Bartimaeus sat down. He leaned forward. With intensity of action, he said, "These followers of his, where do I find them? I met one of them."

"I do not know. The rumor is that they are hiding. They fear that the Sanhedrin will want to put them to death, at least have them imprisoned. So far, Herod has stayed out of this, but his actions will be what he sees as best for him. Who knows what will happen?"

The two men sat in quiet sipping their wine, each immersed in his own thoughts. Finally, Bartimaeus broke the silence. "Do you have a room for me here? I have much to do tomorrow."

"Come," he said, "I will give you one of our finest rooms, and I will have the porter prepare a bath and a meal for you. Welcome home."

9

SAUL OF TARSUS

When Bartimaeus returned to his room after taking a bath, there were fresh clothes folded on the bed including a soldier's uniform and new sandals on the floor. A cavalry sword, longer but lighter than that of the infantry, hung in a scabbard on the back of a chair. There was also a white tunic made of fine cotton for sleeping. He pulled on the tunic and set the clothes that he had worn on a shelf. Of all the worries and concerns that had haunted him for so long, returning to the guard was the easiest and the only one that was finished; he was a soldier again.

His mind returned to the two tasks ahead of him. First, and most importantly, he needed to find Saul. He took a deep breath when he thought of how Saul might react to learning that he was cured by Jesus of Nazareth. Regardless, Saul's acceptance of that was necessary not only to be ritually cleansed but to do so as Gamela demanded. He shrugged that thought off and turned his attention to the other task: to find Thomas, the twin. He was the only person that could tell him of Jesus. He wished that he could immediately start to look for Thomas. He dreaded talking to Saul. Besides, he never talked to Saul; he just listened to him.

There was a knock at the door, and a servant entered with a tray of warm food—bread, a clay pitcher of water, and a brass pitcher of wine. He set them on the table and poured water and wine into brass cups. Then, he left with a sincere welcome home to Bartimaeus.

Bartimaeus immediately realized how hungry he was. He broke off a piece of bread and ate it with a cube of meat from the bowl. The food and the wine were thankful relief to his body, and they brought a semblance of peace to his mind and spirit. After a while, he laid on the bed and pulled the blanket over him.

He rose before daybreak, as he was accustomed, and put on his fresh uniform and new sandals. He picked up the sword and pulled it from the scabbard. It was a fine officer's sword. He felt the sharp blade and fine handle. It felt good in his hand. He held it to the light then picked up the scabbard and thrust the sword back into it. He hung it back on the chair. He would not need a sword today.

He was greeted by many of his friends and comrades as he walked through the halls and entered the dining room. He sat at a table which soon was filled with those that welcomed him back and that wanted to congratulate him. Everyone wanted to know how he was cured, but he just responded that he had been cured a few days ago and that he really did not know how. Although that answer may not have been completely true, he did not know how he had been cured or why. He only knew that a man from Nazareth, named Jesus, had cured him, and that man had been put to death here in Jerusalem.

The dining room was almost empty, and the last person had welcomed him back when Bartimaeus rose and exited the room. He was walking down the hall when he heard a man behind him call his name. He turned as the man in uniform approached.

"Bartimaeus, I heard last night that you had been cured and that you are back. I did not want to disturb you last night. Surely, you wanted your rest, and you must be tired of telling your story. I understand that the Nazarene that was crucified by the Romans cured you. Does that worry you that maybe you were cured by a lawbreaker, or worse, that you may soon go blind again?"

The fact that the man speaking to him had neither greeted him nor wished him well was not lost on Bartimaeus, nor was the man's disparaging grin. The man was well muscled and confronted Bartimaeus as if prepared for battle. Bartimaeus thought that is the nature of the man. Maximus was a Roman citizen that had earned that distinction by fighting many battles for Rome throughout its empire. Maximus had been assigned to Herod's guard at the request of Pontius Pilate, and he was the head of the infantry for the guard. Bartimaeus was the head of the mounted soldiers, but Maximus made it clear to all that he was the second-in-command behind Hezekiah. He was a man that enjoyed the power of authority without any regard for its responsibility. Bartimaeus had often seen Maximus abuse that power with others, especially with the lesser soldiers. Bartimaeus did not care for the man, and that had been well expressed between the two of them in the past.

Bartimaeus recognized the unpleasant sound of Maximus's voice before he turned around. "No, Maximus, I do not worry about such things. I have little concern about those that break our Jewish Laws, and I have no more control now over going blind again as I did the first time."

The man's grin faded, and his voice took on a challenging tone. "I understand that you visited Hezekiah as soon as you arrived. I suspect that he was pleased to have you back so that you can return to coddling those weakling excuses for soldiers atop those stinking animals that you are so fond of. A real soldier fights with a sword or a lance with his feet on the ground." He almost spit out those last words.

"Maximus, I am glad to be back among men that may not always do what is right but that earn the honor and trust of each other. That is something that you never managed to receive or deserve, and for that, you are the lesser man."

The two men pierced each other with their eyes. They had never been friends and had often confronted one another in performing their duties. Maximus was the bigger and stronger man, while Bartimaeus was the lighter, more agile, and skilled fighter. They had never come to fully testing the other, but that was something from which neither would walk away.

Maximus's eyes went to Bartimaeus's belt. He said, "I see that you are not wearing that fancy cavalry sword. Maybe it is too heavy for you or the horses to carry. A real soldier carries and uses a heavy, broad sword sharpened on both edges of the blade."

Without breaking eye contact, Bartimaeus said, "I see that you have your broad sword at your belt as always. Do you still have that dagger concealed under your cloak in the back?"

The menacing smile returned to the man's face. He reached behind him with his left hand and pulled out a long, curved dagger. He held it up toward Bartimaeus. "I took this off the first man that I killed. He did not know how to use it. I showed him. I enjoy showing it to others. Maybe if I am lucky, I will show you someday."

"Maximus, my mother told me not to spit in the water. I may have to drink it someday. Someone better than you may show you a better use for that dagger."

Both men knew that there were to be no more words. Only action was left as an option to either. Both knew and had avoided that. Bartimaeus turned and walked away knowing that someday walking away would not be an option.

Bartimaeus exited the barracks through the main door that faced the new palace of Herod Antipas. A busy street separated the two buildings. To the left, the street led to the temple. He turned to the right and walked toward the Roman fortress. The Romans, once they occupied Jerusalem, had taken possession of the palace of Herod the Great and had added the praetorium where Pontius Pilate lived. He passed by the Gennath gate that led to Golgotha. From there, he turned left past the Roman fortress. It was then a short walk to the Essene quarter with the high priest's house and the Pharisee school.

On the walk, his thoughts went to Jesus. It was only a few days since Jesus, after his arrest, would have followed those same streets from the Sanhedrin chambers at Caiaphas's house, to Herod's palace, then to the praetorium, and from there through the Gennath gate to Golgotha. He could not comprehend how the leaders of the Jewish religion and the rulers of the country could have found reason to execute the man that had mercy on him when no one else had. He shook off the question of what he would have done as a soldier if he had been there and had known of the miracle worker from Nazareth, Jesus. But then, he only knew little of Jesus even now except that he had cured him.

His thoughts returned to Saul. He suspected that he could find Saul at the Pharisee school since he was studying under Gamaliel, one of the most distinguished teachers and Sanhedrin member. If not at the school, he could either learn where to find Saul or, if necessary, leave a message for him.

It was a good walk with no distractions. It provided time for him to prepare to tell Saul about his cure and to seek his guidance as to what he must do to be cleansed. The ritual baths were nearby, and he hoped that he could satisfy all requirements quickly so that he could devote his time to finding Thomas and other followers of Jesus. He had occasionally visited Saul, usually to deliver a message from Gamela, and he was hopeful that he could find him this morning.

He went by the house of the current high priest of the temple, Caiaphas. Adjacent to that house was the building that contained the Sanhedrin chamber. Past that, he turned down a smaller street, and shortly he was at a building that was used by the Pharisees for study and meetings. Bartimaeus entered the modest building and was met by a doorman, who upon recognizing the uniform of Herod's guard, brusquely asked his purpose. Bartimaeus told him that he was looking for Saul of Tarsus. The doorman remained seated while surveying the unexpected visitor. After a feigned display of the doorman's importance that clearly sent the intended message to Bartimaeus, the doorman asked his name. Without further word, the doorman rose and exited down a hallway.

A few minutes later, he returned, sat down, and without looking at Bartimaeus informed him that Saul would join him shortly. Bartimaeus waited and soon realized that the delay was likely meant as a clear message from his brother-in-law. Growing impatient, he stepped out of the doorway. At that, he heard the doorman abruptly scurry down the hallway. In a few minutes, Saul appeared in the doorway.

Without any greeting to his visitor, Saul announced, "I was told that one of Herod's guards was here to see me and what name he had used. He said that you were in a uniform of Herod and that you were not blind. As you can imagine, I doubted that it really was you.

I went to a window to watch who would leave the building. When you stepped out, I saw that it was you."

Saul stopped talking. Bartimaeus waited, but Saul offered no additional explanations or greeting. With none coming, Bartimaeus responded, "I came to tell you that I have my sight back. Gamela wants me to inform you and determine what I need to do to be cleansed."

The two men stood assessing each other. There was no love lost in the encounter, each waiting for the other to make the next overture. Saul stepped through the doorway and said, "Follow me." Saul walked briskly with Bartimaeus following a few steps behind. Once past the building, Saul turned into an alley. From there, they entered a small side gate that led to a courtyard behind the building. Once inside, Saul said, "Tell me how you got your sight back. Tell me everything."

Bartimaeus proceeded to tell him the essence of his cure while intentionally leaving out certain details that he had always gladly shared with others. He noticed that when he said that it was Jesus of Nazareth that had cured him that Saul's eyes blazed with more self-righteous indignation than he had ever seen before. When he was finished telling Saul all that he thought necessary, Saul glared at him as if Bartimaeus had just told a repugnant tale. He spit out the next words. "You got your sight back from that Nazarene. He was an evil blasphemer. You cannot be cleansed!"

Instantly, the years of pent-up rage boiled within Bartimaeus. He wanted to reach out and bring an end to the source of that turmoil and pain. He thought, *After all this, I have been cured, and I am being denied the one source of relief that can restore me to my family and my wife.* If the two men had been crazed animals, they surely would have pounced on each other in a struggle which only one could survive.

Taking a deep breath and blowing it out, Bartimaeus said, "I have heard that this Jesus was crucified. I never met him other than when he cured me, and even then, I did not see him. How can you judge me unworthy to be cleansed? I am not his follower. I do not even know him."

Saul looked him up and down, and Bartimaeus knew what he was thinking. Saul said, "You are a sinner. God punished you for your sins. You were not cured by God. You were cured by a blasphemer. The Sanhedrin judged him according to the Law. He said that he was the son of God. That is blasphemy. The Law demands that a blasphemer be put to death. The Sanhedrin did what the Law commands. The Nazarene blasphemed the name of God. He was put to death as the Law commands."

Once more rage rushed through Bartimaeus's body. He could no longer tolerate being in Saul's presence. "Saul, you and your Laws can go to hell!" He could not trust himself any longer in Saul's presence. He turned and hastened to the gate.

As he was leaving, Saul yelled, "Go, and stay away from me and my family! I will tell Gamela that you have blasphemed, and she is to have nothing to do with you ever again."

Bartimaeus stopped. His right hand instinctively moved to where his sword would have hung. He touched the bare belt, then he drew his hands into clenched fists before him. He dropped his hands and banged the gate open. As he did, he wished that he had never known Saul, and he intended to never have anything to do with him again.

10

THOMAS DIDYMUS

Bartimaeus was anxious to put space between himself and Saul. From the alley, he returned to the main street. He did not have a destination in mind; he simply wanted a diversion for his mind and spirit. He walked with no purpose and delayed at the shops and markets along the way. He looked back on how the journey to Jerusalem had been filled with optimism. He had been reunited with his family, and although not all was as he wished with Gamela, he had a clear path to regaining her heart. His optimism had been dashed when he got to Jerusalem and learned of the death of Jesus. And now, his meeting with Saul was worse than he had feared. On that hung much of his fate with his wife. Worse, he did not know how to solve that dilemma.

Then, this morning, before he embarked on what he intended for the day, he had the unpleasant encounter with Maximus. So far that day, he had twice turned his back and walked away from adversaries. With neither could he find reason nor a remedy for the situation. He shook his head as he recalled that it was only yesterday that he met with Hezekiah. Before that, all had been good. He had been filled with optimism. That optimism was clouded when Hezekiah told him of the death of Jesus. How quickly life's events can turn. He looked back on how serene and simple it had been in that one-room house with Monica. He wondered if all that he was attempting to do could be accomplished. It would be easy to return to Monica, too easy. And if he did, the haunting uncertainty would seize his mind and drag him away from her. He could not bring another heartache to her. Monica deserved better than him.

He wandered aimlessly in the lower part of the city, then turned his direction toward the temple. He had to find Thomas, and although Jesus had been crucified for blasphemy, it seemed plausible that his followers would be found at the temple or that people there would know of them. Along the route, he came upon the hippodrome which was built by Herod the Great and was modeled after the Roman circus. There were no horse or chariot races scheduled for that day, but the manager of the stable, recognizing the uniform of Herod's mounted guard, allowed Bartimaeus to enter.

He went to the stable. It had a long, wide walkway with stalls on each side. There were a few horses standing at their stall doors with their heads hanging over. Saddles and tack hung along the walls. The sounds and smells were a comfort to him, and soon his mind was clear of his wasted effort with Saul and senseless meeting with Maximus. He walked from one stall to another, calling each horse to him, touching it on the head and neck, talking to it, and assessing its fitness and conformation. There was no urgency to be elsewhere. At the end of the line of stalls, he decided that he would go directly to the guard's stable and that a ride would relax and clear his mind.

He picked up the pace of his steps and shortly arrived at the stable. He instructed the attendant to brush and saddle his horse. He mounted and rode past the Roman fortress and its towers and exited the city walls at the Gennath Gate. He had no intention of schooling the horse nor did he have a destination in mind. Rather, he let the horse walk on a loose rein, the horse's head hanging toward the ground and swinging lightly from side to side in rhythm with the strides. He thought how relaxing it is to be joined with such a fine creature and communicating with it in the simplest and purest manner. That communication, when performed by the rider with a bit of skill and practiced with an abundance of patience, could be rewarded in a dance of paired harmony.

Within minutes he walked past Golgotha. He stopped and looked up the rocky trail to the site of the gruesome crucifixions.

He thought that was a barbaric form of death that the Romans had brought to the land. In Jewish Law, stoning was the prescribed means of delivering a death sentence, at least that was quick, if not merciful.

The gate that he had come through and the trail that he was on was the same that Jesus had walked carrying the beam of the cross on which he was to be nailed. He counted the days. It was only six days since Jesus died and nine days since he had been cured by Jesus. So much had happened in those nine days, and he still had no answer to any of it.

He continued his ride around the city walls. In a short while, he was on the east side of Jerusalem. He paused at the entrance to the Garden of Gethsemane. He had learned that that was where Jesus had been arrested by the temple guards. From there, Jesus had been taken through the Sheep Gate, past the temple, and to the Sanhedrin council where he was tried and found guilty of blasphemy. Again, Bartimaeus was haunted with the question of why.

Passing by the temple on the outside of the wall, he came to the road that turned toward Jericho. He stopped and looked down that road. He thought of the comfort that he could have with Monica. All that was necessary to have that comfort was to simply turn down that road. He could be with her again that day. But he thought of Gamela and his family. There was also comfort to be had in returning to the life that was his before tragedy struck them all. He looked at the hills around him. Although rocky, the land was green. It had bushes and small trees. There were grassy patches where rainfall gathered. He saw several children playing as they tended the family's sheep. He recalled the dream that he had about seeing God's love, and he remembered Jesus's words to him that he would see again. He was seeing again, but not only with his eyes. He was seeing things differently now. He wondered if both the dream and Jesus's words were the same message for him, and he trusted, if so, the meaning to that message was to be found in Jerusalem, not in Jericho. With that, he squeezed the horse's sides and continued following the city wall.

It was midafternoon when he reentered the Gennath Gate. He dismounted and walked the horse back to the stable. After leaving the stable, he felt refreshed, and he set off to find Jesus's followers, particularly Thomas. The temple was the likely place to start his search. He had already decided, based on his unpleasant meeting with Saul, that it was not likely that he would be well received by the temple priests or the fanatical Pharisees. He thought that the best source of information would be from the merchants and money changers at the temple. They were there on a regular basis, and it was to their advantage to know people.

Arriving at the temple, he walked around the portico where he stopped to carefully question people about Jesus and his followers. He soon found that men were generally unwilling to answer his questions, especially since he wore the uniform of Herod. Several of the women, not as intimidated by the uniform and being more receptive to a pleasant smile, were willing to talk to him. All knew of Jesus and his followers. Many spoke sadly of his death. He also learned that since Jesus's death, none of his followers had been seen at the temple. One elderly woman said that she had heard Jesus talk and had seen his peaceful ways. She could not understand why others would judge him so harshly. She said that she lived in the Essene quarter and that Jesus and his followers had been seen there. Maybe he should go there to look for them. It was getting late, and he had no desire to return to the area where he had met Saul the previous day. He would go there when he was fresh and in better spirits.

He returned to the barracks and had a servant deliver food to his room. He was in no mood for conversation or to engage with others, and he certainly wished to avoid another confrontation with Maximus. It had been a busy day, and he replayed the events of the past few days. He tried to shut out any further thoughts of Saul and Maximus. Rather, his thoughts kept returning to where he had been that day, especially the Garden of Gethsemane and of Golgotha. He fell asleep picturing Jesus, the man that had cured him of his blindness, being tried and crucified without anyone coming to his defense. He again wondered what he would have done if he had been there. Was there anything that anyone could have done? Mostly, why did that happen to Jesus? Could Jesus not have prevented that? Especially if he had the power to return to life. It was a mystery that he could not understand.

The next day, he awoke early and dressed in the clothes that he had worn from Jericho. He had learned the day before that it was not to his benefit to wear the uniform of Herod when trying to find the followers of Jesus. He followed the same route that he took the day before when he went to see Saul. This time, he headed directly to the area of the ritual baths. He laughingly thought to himself that he would not expect to see Saul or any self-righteous Pharisee at the baths since they would surely think that they had no need to be cleansed.

When he arrived at the baths, there were shops nearby where merchants sold goods. There were also several open canopied booths with tables and benches where food and drink could be purchased. He found one with an unobstructed view of the bath. He chose a booth where a young woman was serving patrons. He sat at a table, and the woman brought him a plate with bread and cheese and a cup of water. He ate slowly, not being in a hurry to move on. She returned to his table several times to refill his water and to ask if he needed anything else. Having established an easy rapport with her, he took a chance to ask her help in finding Jesus's followers. On her return to his table, he said, "Excuse me. I wonder if you could help me."

Smiling, she said, "I will, if I can."

"I have not been in Jerusalem much for the past three years. I was injured and was often in Jericho where I live. During the time that I was away, much happened here. Something that is very important to me." He paused to gauge her reaction. Seeing none, he continued, "I know nothing of this man Jesus, except that he was put to death by the Sanhedrin and the Romans a few days ago. I am trying to find his followers. I was told that they were seen here before he was killed."

He saw her expression change. She furrowed her brow and set her chin. She glared at him and said, "He was a good man. He helped many people. And he spoke kindly to me and to others. He brought comfort to many. His followers are good men." She paused, crossed her arms, then added, "And women too. Even his mother was here with them, but I have not seen them since Jesus was crucified, and I will not say or do anything that would bring harm to any of them." She repeated with emphasis, "Not to any of them."

He immediately sensed her sincerity and the danger that Jesus's followers were in. He leaned back and said, "I hope that you can believe me. I have no intention to harm any of his followers. I did not know Jesus, but he cured me when I was blind. I want to learn about him. I have only met one of his followers. His name is Thomas, and I understand that he may be called Didymus. He is the one that I am looking for."

She eyed him carefully and saw truth in what he said. "I know Thomas. He is a good man. He has taken the death of his friend very badly. I see him every day sitting over there by the pool. Just sitting there looking at it. Sometimes he buries his face in his hands. I think that he is weeping. I do not see the others, but I know they are close by. They were all near here before Jesus was taken. I suspect that they are afraid. I do not blame them."

Bartimaeus measured the trust that he could place in her then said, "I saw Thomas only once and at that time I was distracted. I may not recognize him. Can you help me?"

Without hesitation, she replied, "He is about your age. He is nice to us. We like serving him. If you want, you can come back this afternoon and I will point him out to you. He is here every day. I suppose that he will be back later."

He put two coins in her hand and thanked her. She nodded and smiled. He immediately returned to the guard barracks and made his way to his room without being noticed. He would have several hours before returning and hopefully finding Thomas.

When he did return, she motioned him over and said, "He just arrived and is seated as always." She pointed him out. He thanked her and proceeded to him.

He walked over and sat down beside Thomas. Without looking his way, Thomas said, "I am sorry, but whatever it is, I cannot help you."

Bartimaeus reached out and put a hand on his shoulder. "Do you remember me? We met last week in Jericho."

Thomas turned to him and without expression, he said, "Yes, you are the blind beggar."

"I am sorry that I did not come sooner, but I had many things that I had to do in Jericho first."

"You do not need to apologize. It does not matter when you would have come. It does not matter now."

"It matters to me. I do not know anything about the man that cured me. I never even saw him. I need to know. I remember that he said that I would see. I do see. You know that. But I think that he meant more than just get my sight back."

"He is dead. There is not anything more to know."

They sat in silence before Bartimaeus spoke again. "I hear some people say that Jesus is alive. Some say that he came back from the dead. Even that people have seen him."

"Yes, others say that they have seen him. I do not understand what has happened. I loved him. His father and mine were brothers. I grew up with Jesus in Nazareth. Almost in the same house. We have always been together. That is why they call me his twin. We even look alike. We worked together. We were builders in Nazareth. When he left home, I went with him. We have never been apart. I believed in everything that he said and did. Then they killed him. I should have had them kill me too. I need to go back to Nazareth. I cannot help you. I cannot be hurt anymore."

"You have talked to your friends then?"

"Yes, every day one of them comes here to talk to me. They will not leave me alone."

"Thomas, you are lucky to have such friends. They must love you. When I was struck blind, I lost everything that was dear to me—my job, my home, my family. But through it all, there was one person that did not abandon me. If it had not been for her, I would have lost my mind, lost my will to live. She never asked for anything. She listened to whatever I had to say. She comforted me in my need. Eventually, she was all that I had. I did not realize it then. I needed her. She saved me. When I was blind, I leaned on her. I trusted her in everything. I would never have made it without her. Maybe your friends are like her. If so, I suggest that you cling to them." They sat in quiet, then Bartimaeus added, "In her care for me, I found a love that I thought was lost forever. Thomas, maybe if you let your friends care for you, you too may find the love that you thought you had lost."

Thomas turned to him. Tears welled up in his eyes. He tried to talk but could not. Finally, he managed to say, "He used to call us his friends. He even called Judas, the one that betrayed him, *friend* that night in the garden. What you just said made me remember that."

Bartimaeus stayed and sat with him. Neither spoke. Bartimaeus recalled the times that he, like Thomas, had suffered in his mind, in silence. He remembered the day that Jesus cured him sitting at the wall with Bar-El. He thought how often we need someone; the times that we too must be the source of comfort and strength to one another.

As the sun set, the shops closed, and those at the baths departed. Thomas stood and reached his hand down to Bartimaeus. The strong hand and arm easily helped Bartimaeus to his feet. They stood not releasing their grip on the other.

Bartimaeus broke the silence. "I hope that I can see you again. I need to know more about Jesus."

"Come again tomorrow. I will be here."

They departed, each with their own thoughts of what the morrow would bring.

When he returned to the barracks, Hezekiah was waiting for him and said, "Bartimaeus, I understand that you have been very busy. But the horses are getting more of your attention than your friends."

Bartimaeus laughingly responded, "Yes, but my friends tell me that I communicate better with horses than with them, and lately I can assure you that they are correct. And better, with a horse, I seldom have serious disagreements. Maybe it is best for all that I stay with the horses."

He noticed Hezekiah looking at his clothes. He realized that he was out of uniform, and Hezekiah was probably wondering why. Bartimaeus anticipated the question and said, "Oh, I was looking for someone at the baths, and I did not want to alarm anyone that it was official business. The uniform and new clothes are greatly appreciated. Thank you. Everyone here has been helpful. Well, almost everyone."

Hezekiah shook his head apologetically and said, "I heard about your encounter with Maximus. I am sorry. You two have always had bad blood between you. I should have sent him off to another post. Maybe I will do that yet. But it is best for me to keep an eye on him here. He can be a problem. I will try to keep the two of you separated." They looked at each other and shrugged their shoulders almost in unison and said, "Good luck with that." And both laughed.

Taking Bartimaeus by the arm, Hezekiah said, "I hope that you can spare an evening for old friends. My wife and I would enjoy having you join us for dinner. Rachel will want to see you. There is much to celebrate."

"Yes, of course I will join you, but much has happened today, and I need to be alone tonight."

"When you come, wear that new uniform. Rachel will want to see you at your best." Then he added, "You can leave the sword here. The conversation will be gentle!"

They laughed, and he added, "Gentle will depend if we avoid speaking of certain distant members of my family!"

They embraced and then walked to their rooms. On the way he smiled and was anxious to be with Hezekiah and Rachel again. They were like family, almost like parents to him. He loved them both. They always had stories to tell him of when they were young and good friends with Timaeus and Ariel. It would be good to be with those that he loved like family.

He awoke early the next morning and put on his uniform then went to the stable. He visited briefly with those that he met there. He asked if there was a horse that could use some schooling. They brought out one that they said was a problem lately and no one wanted to ride. He took time to brush the horse and to pick its hoofs. He saddled it and mounted. They rode out the gate to the training arena. As he rode, he had no expectations for the horse. He kept everything simple, working just to gain the trust and confidence of the horse. He found nothing wrong with the horse but recognized that the horse was very sensitive and that it would take a patient and attentive rider. Such a rider would be rewarded with an exceptional horse, one that would do all that was asked of it with trust and confidence. That was all that could be desired between a horse and rider. Bartimaeus let the reins slip through his fingers as the horse hung his head in a smooth, relaxed walk back to the stable. Bartimaeus promised himself that no one else would ride that horse until he found the proper rider.

He left the stable with a light heart and an easy step. He wondered whether he or the horse, both of which had started the morning a bit tense and uncertain, had come away more relaxed and at ease. He was glad that the horse had worked its magic on him. He hoped that he had done the same for the horse, and he believed that he had.

After leaving the stable, Bartimaeus went directly to the baths. He sat at the table, and the young woman from yesterday brought him food and drink. When Thomas came into sight, Bartimaeus rose and walked toward him.

They met, and Thomas spoke, "I did not recognize you until you stood and started walking toward me. You are a soldier for Herod."

"Yes, but not really much of a soldier. My family raises the horses. That is why I was in Jericho last week."

He sensed an ease with Thomas that was not there the day before. Thomas continued, "After you left, I thought about what you said. I thought about the woman that you told me about. She had not deserted you when you needed someone. What struck me the most was that you called me friend. I thought about how many times Jesus had called a stranger friend. And he called us his friends. Even as a child in Nazareth, he often called others his friend. I thought about my friends. I had abandoned them in my grief, but they did not abandon me. I know that they want to help me. They are my friends. I have been selfish. Some of them came to me last night. They asked me to join them for dinner tonight. I am going to do that. It has been almost a week since Jesus died. It will be good to talk to them, to be with friends."

Bartimaeus smiled. "That is good. Can I see you here tomorrow...friend?"

Thomas took ahold of Bartimaeus's hand, and with the other clutched his elbow, he replied, "Yes, I will see you tomorrow...friend."

11

JOSHUA

The next day, Bartimaeus waited for Thomas at the baths, but he did not return. The previous evening and that morning was a time of hopeful expectation that he would finally get answers to his questions and, most importantly, learn of this mystery man, Jesus. While waiting for Thomas, Bartimaeus casually asked people if they knew of Jesus and, if so, their reaction to his rejection by the Sanhedrin and execution by the Romans. To some, Jesus had been found guilty of blasphemy by the religious leaders, and since they could not carry out the prescribed death sentence, they had Herod Antipas and Pontius Pilate do that for them. To them, that was lawful and proper. For others, they shook their heads and told of the good works that they had seen Jesus perform. He was aware of Jesus's good works, and no one that he talked to told of any evil that Jesus committed. He wondered why a good man should be put to death. What puzzled him more was that some saw the goodness in Jesus while others rejected Jesus based on the word of others. Where was the truth to be found?

While waiting for Thomas, he thought of life's ironies. Less than two weeks ago, he had been set free of terrible suffering of body, mind, and soul. For three years, he had been blind, and as a result, he had been stripped of his manhood, his life's work, and reputation among others. Worse, he had those most dear torn from him. Now, after being cured, everything in him shouted at the injustice of being denied the joy that should be his. Why did Gamela continue in her doubt of his faithfulness to her, to deny him his children? Why is the source of his cure regarded as a lawbreaker and criminal? And why did the religious leaders and civil authorities see fit to have this man crucified? Even the man that he served, Herod Antipas, had played his role in the death of Jesus. He was still unable to learn anything about Jesus. His only hope was with Thomas, and he was not to be found.

In talking to others, he learned that when Jesus died, there was a terrible storm and that the earth shook. He knew those to be the events that he had witnessed as he walked with Susanna and her family to his home. He also heard rumors that the curtain before the holy of holies in the temple had been torn at that time. He wondered if those were a sign from an angry God. Or maybe a sign of an evil power being released or being vanquished in the world. Those events and questions added to the mystery of this man, Jesus, and he could not be at peace until he found the truth. The truth that would set the course for his life. A truth that would truly set him free.

He stayed at the baths until sunset. The market closed, and the baths became deserted. He slowly found his way back to the barracks. He needed a diversion and some companionship, so he went to the common area. He mingled with his friends and met some new ones. All were glad that his sight had returned. They knew the story by now, and other than passing comment, that had become a moot point. One of the new, young soldiers introduced himself to Bartimaeus. His name was Joshua, and he said that he was very glad to meet Bartimaeus and that he was also from Jericho, and he knew of Bartimaeus's family horse farm. He said that he often saw Bartimaeus and his brother training the horses and that he dreamed of being a mounted soldier someday. He was about ten years younger than Bartimaeus, and the two found much in common and spent enjoyable time talking.

When the men went to dinner, the younger man kept up a running dialogue about horses and riding which Bartimaeus thoroughly enjoyed. That was a welcome diversion to keep his mind off other troubling matters. Toward the end of the evening, Joshua informed Bartimaeus that, although he had no experience with horses, he would request Hezekiah to allow him to try out for the mounted unit. Bartimaeus sat back and considered what Joshua had just said. What he was suggesting would be unusual. Most of the mounted soldiers had prior experience with horses. Neither he nor his brother had needed to make that request. Rather, Hezekiah had expected them to be mounted soldiers when they joined the guard. Bartimaeus appreciated Joshua's attitude and enthusiasm. He smiled and nodded his head. He said, "That would be good. I hope that you are successful. I will be starting training at the stable soon. Come by when you are free from your other duties. You said that you have never ridden before. Is that correct?"

He responded, "That is right. Only in my dreams."

Bartimaeus stood and stuck his hand out to the younger man. "I will put you on a horse and see if you can stay on or if you fall off."

Joshua rose and pumped Bartimaeus's arm. "I will. I will see you at the stable as soon as I am able. Thank you."

That evening visiting old friends and making a new one had refreshed his spirit. His visit with Joshua had him thinking of training the horses and riders. He was excited to get back to what he enjoyed. He would return to the stable the next morning. It was time. He thought of Joshua and hoped to see him again.

12

THOMAS AND MATTHEW

The next day, after returning to his duties at the stable, he was ready to return to the baths and renew his search for Thomas. The previous evening with Joshua and the morning with the horses had left him optimistic, and he anxiously set a fast pace. As he came through the street into the opening, he could see the baths area, and he strained to look for Thomas, but he was not to be seen. He walked to the center of the open area and carefully scanned every face. He saw the area where he had met Thomas two days ago, and he went there and sat down. He presented a strange sight sitting at the baths in his guard uniform, and he garnered questioning looks and suspicious stares from many.

The sun was setting when two men entered from a side street. They stopped and looked his way. They both had scarfs covering their heads and much of their faces. One of the men, looking his way, turned to the other nodding. Bartimaeus stood when they proceeded toward him.

When they got close, one of them pulled the scarf from his head and, with a smile, stretched out his hand. It was Thomas. He said, "Bartimaeus, thank you for coming today. I am sorry that I missed you yesterday. I was delayed by a visit from another friend. A friend that you already met but you do not know yet." With a contented smile, he turned to look at the other man then turned back to Bartimaeus.

He said, "Bartimaeus, I want you to meet Matthew. He is one of Jesus's followers and my very good friend. Thank you for reminding me of my friends the other day. After we parted that day, Matthew found me. The words that you spoke made me listen to what Matthew said. He told me again of those that have seen Jesus, and he told me that they had seen Jesus in the upper room where they are staying. He convinced me that I needed to be with my friends. I went with him last night. It was good. Everyone was glad to see me. They were all so happy. They told me of seeing Jesus. They said that he had returned. It was good to feel their happiness, but I did not believe what they were telling me. I was afraid of being hurt again. What if they were wrong? What if it was not Jesus that they saw? Forgetting what you told me about being with friends, I started to go to the door when suddenly Jesus appeared in the room. I could see him. He glowed. He was beautiful. He called me by name to come to him. He held out his hand and showed me the marks of the nails. He opened his cloak and showed me the wound in his side. I knew that it was him. I knew then that he had risen from the dead. That he truly is God. He is both man and God. I called him my Lord and my God. He said that I believed because I saw him. Then he said, 'Blessed are those who have not seen yet believe.'"

Thomas stopped and looked as if reading Bartimaeus's mind. "You never saw him. I hope that you believe what I am telling you. Jesus told you that you would see. I hope that you see that he is God. Only God could do what he has done. Only God could return to us after being crucified. He is our Lord."

Bartimaeus replied, "I believe what you are telling me, but I really do not know what to believe, if that makes any sense. You have known him all your life. You have seen all that he has done. You have seen him alive again. I have not. I want to believe. Will you teach me?"

"Yes, yes. Of course, I will teach you. I want to tell you all about him. And Matthew will help. He is very good at telling stories about Jesus. All day today he was reminding us of the stories and the words that Jesus said. We talked about what Jesus's words meant.

Jesus called God his Father. Now we know that Jesus is God, the Son of God. Those words have meaning to us now."

For the first time Bartimaeus felt like he was finally going to learn about Jesus. He wanted to hear all that he could. He wanted to start then. Matthew saw the look in Bartimaeus's eyes. "Yes, we will tell you everything. We want to tell everyone. But we leave tomorrow for Galilee. Jesus told us to go there, and he will see us again. We leave early tomorrow morning." Thomas put his hand on Bartimaeus's shoulder. "I will find you when I return. I promise, my friend."

13

BARTIMAEUS AND JOSHUA RETURN TO JERICHO

After Thomas and Matthew departed, Bartimaeus had a lonely, longing inside of him, a longing that could not be satisfied by anyone at the barracks. Normally, when he had such feelings and was away from those that he loved, he could quell those feelings at the stable. Even if he did not ride, for him, that tranquil environment would quiet his empty heart. That evening, he had no desire to be with others. His longing was for Gamela. That was a feeling that he had not had in a long time. He thought of the times when he and Gamela had been together in Jerusalem. That was in the early years of their marriage before they had children. She would travel with him to Jerusalem in a chariot. He would drive a team of horses with her standing at his side holding tightly to his arm. In Jerusalem, they would stay with Hezekiah and Rachel. Although they enjoyed their time with their hosts, they mostly enjoyed their time alone. When they could, they would walk the streets in the evening, stopping to shop or to enjoy a simple meal together, just the two of them. After a few weeks, she would return to Jericho, but Bartimaeus would stay in Jerusalem. At those times, Gamela would travel under the protection of an escort of soldiers provided by Hezekiah. Hezekiah arranged those escorts as if he was protecting his own daughter. Gamela would tease Bartimaeus that Hezekiah cared for her better than he did. Bartimaeus would act jealous, and they both would laugh. They both knew, and cherished, the love that was given to them by Hezekiah and Rachel. That was a simple time with precious memories.

Not being in a hurry, he decided not to return directly to the barracks. He left the bath and passed through the nearby Essene Gate. Once through the gate, he walked on the trail outside of the wall. It was not long before he came to the turnoff to Jericho. He remembered being there just a few days ago. Then, he had been tempted to take that road and return to Monica. This evening, his thoughts were of Gamela, and he longed to return to her. But he knew that the comfort that he sought would not be found at the end of that journey. He continued his walk and passed the gates that led to the temple. Soon, he came to the footpath to the Garden of Gethsemane. He turned and walked up that narrow, rocky trail through the olive trees. His thoughts went to Jesus and his apostles. Jesus had been arrested in that garden less than two weeks ago. On that evening, his apostles had abandoned Jesus and fled.

It was a pleasant evening, but he was glad that he had worn his cloak. He left the path and sat with his back against an old olive tree. Although not needed for warmth, he wrapped the cloak about him. As he did, he recalled sitting at the wall of Jericho when Thomas had taken him to Jesus. At that time, he had left his cloak on the ground in his hurry to go to Jesus. He did not want anything to delay him. His thoughts went to Bar-El, and he hung his head to his chest. He hoped that Bar-El had forgiven him for not asking Jesus to also cure him. He folded his arms tightly about his chest and frowned. He felt that he had abandoned Bar-El, and he wondered how he could have done so.

He leaned back and looked up at the night sky. There was no moon, and the stars shined brightly in the total blackness. His thoughts returned to the followers of Jesus. They had abandoned Jesus on that moonlit night. He pondered what it is that causes men to think only of themselves and to abandon others in time of need. As a soldier, he was instructed to band together against an adversary. If soldiers understood that fundamental principle, why did not others? Why not for friends? Why not for those that are most loved?

Those were questions that he could not answer. Jesus did not know him, yet he had cared for him. He was told that Jesus often did the same for others. He leaned back and closed his eyes. He wondered what Gamela was doing, and he again dreamed of being with her.

It was late before he rose to return to the barracks. He entered the city through the Golden Gate and walked past the temple. Soon, he knocked at the door of the quiet barracks, and the watchman welcomed him.

The next morning, Bartimaeus met with Hezekiah. Understanding Herod's complicity, if not his tacit participation in the execution of Jesus, Bartimaeus could not speak candidly to Hezekiah of his desire to learn of Jesus. Rather, he simply told Hezekiah of his meeting with Saul and of his intention to comply with the requirements of ritual cleansing so that he could return to good graces with Gamela. Hezekiah was very supportive. He told Bartimaeus to take whatever time necessary and that he could adjust his duties with the guard as needed. Bartimaeus explained that there was not anything specific that he could do in that regard. Although he made it sound like he expected to remedy the situation with his brother-in-law, Saul, he realized that the path to reconciliation with Gamela lay in learning of Jesus. That could only be done through Jesus's apostles. They had returned to Galilee, and he did not know when, or if, they would return.

He had two paths before him. If, in meeting with the apostles or by other means, he determined that Jesus truly was a blasphemer and a false prophet, then he could presumably reconcile with Saul and be cleansed. That was a clear path to returning to Gamela. Although that path meant rejection of Jesus, something in which he found no comfort. The alternative path was one in which he could not justify Jesus's crucifixion by the authorities. A path that would lead him to believe that Jesus was doing God's will and that Jesus was a prophet or even the Messiah sent by God. With that path, it was likely that Saul would not change his posture toward him as a sinner. If so, that would continue to be an impediment to reconciling with Gamela. There was nothing that he could do in either eventuality at this time. He must wait until Thomas and his friends returned to Jerusalem, if ever. He also realized that any association with the apostles could put him, and possibly Hezekiah, at risk with Herod and the Roman authorities. He decided that any future contact with Thomas and his friends that he would not wear his guard uniform. That would be best for all involved.

After telling Hezekiah all that he thought necessary at that time, Hezekiah told him that he would arrange a meeting with the senior officers to inform them that Bartimaeus would return to his duties of training the mounted soldiers and the horses. Hezekiah invited Bartimaeus to join Rachel and him for dinner that evening. Rachel was anxious to welcome Bartimaeus home. They parted with Bartimaeus thanking Hezekiah for not abandoning him through his ordeal of the last three years.

As Bartimaeus started to walk away, he stopped and turned back to Hezekiah. He said, "I know that I never said this before. I wish that I had. I have been seeing things differently lately." He stopped, then added, "I hope that you know that I always loved you like the father that I never had." There was silence, and Bartimaeus immediately regretted saying that. Maybe Hezekiah did not share that feeling. Bartimaeus was about to walk away when Hezekiah spoke.

"You did not need to say that, then or now. I could never be the man that your father was. I did for you and Barariel what your father would have done if he were here. That is all that I could do. All that I must do." There was silence as the two faced each other. Hezekiah continued softly, "But thank you for telling me. I will tell Rachel what you said. That will make her happy." Bartimaeus nodded to him then turned and walked away.

He spent the rest of the day at the stable and the training arena appraising both the horses and the new riders. Most of the horses came from his family's horse farm and those he knew well or had previously trained them. A few horses had been added in the last three years, but those were not completely unknown to him since he knew of their breeding. Likewise, he knew most of the mounted soldiers, but there were a few younger soldiers that were new to him. He thought of Joshua and his desire to join the mounted unit. He had taken an immediate liking to him when they previously met at the barracks. That Joshua was from Jericho and had grown up tending animals, although not horses, was also in his favor. He would put in a good word for him with Hezekiah. It would be good to bring a young, inexperienced rider along that was fresh and that did not come with riding techniques or habits that he had to correct. He looked forward to the young man joining him. Maybe Joshua would share his passion for horses. Maybe Joshua would help to fill the void that the death of Barariel had left. He hoped so.

He had a pleasant evening with Hezekiah and Rachel. Hezekiah informed him that the other soldiers were glad to have him back and resuming his duties. They talked about Joshua, and Hezekiah said that he would look into having him assigned to the mounted unit. Rachel soon demanded that they no longer spoke of the guard, and their attention turned to happy times together.

Hezekiah and Rachel had three daughters but no sons. Maybe that contributed to the almost paternal attitude that Hezekiah had toward him. Two of the daughters were married. Only the youngest joined them that evening. Although a few years older than his daughter, she reminded him of Mariam, and it was medicine for his soul to be with her.

Within a few days, he was fully into his schedule. He rose early while still dark and arrived at the stable. He would leave a schedule of the horses to be worked each day, and the first would be saddled and ready when he arrived. He typically worked with eight horses each day. The younger ones required a bit more time, and he enjoyed seeing them advance in their movement and acceptance of his aids. He liked to rotate the veteran horses through his routine, checking on their conditioning and working on improving their movement or correcting a bad habit that had developed. The training of the horses continued through the morning, then he would take a well-needed break. The afternoons were spent with the younger soldiers, typically on well-trained horses. Usually there were three or four riders in those training sessions. After those scheduled rider training sessions, he would stay at the stable to work with any of the veterans that wanted his advice and help with a horse or to tend to a horse that may be recovering from an injury or lameness. He enjoyed being with the horses and with the men at the stable that cared for the horses. Often, they were older soldiers that could no longer serve on active duty but found comfort with men and horses that had been their lives' work. Bartimaeus's closest companions had always been the riders that shared his affection for these magnificent animals and shared his passion for the subtle art of communication and willing partnership between two fellow creatures.

It was a few days into his normal routine when Joshua arrived at the stable and excitedly told Bartimaeus that he had been instructed to go to the stable for training, and if he had the talent, that he would join the mounted unit. Bartimaeus congratulated him and poked fun at him for thinking that a sheepherder from Jericho could ever learn to ride; maybe at best, he could learn enough to not fall off.

For the next several weeks, Joshua spent all his available time at the stable. He not only attended the schooling sessions for which he was scheduled, but he stayed to watch other riders and listen to Bartimaeus's training sessions. When he did not have other duties, Joshua would be at the stable in the morning when Bartimaeus was working with the younger horses. He wanted to learn all that he could about training a horse. He would also be at the stable in the evenings to learn about the care and feeding of the horses. He was particularly interested in the treatment of injured or lame horses. He wanted to learn anything and everything about not only riding but tending to horses.

Joshua was talented but more importantly a dedicated student. It did not take long before he was a solid and reliable rider. The fine nuances were yet to be learned, but he could ride with confidence and skill. There was no doubt that he would be a fine horseman. The days and weeks of practice and learning from all that Bartimaeus taught him was showing in his skills and accomplishments. He was already a better horseman than some of the veterans.

The cool days of spring had turned into early summer. Bartimaeus was arriving earlier at the stable to work the horses, and the afternoon sessions with the riders were becoming long, hot work. It had been more than a month since he had returned to Jerusalem, and he had no communication with Gamela or his family or Monica during that time. He looked for a reason for a return visit to Jericho and a break from the rigors of work and the noisy bustle of Jerusalem.

For Bartimaeus, horses should be in pastures, not confined to a stall. But in Jerusalem, that was not possible. The best that he could manage was to rotate a few horses at a time from duty in Jerusalem to the farm in Jericho. This was also a good opportunity for the men to spend a long day in the saddle without the rigor of training. Usually, he would take several men with him to deliver horses to his farm and to bring fresh ones back. But that required more responsibility on his part to manage the men who typically would stay at the quarters of Herod's summer palace. There were two veteran horses that could use a few months of pasture turnout, and he used that as a reason to return to Jericho. He was pleased with Joshua's progress, and since Joshua had family in Jericho, that solved the problem of Bartimaeus needing to manage Joshua's stay while in Jericho. When he told Joshua of his plan for him to travel with him to Jericho, he was delighted. That not only provided an opportunity to visit home and family, but it provided more time to learn from Bartimaeus and to visit the horse farm.

The two of them left early one morning and arrived in Jericho midafternoon. They went directly to the horse farm. Once there, Bartimaeus introduced Joshua to Ezra and to those that tended the farm. Saul David was working with Ezra and was glad to see his father. After a short greeting, Saul David said that he would go tell his mother and Mariam that his father was home. Bartimaeus instructed the workers to turn the horses out for a well-deserved rest. They were to select two horses for the return to Jerusalem in two days. With that done, he took Joshua with him, and they walked to Gamela's house.

Gamela and Mariam were waiting when they arrived at the house. Mariam was anxious to hear of any exciting news from Jerusalem, but her eyes often strayed to the young, handsome man that was with her father. Gamela was very welcoming to Joshua and invited him to stay for dinner. She also said that he could stay with them at their house. Joshua thanked her and explained that he was anxious to return to his home and to visit his family. All understood, and after a brief discussion by Bartimaeus with Joshua about their return to Jerusalem, Joshua said goodbye to all and departed for the walk to his home.

Bartimaeus had a brief visit with Gamela and the children then said that he must go to his mother. Joining Ariel, the two sat outside in the shade of a tree, and he told her all that had happened since his return to Jerusalem. He started by informing her of his meeting with Hezekiah and his return to training the horses and riders as before. Then he told her about Joshua, his progress with training and his growing fondness of the young man. He then told her of his disappointing meeting with Saul. That, of course, meant that he would not have good news for the ritual cleansing and reconciling with Gamela. Worse was the news of the man that had cured him, Jesus. He told her that the Sanhedrin had denounced him as a blasphemer and had him put to death. Ariel was truly saddened to hear the details that he told her.

He informed her of his meeting with Thomas and Matthew and the story that they told him about Jesus returning from the dead. She was receptive of the idea that God can work such wonders and even recounted some stories from the scripture of remarkable and mysterious events that their God had performed in the past. It was uplifting for Bartimaeus to hear his mother talk in such positive manner. They concluded by discussing how and what he would tell Gamela, and how she was likely to take news of Saul's opinion of Jesus and therefore the stalemate in Saul's stand regarding him. They ended with her optimistic words that Gamela would certainly realize that her husband was a good man, a faithful husband, and a much-needed father. It was good to be with his mother, and he returned to his house thankful that he was home.

When he returned to the house, Gamela sent the children to Ezra's house to visit. He then proceeded to tell her of all that had happened. That telling was much the same as with Ariel. However, for Gamela, he told of the meeting with Saul in a more positive tone, and he downplayed the meeting with Thomas and Matthew. He tried to convey a spirit of optimism and that he simply needed to resolve the question of who Jesus was and to convey that to Saul to get his acceptance. Finally, he ended with an expectation to have all this behind him and for them to return to the way things were before his accident. She agreed that she, too, was optimistic and looked forward to resuming their life together.

Bartimaeus spent the next day with Ezra at the stable appraising the horses and making plans, as needed, to continue to provide mounts for Herod's guard. The next morning, he said goodbye to Gamela and the children, then he went to Ezra's house and did the same. He left the house with arms locked with Ariel as they walked to the stable. Two horses were saddled and ready. He told his mother that he would visit Susanna on the way out. He gave her a final hug and kiss then mounted and led the other horse down the road to Joshua's home.

He gathered Joshua and told him of his plan to visit his sister in Jericho, and they departed. He knew that he would also visit Monica, but he would not mention that until after they left Susanna's. When they arrived in Jericho, they went to the stable and told the man that they would be back in a short while. The man recognized Bartimaeus but said nothing.

They walked to Susanna's and entered. As always, he and Susanna laughed and saw humor in so much of what each had to tell. She shook her head and remarked that Saul should let his sister live her own life. She was much more interested in what Bartimaeus told her about Jesus, but he was careful of what he said with Joshua there. She was shocked to learn that Jesus had been put to death in Jerusalem. She was angry when he told her about the Sanhedrin's actions and about the barbaric cruelty of the Romans. She wished that God would once more smile upon His people but mostly that the people would return to God as the prophets had so often warned them. There was sadness in her voice when they parted. He did not say anything to her about Monica, but he suspected that she knew that he planned to visit her, too.

It was a short walk to Monica's. He told Joshua that he had another family member to visit, then they would be on their way. Joshua assured him that there was no urgency. He enjoyed meeting Bartimaeus's family, and he could feel the warm affection that Bartimaeus and Susanna had for each other.

They arrived at Monica's house, and he knocked on the door rather than walking in. She opened the door, and their eyes were instantly fixed on the other. She took a little step forward then stopped. Her eyes went to the man standing behind Bartimaeus. She lowered her gaze as she realized the reason that he knocked before entering. If he would have been alone, she would have rushed to his arms, and that is what she desperately wanted to do. She let her arms drop to her sides, and she did not let her expression betray her emotions and needs. She instinctively shot a glance at Joshua to see if he was reading any of the feelings that she was desperately trying to hide. Seeing none, her eyes went back to Bartimaeus. She spoke, trying to keep her voice still. "Bartimaeus, what a wonderful surprise. I was not expecting you." She stopped and felt her lip quiver. She looked away from him and continued, "I have been thinking of you and wondering how you are doing in Jerusalem."

He nodded and replied, "It has been good. I am back with the guard." He glanced toward Joshua and said, "This is Joshua. He is new with the guard. I have been training him. We arrived only a few days ago, and we took the horses directly to my farm. He is from Jericho. He stayed with his family. I stayed at home. There is never enough time when I get home. You know how that is."

She responded, "Yes, I know that you are very busy at the farm with the horses…and with your family." She moved her eyes to Joshua and said, "It is nice to meet you. You are lucky to work with Bartimaeus. I know that he is good with horses." Then she added, "And people too. Please come in."

Bartimaeus turned to Joshua and saw a big boyish grin on his face. He was looking directly at Monica, and Bartimaeus had to grab his arm to break the trance and get him to move through the doorway. Inside, Monica scurried about making her guests comfortable. As soon as she could, she pulled up a bench across from Bartimaeus, put her hands in her lap, and said, "Well, tell me everything that has happened. Do not leave anything out."

She beamed at him and sat as attentive as a child waiting for a present. He told her of his return to work and how much he enjoyed that. He also gave her an abbreviated telling of his meeting with Saul.

Finally, he told her of the shock that he had when he learned that Jesus had been put to death before he had a chance to meet him. Then he provided the same, safe version of his account with Thomas that he had given Susanna. She had questions about Jesus and why he had been put to death. That troubled her, but she did not pursue that since Bartimaeus had no details other than what he had learned from others.

He asked how she was doing, and she responded that she was fine and busy. She told him that she often visited Susanna and had begun working for Susanna's husband. It helped her to stay busy, and it provided money to support herself.

After they had each finished updating the other, there was silence. He longed to continue talking, to listen to her stories, to spend the day with her, to not return to Jerusalem until the next day. He frowned and regretted that he had brought Joshua with him. At that, he turned his head toward Joshua and noticed that he was still smiling at Monica. She simultaneously turned her attention toward the stranger, and when she saw him smiling at her, she looked away. Bartimaeus noticed her reaction, and with a look of strong reproach toward Joshua, the young man stopped grinning and looked away from Monica.

The three sat for a moment in an awkward silence before Bartimaeus stood and, stretching his hands toward Monica, announced that they needed to be on their way. Monica rose and took both of his hands in hers. There was no joy in either of their voices as they spoke. Joshua, with a straight face and moving toward the door, thanked Monica for her hospitality. He opened the door and walked out. Bartimaeus and Monica stayed frozen, each knowing what the other wanted, what the other needed, but which neither could give. They squeezed each other's hands. He turned and walked out. She went to the door, stepped out, and watched them walk away.

Joshua stayed a few steps behind as Bartimaeus set a fast pace to the stable. Bartimaeus paid the man and mounted. Once through the gate, he spurred the horse to a fast canter and rode until out of sight of the walls of Jericho. He pulled up, and Joshua shortly joined him. They rode on in silence.

Eventually, Joshua felt safe to talk. "You said that we were visiting a relative. Monica is not your sister. Who is she?"

"She is my brother's wife." Not another word was spoken.

14

THE APOSTLES RETURN TO JERUSALEM

When Bartimaeus and Joshua returned to Jerusalem, it was nearly seven weeks since he was cured by Jesus. He looked back on all that had happened during that time but regrettably concluded that none of the most important goals had been accomplished. Further, he had no assurance that he would learn of Jesus, and without that, his reconciling with Gamela was doubtful. Every day he walked to the bath hoping to find Thomas. The waitress had become accustomed to his arrival, and seeing him, she would just shake her head. Thomas was not to be found.

It was a few days before the Hebrew great feast of Shavuot, the festival of the first fruits. During that feast at the end of the grain harvest, many Jewish travelers from around the world converged on Jerusalem to offer the first fruits of their labor from the fields at the temple as the Law commanded. During that time, the streets and bazaars were filled with people. Other than his daily walk to the bath, Bartimaeus kept himself confined to the barracks and to the training stable. Many of the soldiers, especially those that were Jewish, took advantage of the festival to enjoy the varied sights and sounds of Jerusalem and the added emphasis on the activities of the temple.

It was late one afternoon when a group of soldiers came to the stable looking for Bartimaeus. When they found him, they were anxious to tell him of what they had seen at the temple. They said that there were several men that they believed were Galileans. One of the soldiers said, "They are telling everyone about this Nazarene named Jesus that was crucified here in Jerusalem. They are saying that he has come back to life, that he has appeared to them. Is that not the man that cured you in Jericho? It is amazing. A huge crowd is gathered there. And listen to this: everyone there says that they understand them in their own language! The Galileans are saying that Jesus is the Son of God. Many in the crowd had heard Jesus talk in the temple and had seen his miracles, and they believe what they are hearing. They are asking what they need to do and are told to be baptized in the name of Jesus, the Christ of God. You should go and listen to them."

Bartimaeus handed the bridle that he was holding to one of the men, and to the one that was talking, he said, "Take me!" The men that entered the stable, and all that were in the stable followed Bartimaeus as he departed for the temple. When they arrived, there was a huge crowd all with focused attention on one man speaking from the steps leading up to the temple. He was older than Bartimaeus with a full beard and a bald head. But Bartimaeus was not interested in him. He wanted to find Thomas. He began to work his way to the front through the crowd. Seeing his intent, his soldier friends took advantage of their authority as well as their strength to forge a path for Bartimaeus. Soon he was standing at the bottom of the stairs where the man was speaking. From there he scanned the faces of the other men that were with the speaker, but Thomas was not there. He noticed off to the side were other groups, presumably around other speakers. He headed in that direction. When he got there, he found two or three men in the center answering questions from those in the crowd. Finally, after several attempts, he found Thomas in the center of one of the groups. By now, the soldiers that had accompanied him had drifted off on their own. He was left there in the crowd listening to Thomas and the others talk about Jesus and answer questions. Little by little those in the crowd went away, usually in groups of two or three men talking amongst themselves. He heard many comments telling of their experiences with Jesus, telling of what they had heard, and of the miracles that they had seen. Eventually, there were only a few talking with Thomas. Finally, all left. Thomas looked up and saw Bartimaeus. Thomas opened his arms and walked over and embraced him. "My friend, it is good to see you. So much has happened since I last saw you that it will take many days to tell you. I am sorry that I was not able to return to you sooner, but as I said, it has been very busy."

Bartimaeus looked from right to left then responded, "I can see that much has happened, and many people want to hear about it." He looked toward the bearded man that was still addressing the crowd. "Who is he?"

"That is Peter. There is no holding him back once he has his mind set. He is on fire to tell everyone about Jesus. He is our leader. We know that from what Jesus told us. Jesus is alive. We saw him here in Jerusalem then many times in Galilee. We were with him when he returned to heaven, but he assured us that he would always be with us. And after what happened with us earlier today, we all know that he is with us. There is so much that I want to share with you, that we want to share with everyone."

He took Bartimaeus by the arm. "Come, I want you to meet the others. I have already told them about you. I told them that you called them my friends. That was what convinced me to return to them. They are my friends."

They went to where Peter and the others were gathered. Thomas introduced Bartimaeus. He said, "You already met Matthew. This is Bartholomew, and Philip, and Simon, and Jude, and Matthias, and James." He then turned his attention toward Peter and said, "The one standing next to Peter is his brother Andrew. On his other side is another James, and the young man with him is his brother, John. They all have much to tell you. You will enjoy getting to know them."

With that, Peter and the others joined the group, and Thomas introduced Bartimaeus to them. Peter welcomed him and thanked him for sending Thomas back to them. Peter turned and looked back at the temple. There was a group of priests and temple guards looking their way. Returning to look toward Bartimaeus, Peter said, "So you are a guard for Herod! It is unlikely that we will be calling him our friend." He glanced back toward the temple at those looking their way. "But it may be good to have someone like you with us. We will be attracting the attention of those that do not want others to hear what we have to say. But we will place our trust in our God, not in swords. Now, let us go home. We have much to do before tomorrow."

Peter started off with the others following. Thomas was still with Bartimaeus. "Walk with me. I will show you where we are staying. We will be here again tomorrow. I hope that you can join us."

"Yes. I will be here. I have waited for this."

From the temple they passed the palace of Herod Antipas and from there followed the same route that he took to the bath. They stopped at a large inn near the bath, and Peter and the others entered.

Thomas said, "We are staying in the upper room. I will invite you to join us another day. Until then, I hope to see you tomorrow." With that, Thomas embraced him and entered the inn.

Bartimaeus's soldier training and his instincts told him that they had been followed since leaving the temple. He returned the way they had come. At the first street, he turned and followed the temple guards and priests that had been following them. He saw them enter a gate into a courtyard with a large impressive house. It was the guard's responsibility to know the important buildings, and he knew this one. It was the home of the chief priest, Caiaphas, and it joined the meeting place of the Sanhedrin. This is where Jesus had been found guilty of blasphemy and condemned to death. Bartimaeus sensed that evil and ill fortune would soon come to his new friends.

That night as he lay in bed, he recalled the words of Peter that day. Peter had called Jesus the Christ, the Son of God. And he thought of Thomas's earlier declaration of *My Lord and my God* when he saw the risen Jesus. His mind went back to his encounter with this same Jesus. He remembered the excited clamor of the crowd in Jericho and the crowd yelling that Jesus was coming. He remembered his words, *Jesus of Nazareth, son of David, have mercy on me*. He repeated those words over and over in his mind. Then he stopped and realized that now the words in his mind were different. He was now repeating, *Jesus of Nazareth, Son of God, have mercy on me*. He wondered what had caused him to unknowingly change the words that he was thinking. He had no answer, but he thought that it truly was the better plea. He spoke the words, *Jesus of Nazareth, Son of God, have mercy on me*, and with that prayer on his lips, he fell into a deep, peaceful rest.

15

To See Again

Bartimaeus was out of bed the moment that he opened his eyes. He was refreshed. He had not felt this peace, this alive since before his accident and blindness. With the fall from the horse, it was not only his sight that he lost. Soon after the fall, he learned how much more would be lost. His sight had returned, but there was still much more to regain. He could not forget the words that Jesus spoke to him: *Oh, yes. You will see again.* But it was not just the words that Jesus spoke; it was the way that he said them. Was there something else that he would see?

The day before at the temple, he had listened to Peter tell the crowd about Jesus. He had watched as Thomas and the others were busy teaching the crowd and answering their questions about Jesus. But he still knew little of this mystery man, Jesus. On the walk from the temple to the inn yesterday, Thomas told him that Jesus had appeared to them several times when they were in Galilee. Bartimaeus had asked Thomas if he would be able to see Jesus, but Thomas answered him that he did not think that was possible. Thomas then told him that the last time that they saw Jesus he was lifted into the sky. They all believed that Jesus returned to his Father in heaven, and he would not come back to them. But before Jesus left, he said that he would send the Spirit of God to them, and after that, they would understand what Jesus had said and done.

Thomas had also told him that evening as they walked to the inn, that after Jesus returned to heaven, they had stayed in Galilee only a few days before they returned to Jerusalem. The first night back all were together in the upper room of the inn when suddenly they felt a powerful presence in the room. It was like a wind, but the doors and windows were closed. It was dark, and lamps were lit. Then the lamps went out, but it was not wind that put them out. A light appeared that filled the room. Then the light seemed to enter each of them and continued to fill the room. Thomas said that there was an overwhelming sense of peace and good throughout the room. After a while—he did not know how long—the room gradually darkened, but the peace remained. That peace radiated from each of them. All remained quiet, then, one by one they would recall something that Jesus had done or said, and they would speak of it joyfully as if they had just discovered a prize. They spent the entire night recalling, telling, and explaining to each other what they now knew of Jesus from deep inside of them. Thomas told him that the next morning they were no longer afraid. They wanted to go to the temple and tell the people about Jesus. He said that Peter is like a new man; that even though many of the people at the temple had seen and heard Jesus themselves, they now understood what Jesus had said and done after listening to Peter.

Bartimaeus had remained silent while Thomas spoke, and he did not ask questions of him. He wondered as Thomas was telling him these things if this is what Jesus meant about seeing. Did Jesus's followers finally see what Jesus had done? Did the people listening to Peter now believe in Jesus? If so, when would he see as they now see? When would he believe?

The next morning after meeting the apostles at the temple, he was late arriving at the stable. He worked the horses that were scheduled for training, but he told the riders that they were to work the horses themselves that day. He was anxious to return to the temple. When he arrived at the temple, Peter was again standing on the steps telling the crowd about Jesus. There was a large crowd listening to Peter, and the other apostles were with smaller groups telling them about Jesus and answering questions.

Bartimaeus noted that the big Galilean fisherman spoke very boldly and quite convincingly of Jesus of Nazareth. He certainly did not speak like an unschooled fisherman. Similarly, the other men were speaking so that all understood and wanted to hear more. But there was one group at the temple that was not receptive to what was happening and the reaction of the people. Bartimaeus noticed that some of the temple priests were with temple guards, and they were pointing at Peter and the others. Bartimaeus well knew the power that the temple priests had and the influence that they could bring to bear on Herod, and through Herod, on Rome. He knew that the religious powers in Jerusalem were not about to let their power and authority be usurped by these Galilean followers of the Nazarene of which they had already disposed.

As evening was coming on, Peter dismissed the crowd, and he called John to him. The two walked into the temple while the others continued talking to many that had not gone away. When Peter and John came out of the temple, the others joined them as they proceeded to the inn. Bartimaeus followed close behind anxious to hear all that he could about Jesus.

Peter and John, in the lead, passed close by a pillar, and a beggar stretched out his hand to Peter who stopped and turned to the man. The others drew close. For Bartimaeus, this was a scene that he knew well, and he wondered what Peter would do. Peter walked to the beggar. He stood looking at the sadly familiar and desperate sight before him. The man reached out and tugged at Peter's cloak. "Have mercy on me," he pleaded. "Help me! I am cripple and can no longer feed my family. We are starving."

John stepped forward and, kneeling next to the man, said, "We would help you if we could, but we have no money."

Peter said, "Look upon us. We have no silver or gold. But what we have been given by the Master, we give freely to you."

The beggar stretched out both hands to Peter as if to say, "If not silver or gold, what is it that you will give me?"

The beggar's wish was answered when Peter boldly said, "In the name of Jesus of Nazareth, the Christ, arise and walk."

BARTIMAEUS, THE BLIND BEGGAR OF JERICHO

The beggar looked at Peter with disbelief. He had heard wishes and good tidings before. Then the hard, calloused, strong hand of Peter reached down taking hold of the beggar's hand, and with a mighty pull, like so many times pulling the net full of fish out of the water, he raised the man to his feet. The man stood bewildered. He knew that he should fall to the ground, but he did not. Peter took the man's other hand and stepped back. The man, being pulled by Peter, leaned forward until he was about to fall, took a step forward. Peter again stepped back, and the man followed with another step. Peter dropped his hands and stepped away. The man looked at Peter then at John, who to the beggar's dismay, did not look surprised. Instead, he wore a smile of understanding at what had happened. The beggar looked back to Peter who stood, eyes closed, lost in serenity. The man himself erect as if testing his balance then leaped toward John and clung to him as tears began to stream from his eyes.

All around were in stunned silence. Many knew the man and his helplessness; now he stood and walked. A few voices were heard, "Praise God." Then a chorus of shouts and praises to God.

When the man dropped his arms and stepped away from John, Peter said to him, "Go to the temple and thank God and thank his Son Jesus Christ." The man nodded and walked toward the temple. Others in the temple and nearby heard the commotion and joined the crowd that was growing about Peter and John.

Peter, with John beside him, once again spoke with boldness and conviction. He raised his voice to quiet the clamor. "Men of Israel, why do you wonder at this as if a man has done this? It was not us that enabled this man to walk." Then starting with Abraham and going through all the prophets, he told the story of God's plan for their salvation. He ended by telling them that God had sent his Son, Jesus, who had been put to death by their leaders. But God raised him from the dead so that all may be converted from this world and believe in Jesus, the Son of God.

There was nothing more for Peter to say, and all were silent. The crowd separated as Peter and John walked away with the others following them. Bartimaeus looked back at the temple where a small group of men remained huddled together. No one knew better than

Bartimaeus the power that could be loosed against these outspoken and emboldened Galileans. Even then, those men gathered at the temple had hatched their plot against Peter and John and anyone that would preach in the name of Jesus.

Bartimaeus caught up with Thomas as they proceeded to the inn. This time Thomas invited Bartimaeus to join them at the inn. Entering the upper room, there were others, including many women, already there. Bartimaeus stayed to the side as those in the room were told the tale that just transpired. Others entered the room, and soon it was full. Thomas noticed Bartimaeus standing alone and came to him. "I am sorry to abandon you, but everyone wants to be told about what happened today."

As they were talking, two men joined them, and Thomas introduced them. "Bartimaeus, this is Nicodemus. He is a priest in the temple and one of the early followers of Jesus, and this is his son, Chuza. Like you, Chuza has served Herod. Chuza served Herod the Great, while you serve Herod's son, the Antipas. We have yet to learn which will be judged worse."

Chuza added, "When Herod the Great died, I told my father that I no longer wanted to work at his palace. As a young boy, I was a servant to Herod. I did not do anything important. I served wine and food to him and his guests. I see that you are in this new Herod's guard. I hope that you do not have to deal with him directly. Why have we been punished by God with such terrible rulers? I am curious. How did you come to be in his guard?"

"I suppose that you could say that I was born into it. My father was in Herod the Great's guard. Mainly, our family has provided the horses for the guard, and we train the horses and the riders. I really do not do much as a soldier."

"So did your father encourage you to join the guard?"

"No, I never knew my father. He disappeared shortly after I was born. Actually, there were two of us. I have a twin brother who was also in the guard."

"It must be nice serving with your brother. What is his name?"

"He was named Barariel after my mother. But he was killed a few years ago by a band of Jewish zealots plotting against Herod."

"You said that your father disappeared. So you never knew him, but you were named after him. Your name is Bartimaeus. So you are the son of Timaeus."

"Yes, it is a good name. My mother told me many good tales about my father. He was a good, strong man. I hope that I can be like him."

While Bartimaeus continued talking, Chuza watched intently with a puzzled look as if trying to remember something long forgotten. When Bartimaeus stopped talking, he felt that there was something more that Chuza was about to add when their attention was suddenly drawn away. There was a loud banging on the door, and it was thrown open. A band of a dozen or more temple guards pushed into the room. After them came several temple priests who stepped forward but stayed behind the guards. The priests looked about the room, then one of them pointed at Peter and at John. The guards pushed their way through the crowded room and, forcibly grabbing Peter and John by their arms, said, "Come with us. You are under arrest."

16

PETER AND JOHN

Bartimaeus did not sleep well that night. He could not free his mind from thinking of the temple guards arresting Peter and John that evening. He played over in his mind the chain of events that had occurred. First, there were the eleven apostles at the temple telling the crowd about Jesus. They spoke of what Jesus had said and what he had done, but now they understood Jesus's words and deeds. Peter proclaimed that in a strong, clear voice for the people to hear. There was a rumble by the crowd when Peter declared that Jesus had risen from the dead three days after he had been brutally crucified. The apostles, mingling with the crowd, assured the people that what Peter said was true, and that they, as well as others, had seen Jesus. Peter told them that they had returned to Galilee where they had again seen Jesus and how, before their eyes, they had seen Jesus taken up into heaven. Peter and the apostles answered many questions of the people and explained that the prophets had foretold all that was to happen when the Messiah came. Jesus was the Messiah and the Son of God. Peter and John had then drawn off into the temple to pray, and when they came out, the lame beggar had asked them for alms. Rather than giving him money, to the man's surprise and amazement, Peter had cured the man.

    He thought that Peter's cure of the lame beggar was so very like his own cure by Jesus in Jericho. At that time, Bartimaeus had asked for mercy of Jesus, not expecting a miraculous cure, yet he received what he most desired and least expected. The lame beggar had asked for alms from Peter and John, but the beggar also received what he most desired and least expected. If the words and deeds of Jesus had resulted in his death, then might not Peter and John also be under the same peril?

After Peter and John had been arrested and taken from the room, there was emotional outcry from those in the room as to what should be done. Some wanted to chase after and rescue their two friends. They recalled how they had fled and hid when Jesus was arrested. They did not want that tragedy to happen again. There was bold and fearless talk of what they could do and how God would give them the power to prevail. Finally, Nicodemus spoke out. He said that he was a member of the Sanhedrin and that there were now some temple priests that were believers in Jesus, and since his death and reports of his resurrection, they wanted to learn more of Jesus and the possibility that he was the Messiah or maybe even the Son of God as he claimed. Regardless, Nicodemus doubted that there would be the will of the Sanhedrin to condemn Peter and John as had been done with Jesus. Further, he assured those gathered in the room that he would leave immediately to the house of Caiaphas and do all that he could to see that Peter and John were not harmed.

Bartimaeus added that he would inform his friend, Hezekiah, of what had happened and would ask his assistance in being informed if the Sanhedrin planned to render Peter and John to Herod on charges of civil disobedience or preaching insurrection against either Herod or Rome. With those thoughts of the previous day on his mind, Bartimaeus dressed for a meeting with Hezekiah. He would not be going to the stable. He put on his finest tunic and strapped on his sword and threw his cloak over his back. He would be prepared, as best he could, for what was required to protect his friends.

It was early morning, and Hezekiah would not be at the barracks, and for the purpose of what he wanted to talk to Hezekiah about, it would be better to meet him at his home. When he arrived at the home, Hezekiah was having breakfast with Rachel and their daughter, and he was invited to join them. Bartimaeus had not had breakfast, and he always enjoyed time with Rachel and their lovely daughter. Over breakfast, Rachel informed him of news of their other daughters, and she asked about Gamela and his children but did not press that subject. When they had finished eating, Rachel and her daughter excused themselves. He then told Hezekiah that he had some personal matters to attend to and that he would not be at the training stable that day, but there was another matter that he wanted to discuss with him. Hezekiah nodded, and Bartimaeus proceeded to tell him of the events at the temple the previous day, concluding with the arrest of Peter and John that evening. Hezekiah told him, that to the extent possible, he would keep Bartimaeus informed if there was anything that he learned of an attempt to have Herod involved in the arrest of Peter and John, or if he learned of anything regarding the preaching of the apostles at the temple.

Hezekiah asked Bartimaeus how his inquiry into Jesus was progressing, and Bartimaeus told him of what he had learned by listening to Peter and the others. They talked of the miraculous cure by Peter of the lame beggar, but Bartimaeus did not comment on the similarity of that to his own cure, but he felt that Hezekiah had noted that on his own. As Bartimaeus was departing, Hezekiah said that he wanted to know more about Jesus and that Rachel would also be interested. Hezekiah invited Bartimaeus to join them for dinner so that he could tell them what he knew of Jesus.

From there, Bartimaeus went to the upper room at the inn. There was no information about the disposition of Peter and John nor had Nicodemus returned with any news. He visited with several of the apostles, but for the most part, all in the room were in small groups waiting to learn of their friends. Finally, they heard voices approaching from the stairs, and the door opened. Nicodemus was the first to enter with Peter and John close behind. They appeared to be exhausted but relieved to be back with friends, and they looked unharmed. They were given water and food which they needed. All in the room waited for one of them to tell what had happened.

Finally, Nicodemus spoke. He told them that Peter and John were taken to the chamber of the Sanhedrin in Caiaphas's house and put in a small room with no window. Nicodemus convinced the guards to allow him to stay with the two. A guard was posted outside the door, and they heard voices periodically through the night and into the morning. At midday, they were taken to the chamber room. Although on short notice, all members of the Sanhedrin were in attendance. Caiaphas sat in the high chair with his father-in-law, Annas, at his right. When the three entered the chamber, Nicodemus took his seat. Caiaphas, without notice to Nicodemus or anyone else, immediately verbally accosted Peter and John. After citing their unapproved preaching and the healing of the lame beggar, Caiaphas rose to his feet and pointed directly at Peter, demanding, "By what right, by what power, and in whose name have you done these things?" At this, Nicodemus paused in his narrative and turned to Peter. With both arms directed toward Peter, he continued, "This man, Peter, sitting here with us, with the boldness of the prophets of old, the wisdom of the patriarchs, and the thunder of God's spirit spoke directly to Caiaphas."

All were focused on Peter as Nicodemus related what Peter had said: "If we are here today because of the good deed done to a poor, lame beggar that was made whole, let it be known to you and to all the people of Israel that this was done in the name of the Lord Jesus Christ of Nazareth, whom you ill-judged and had crucified. This Jesus, God raised from the dead. In the name of Jesus Christ, the lame man was cured, and in his name we preach."

Looking back to those in the room, Nicodemus continued his narration, "There was quiet in the chamber. No one dared speak. Such boldness of speech appalled some of the council members but clearly caught the attention of others as they leaned forward in concentration of Peter's every word. Caiaphas then ordered Peter and John to be removed. He certainly did not want to hear any more testimony from this fisherman who had become a skilled orator." With a pause to let his words settle on the listeners, and with all straining forward, intent on every word, Nicodemus continued, "After Peter and John were removed, Caiaphas told those present that they had heard directly from the lawbreaker and that this cannot be allowed to continue. Many cried out asking what they shall do. Others added that there were now many believers of Jesus, even thousands. They could not put all that believed in Jesus to death. Caiaphas then said that soon all in Jerusalem will know of the cure of the lame beggar. He said that Peter and John must be severely warned of what would happen in the future if they were to preach in the name of that Nazarene again. With that, Peter and John were led back into the chamber, and in anger, Caiaphas ordered Peter and John to no longer use the name of Jesus." Turning once more toward Peter, Nicodemus continued, "Then Peter spoke boldly, and he said to those present, 'Is it right for us to listen to you or to God? We cannot do anything but speak of what we have seen and heard.' Caiaphas stared at Peter and John, then after a final warning, he ordered the guards to throw out those damned fishermen."

Peter's brother, Andrew, then spoke and noted that all in the room had been praying for the safe return of the two. Then he led all in a prayer of thanksgiving and praise to God for the safe return of their friends. After that, all in the room gathered in small groups, and there was discussion of what this meant and how they would respond to the threat. All agreed that they must and would continue to preach in the name of Jesus and to teach others of the promise of everlasting life through Jesus, the Son of God.

Before leaving, Bartimaeus noticed Chuza with his father and several of the women. He joined them. Chuza commented that Bartimaeus was in his finest guard uniform and that he had his sword with him. When asked about carrying the sword, Bartimaeus told them of his intention to do whatever necessary that no harm would come to Peter and John. In fact, he had met with Hezekiah that morning to learn if there was any action by the Sanhedrin with Herod in regard to Peter and John. With that, Chuza asked him about Hezekiah, and Bartimaeus told him that he was a longtime family friend and that Hezekiah had served in the guard with his father. Chuza nodded his head a few times then said, "Yes, I remember seeing Hezekiah in the king's chamber meeting with Herod the Great." He stopped and looked at Bartimaeus then added, "But that was a long time ago. Much has happened since then, for all of us. Some of it best forgotten."

17

THE APOSTLES ARE ARRESTED

After the arrest of Peter and John and their trial before the Sanhedrin, Bartimaeus spent more time with the apostles and the community of followers of Jesus. He continued to go to the stables in the morning to train the young horses and to work with a few of the riders. In the afternoons, he would go to the temple where Peter continued his preaching about Jesus and where the apostles were talking to groups about Jesus and answering their questions. In the evenings, the apostles would return to the inn where women prepared meals and the community ate together in common.

More people were coming to the temple every day, and soon the crowd of believers at the temple had grown to thousands. Those that believed and accepted Jesus as the Son of God were baptized by the apostles as Jesus the Christ had instructed them in the name of the Father and the Son and the Holy Spirit. There was a spirit of love and mutual concern among the Christians, as they now called themselves, and they cared for each other as brothers and sisters.

As a soldier, Bartimaeus had seen certain men grow in leadership and strength of character. He marveled at the apostles, especially Peter, with his burning passion and clarity of purpose. All the apostles spoke boldly of what they had seen and what they knew of Jesus. They recalled his teachings and his deeds with a new insight. As Bartimaeus watched, as he listened, he recalled Jesus's words to him: *"Yes, you will see again."* On the night that Peter and John returned after being arrested, he had listened to Nicodemus tell of the trial and of Peter's words. After that, he believed that the carpenter from Nazareth, the man that cured him, that worked miracles, that had been put to death, and that had risen to life was truly the Son of God. Although he could not understand why God and the Son of God would do as they did, he accepted it. That evening, after Nicodemus spoke, he asked Thomas if he could be baptized. When Thomas poured the water of baptism on him, he felt in his heart the words that Thomas spoke when he first saw Jesus in that same upper room of the inn. Bartimaeus, like Thomas, also proclaimed, "My Lord and my God."

Every day people flocked to Jerusalem from nearby towns like Bethany and Bethlehem to hear the apostles and to be baptized. The cures by Peter and John and the baptisms of many followers were not unseen by the temple priests and especially the high priest, Caiaphas, and old Annas. Many of the members of the Sanhedrin were appalled at the scene and fretted at the number of Jews that were choosing to follow Jesus. It was not long before another meeting of the Sanhedrin was called including indignant Pharisees that had long rejected Jesus and his teachings and the Sadducees who did not believe in life after death. Although those groups did not agree on all matters of their Jewish religion, they did agree that Jesus was a threat to their way of life. Behind closed doors, the powerful leaders of the Jews resolved that the apostles were a threat and were drawing followers to Jesus who they referred to in a disparaging way as "that Nazarene." They vowed to destroy the leaders, and with no leaders, the sect of followers would dissolve. That afternoon as the apostles left the inn and were on their way to the temple, they were arrested and hustled through the streets to a prison and cast into a cell.

Bartimaeus was at the stable when a messenger arrived who informed him that he was to go to the inn. When he arrived, Nicodemus told him what had transpired. Nicodemus related that he and other priests that believed in Jesus had not been invited to attend the Sanhedrin meeting. He said that there were other priests of the temple that did not agree with Caiaphas in this matter. He said that there was concern because at the trial of Jesus, there were those that told lies about Jesus, and they were afraid that the same may happen to the apostles. Nicodemus told them that there was limited action that the Sanhedrin could take and that possibly Herod's assistance would be solicited. Others in the room said that they should not do anything that could make the matter worse for the apostles, and there was no decision as to the course of action that should be taken. Some of the women began to sing psalms, and soon calm settled into the room. No more was said as to what should be done.

That night, Bartimaeus was sitting on the floor with Nicodemus and Chuza when they heard soft voices outside the door, and the door slowly opened. There were a few lamps lit, enough to see movement. Into that darkness, the apostles slowly and quietly entered. Those that were awake rose to welcome them, and those that had been sleeping joined them. The apostles were surrounded, and all were asking what had happened and how they had managed to be freed.

Holding his hands up and asking for silence, Peter told the tale. "As you know, we were arrested by the temple guards as we were on our way to the temple. They did their best to surround us so that the people would not see us. They took us immediately to the prison and locked us in a cell together. We were crowded in there and were told nothing. But we did not fear. There was no fear in any of us. We placed our trust in our Lord. We even talked of the privilege of suffering as our Master did. No one came to us nor were we given anything to eat or drink. Night came, and we laid down together on the floor of the cell. There were no windows and no lights anywhere. No one was seen. There was no sound. Without any banging of the iron bolt or creaking of the hinge, the door simply swung open. We walked out of the cell, but there was no one there. We walked down the corridor into a large room. There we saw a person surrounded in radiance, an angel. The angel told us that we were to leave, and in the morning, we were to go into the temple where we were to proclaim Jesus and him crucified and risen to life. He said that we were to go into the temple. We were not to stay in the portico as we had done before."

The women gathered blankets and cloaks and pulled the weary apostles away. They said that the morning would come soon enough and that the apostles needed to rest. When they woke, the women had prepared breakfast and had fresh bread for them. They ate, and before departing for the temple, they were blessed by all. Then the apostles, with all in the room joining them, walked into the street, and headed to the temple with a psalm of praise on their lips.

Word of the prior day's arrest of the apostles had spread through the city, and their appearance in the streets soon had a crowd following and joining in the psalm prayer. They arrived at the temple, and rather than stopping at the portico, they went directly inside where Peter commenced, in a strong voice, delivering a message of Jesus the Son of God and of their deliverance from prison by an angel sent from God. The temple was full, and people packed the outer portico and steps. The temple courtyard was filled with a huge crowd, and no more could enter through any of the gates. Soon, some of the temple priests with guards in front pushed their way through the crowds frantic to get to Caiaphas to inquire as to why the apostles had been released from prison.

Before the priests from the temple arrived, Caiaphas had already received report that the prisoners had mysteriously disappeared from their dark cell sometime that night. The prison officer had assured Caiaphas that the apostles had certainly been placed in the cell the previous day and the cell door secularly locked. There had been guards in the prison continually, and there was no report of anyone entering or leaving the prison. There was no explanation of how the prisoners had disappeared. The prison officer swore that he had inspected the cell with the prisoners inside himself. He assured Caiaphas that there was no way for them to escape—but they had! When the priests arrived at the house of Caiaphas, they informed him of the crowd at the temple and that the apostles were now inside the temple preaching to the people. News of the mysterious escape of the apostles and the crowd that now gathered to listen to them incensed Caiaphas. Now, he was afraid that there would be rioting. He sent word to assemble the Sanhedrin and to arrest the apostles and bring them to the council chamber once more. In a rage, Caiaphas shouted that this time judgment would be swift and harsh. That this rabble could not be allowed to continue to incite the people over this false Nazarene prophet. He swore that if he could not do this, then he would see that Herod or Rome did.

With the Sanhedrin assembled, the mysterious facts were made known to all; the men that had been arrested and jailed yesterday were, in fact at that very moment, teaching the people about Jesus, and this time they were inside the temple! Once the captain of the temple guard, along with senior officers, were in attendance at the council, Caiaphas issued his proclamation: "Those men must be stopped immediately." An order was given to the captain: "Take your men and go to the temple and bring those fugitives back to the council." But Caiaphas added, "Do this without violence," for he feared what the crowd would do when the guards took the apostles away. Clearly, Caiaphas was realizing that what he had attempted to solve less than two months earlier with the death of Jesus had not worked. He had no choice now but to deal severely with Jesus's followers.

Soon, the apostles were dragged before the Sanhedrin. Peter, with John beside him, stepped forward to Caiaphas and the council. Caiaphas, weary and bewildered, pointed at Peter and shouted, "You were commanded to no longer preach in the name of the Nazarene. Yet you are continuing to do so, and now inside the temple. You are filling the people with this false teaching." His voice cracked with anger. "You are blaming us for the death of this Nazarene. You threaten to bring the blood of this man down upon us. This must stop." There being no answer or reaction by Peter, or the others, Caiaphas demanded, "What have you to say for yourself?"

Peter spoke plainly to Caiaphas but stretched his hands out to all as he said, "We must obey God, not men." The judges stared silently. There could be no reply. Hearing no response from the council, Peter continued, "You put Jesus to death on a cross, but the God of our fathers raised him back to life. We have seen Jesus, and we saw him return to his Father in heaven. We are witnesses to this. And God sent his Spirit to strengthen us and to give us what we are to say. We have no choice. We must obey our God."

The council members remained silent. Even shrewd old Annas sat beside Caiaphas stroking his long gray beard. In the quiet, a man rose to address the assembly. He asked for the prisoners to be removed from the room. When they were gone, the man came forward to stand in front of the judges. All knew him. His name, Gamaliel, a high-ranking Pharisee and doctor of the Law. The Sanhedrin settled back to listen since his wisdom and judgment was renown. Gamaliel then spoke as a man of common sense without emotion. He started by reminding the assembly of another man that had recently aroused the people with his teaching and had garnered many followers of his message, but when put to death, all that had believed in him had been scattered, and nothing more had come of him. Then he talked of those that follow Jesus and said, "Let them be. If the work that these men do is of their own or of other men, then it will come of nothing. But if it be of God, we cannot work against it, and perhaps we would find ourselves fighting even against our God."

Whether it was the crowd that they feared or the mystery of the apostle's escape from prison, which they still had no answer, or whether it was the logic of Gamaliel's words, the Sanhedrin and the judges consented. Adding to the judges' word of final consent, Annas raised his hand and, in a gravelly voice, added, "They must be ordered to stop all preaching. And they must be sent back to Galilee. Let us put wise Gamaliel's words to the test. Have them all whipped with a double strap, twenty-six to the back and thirteen to the breast. Let us see if this teaching be of God or, if of men, they will run home like beaten curs."

As the assembly was leaving, the man that had been sitting next to Gamaliel approached his teacher. He said, "Rabbi, your wisdom cannot be doubted, but these men continue to preach blasphemy. They break the Law and must be stopped. What if they persist? What then?" To this Gamaliel had no answer. He simply put his hand on the other's shoulder, and they walked out. That man was Saul of Tarsus.

18

CHUZA'S STORY

The beatings that the apostles received made the fire of love for God and his Son burn more intensely in their hearts. There were those in the Sanhedrin that had disagreed with Annas's wish to beat the apostles, but the judges were handpicked by Caiaphas, and the majority of the seventy-one members went along with the cruel dictate. Immediately after the Sanhedrin dismissed, Nicodemus hurried to the inn to convey the terrible news. Once those waiting at the inn had recovered from the shock of the Sanhedrin's action, there was a scramble to gather jugs of water, clean cloth, and oil for the wounds. Some of the stronger men went to the prison to help the apostles after they were released. Soon, it was common knowledge among the people of Jerusalem of what had been done, and many lined the streets as the apostles made their way to the inn. The crowd was mostly quiet. An occasional prayer of blessing could be heard. Many shook their heads and muttered their disgust at this display of evil. Even those that were not followers of Jesus had kind words and sympathy for the cruelly beaten men.

It took many weeks for the whip lashes to their bodies to heal. But the marks on their hearts were indelible. The apostles wore those marks deep within their soul happily and humbly out of love for their Lord and Master. Despite the dire warning and inhumane punishment, the apostles lived out Gamaliel's verbal proviso. Once physically able, they returned to the temple preaching the good news of

Jesus Christ and him crucified and risen. That action heightened the intent by Caiaphas and Annas and other ardent opponents to Jesus to eradicate his followers. One of those ardent opponents to Jesus was Saul of Tarsus, an avid spokesman for an all-out campaign, even unto violence, to carry out the strict letter of the Law.

From the time that Bartimaeus stood at the gate of Jericho with his eyesight restored, he had looked down the road that Jesus had walked trying to see the man that made mercy on him. He had come to realize that Jesus did not simply have mercy on him. That was easy; many good people had mercy on him. But Jesus had done more. He made mercy on him much as a person would make love to another. Jesus did so willingly with no expectation of return. Jesus had made mercy on him out of an abundance of love for him when others saw him as unlovable, and that, to Bartimaeus, made all the difference in the world. From that point, Bartimaeus had sought to find the man, Jesus of Nazareth, to thank him, to come to know him, maybe even to call him his friend. But all of that was seemingly dashed when he learned of the death of Jesus. After returning to Jerusalem and learning of Jesus's death, the darkness of that unattainable longing would well up inside him and grip him with a helpless, unrelenting void. In that distress, he would once more cry out in his heart as he did that day at the gate of Jericho, *Jesus of Nazareth, son of David, have mercy on me.*

It had been through Thomas, the twin, that he had come to know Matthew. After that, he came to know all the apostles. They had welcomed him, and it was only through them that he was able to answer his questions. Only through them that he was able to learn of Jesus of Nazareth. He was attracted to these simple men. They did not talk about Jewish Law or dwell on sin. He learned that Jesus often told people that their sins were forgiven, and that Jesus would often say to those that were forgiven to go and sin no more.

Each of the apostles had much to tell him. It was Peter that spoke so boldly, so unequivocally about Jesus. It was through the faith of those simple men that Bartimaeus found his faith and cried out like Thomas, *My Lord and my God.* After that, the prayer that he used to dispel the doubts and fears and anxiety that would well up inside him was, *Jesus of Nazareth, Son of God, have mercy on me.*

Most days, except when his guard duties called him elsewhere, would find Bartimaeus at the temple or with his friends and new companions in the upper room of the inn. The soldiers saw his daily excursions to the temple and his late return to the barracks. Some asked him about his seemingly newfound religious fervor, and he openly told them of his intent to learn about and to follow the way of Jesus. Soon, a few of them accompanied him including Joshua, who quickly became well known within the community of believers. Bartimaeus did not try to outwardly influence those that he served within the guard, but many saw a change in him. Even some of the Gentiles in the guard become followers of Jesus through him. Joshua and a few others were now constant companions with Bartimaeus, and they supported each other in this new way of living. Occasionally those soldiers would discuss among themselves their chosen profession and that they served a king that openly flaunted the Jewish Laws and customs. More so, they wondered if being a soldier was in keeping with being a follower of Jesus.

One evening Bartimaeus with Joshua and several other soldiers asked Matthew about that. Matthew told them that he was not sure, but he told them that once a Roman centurion had asked Jesus to save the life of the soldier's dying daughter and that Jesus had done so. Matthew said that the apostles were surprised that Jesus did that for a Roman soldier. Jesus responded to them that the centurion came to him because he believed in him. After hearing that from Matthew, the soldiers no longer questioned what they did, and they found comfort in that story.

One evening at the inn, Chuza approached Bartimaeus and said that he had something that he wanted to talk to him about. They went out of the inn, and Chuza asked Bartimaeus to walk with him to the bath. It was a short distance, and the two men walked in silence. Chuza was Bartimaeus's senior, and Bartimaeus gave him the courtesy of that silence. When they arrived at the bath, Chuza motioned for him to sit with him.

Chuza turned to face him and said, "Bartimaeus, it has been some time since first we met. After that, I sought to learn more about you. As you know, we have something in common. We both worked for a Herod. I, as a boy, but old enough to clearly understand the intent of a man's words, was a servant to Herod the Great. You serve his son, Herod Antipas. Neither of those men can be honored." He stopped to weigh any reaction that his words may have produced. Receiving none other than a slight shrug from Bartimaeus, he proceeded. "As a young servant, I was of no consequence to Herod. He would speak to others in my presence without any concern of what I heard. Even if I were to speak of what I heard, which out of fear I would never do, he would simply lie if he so chose to cover it up. I heard him lie many times. His only interest was himself. He cared for no one and nothing but himself. To Herod, uncompromising loyalty to him was the only measure of any man. I heard and saw many terrible things. I often told my father of the terrible deeds that I saw and heard in the king's chamber. One evening, after telling my father one of those terrible stories, he told me that I was not to go back. My father took care of arranging that with the chief steward of the palace. Besides, Herod did not care about me. Some other boy would pour the wine for him. Shortly after I left, Herod died."

Chuza paused again, measuring Bartimaeus's reaction and whether he should continue. "Sometime after meeting you, I recalled a conversation that I overheard between Herod and a soldier thirty-three years ago. I clearly remember this because after that happened, I knew that I could no longer serve Herod. At that time, I did not tell my father what I had heard because it would have greatly disturbed him. But I did tell my father about it the other day. After hearing what I had to tell him, he said that I must tell you. This is something that happened when you would have been just a baby. And it is over. Nothing can be done about it now. You know my father, Nicodemus, he is a wise and honorable man. A good man. A good priest. We need more like him. Caiaphas and Annas are not good priests. How do men like that get power?" He answered his own question, "I suppose because evil men want power. Maybe it is because power itself makes some men evil."

Chuza looked off to the side and sighed then, turning back and looking squarely at the other man, continued, "Bartimaeus, my father wanted me to tell you this as soon as I told him. I could not do that until now. I see in you a good man. A man of peace in your heart. But I have something to tell you about your father, Timaeus."

Bartimaeus tensed, and his hands went to his knees, and he leaned toward Chuza. "What do you know of my father?"

"I never saw your father. I do not know him, but I heard Herod and another man talk about him."

"What could Herod have to say about my father? Surely, he was a good soldier. Neither I nor my brother would have been allowed to enter the guard if there was a stain on our family."

"It was not what your father did. He did nothing wrong that I know. What I must tell you is something that others did that was wrong, something terribly wrong. Your father knew of it. Herod was afraid that if your father told of this to others that not even his lies could quiet the horror of it."

Chuza went on to tell Bartimaeus what he had heard and seen in Herod's chamber. He related that three astrologers from the east had come to Herod's court and had been allowed an audience with the king. Herod relished such visitors. Herod needed to feel important, to think that others came to him and sought his advice because he was wiser than other men. Those three were learned men, men of clear distinction from other men. They were not Jews. They said that they had seen signs in the sky that told them that a new king of the Jews was to be born. A king that would reign not only for the Jews but over the world. They came to Herod to learn where this king was to be born.

Herod had at first scoffed at them that there was not to be a new king born. He was not to have another son born to him. Herod had no regard for the sons that he already had. To Herod, his sons were not worthy to follow him as king, and there was no intention of having another son. But Herod must have worried that if these learned men could by chance be reading these signs correctly, that such a child would be a threat to his heritage. He would not tolerate a future king not being from his loins. That would diminish his self-perceived greatness. So Herod asked the learned Jewish scholars about the prophecies as to where the great king, the messiah, was to be born. He was told that it was Bethlehem.

With that knowledge, Herod had given an order to a palace guard that the male babies of Bethlehem were to be killed. The plan was for hired assassins to carry out the killings. But that soldiers from the palace guard would be used to help the assassins get the babies away from their parents quietly, without arousing suspicions. The guard soldiers were not to perform that atrocity, nor were they to know what the hired men were doing. The soldiers that were selected for this assignment were not from the Bethlehem area, and most were not Jews. Chuza told Bartimaeus that the man in the guard that Herod had given that order to had selected Timaeus to lead that group of soldiers to Bethlehem to carry out that order and, unknowingly, to aid the assassins in their terrible deed. However, Timaeus found the slain bodies of the babies, and he discovered what was done. In a rage at what he had been made a part of, Timaeus had returned to Jerusalem that night. Timaeus went to the man that gave him that order, and he swore that he would tell of this atrocity to bring Herod down. That man told Herod of what Timaeus intended to do. Hearing of the threat against him, Herod ordered that Timaeus was to be killed before he could tell the tale to anyone. Chuza told Bartimaeus that a few days later he heard that man tell Herod that Timaeus had been killed as he was returning home to Jericho.

When finished telling that tale, Chuza said, "I could never forget knowing that Herod had ordered the killing of those babies in Bethlehem and that he ordered one of his soldiers, Timaeus, your father, killed to keep others from learning of that terrible deed."

Neither moved nor spoke. Bartimaeus rose and walked a few steps away. His back was to Chuza, and he dropped his head and shook it in disbelief. He turned and demanded, "And the name of the man that gave this order and had my father killed?"

There was a long pause before Chuza spoke. When he did, he said only one word, "Hezekiah."

Bartimaeus had stopped wearing his sword, but his hand instinctively went to his side. He looked at Chuza waiting for some explanation, something more that he must know to vindicate the man that had been a willing participant in such a barbaric act that had ordered the death of Hezekiah's own friend, the death of his father. But there could be no explanation, no possible justification for such an act. His only thought was how could a man that he loved, a man that had told him of his love for his father have been responsible for his father's death? Only one person could have those answers. Bartimaeus turned to walk away.

Chuza called to him, "Wait, Bartimaeus. Stop before you do anything. Let others talk to you before you leave. Let us find Thomas or Peter. They will help you with this." Chuza tried to hold on to Bartimaeus's arm, but he pulled away and walked off.

When Bartimaeus arrived at the barracks, he went to his room and pulled the sword out of its scabbard. He passed a few others on his way to Hezekiah's office. He did not stop to answer their questions but burst into Hezekiah's room.

"Hezekiah, I know what you did! You, of all people! My father was your friend. You had him killed. You killed my father." By the time that Hezekiah rose to his feet, Bartimaeus had rushed to the other side of the table and had his sword pressed hard under Hezekiah's ribs pointed up to his heart. "How could you do that?"

"Bartimaeus, many times I have wanted to tell you. I could not when you were young. Then I could not bear to hurt you more when you were blind. Every time I was near you or your brother, my shame was too much to bear. I tried to make up for it. I tried to be a father to you."

"I suppose that you are going to tell me that it was not your doing. You only did what you were told. That you are a soldier!"

"No, Bartimaeus. I have long accepted the fact that I allowed this to happen. I could have stopped it, but I did not. I have regretted that every day since. I do not blame you for wanting to kill me. I have wanted to die many times since then. I can assure you, killing me will not end your pain. It will not make enduring this any easier. Although I do not deserve it, for your sake and for those that love you and need you, forgive me. Have mercy on me."

"Have mercy on you!" he said and could feel his grip on the sword tighten as he pushed even harder on the blade and saw Hezekiah's eyes close. "Mercy! What mercy did you show my father, your friend? What mercy did you show my mother? What mercy did you show my sister and my brother? What mercy have you shown me?"

The door was open, and several soldiers had entered but stayed on the other side of the table. All remained motionless. Bartimaeus spoke softly so that only Hezekiah could hear, "Have mercy on you, hell! Have mercy on me." With his free hand, he pushed Hezekiah away and stabbed the sword into the table. He pushed his way past the others and out of the room.

Joshua was standing in the hall, and as Bartimaeus pushed by him, without stopping or looking, he said, "I am going home."

Maximus's room was adjacent to Hezekiah's. When Maximus heard the commotion in the hall, he had come out of his room in time to see the men in the hall separate to allow Bartimaeus to pass through. He stood there watching until Bartimaeus disappeared down the hall toward his room. Hezekiah's door remained open, and the men that had entered were leaving, talking to each other. When no more men exited the room, Maximus stepped in. Inside, he watched as Hezekiah lowered himself onto the edge of his chair and placed his head into his hands. As Maximus gazed upon the man crushed and broken, he thought how old and weak Hezekiah had become.

19

GOING HOME

After Bartimaeus stormed past the stunned onlookers in the hallway, Joshua went to Hezekiah's room and looked through the open doorway. He saw Maximus standing in the middle of the room, legs spread and arms crossed, surveying Hezekiah slumped at the table with his head cradled in his hands. Joshua waited as if his presence could bring solace to the man sitting at the end of the room. Maximus turned and walked toward the door. He stopped long enough to cast a repugnant grin at Joshua, then strode into the hallway and back to his room. Joshua entered the room but stopped sensing the pain emanating from Hezekiah. He backed out and pulled the door closed leaving Hezekiah alone. Then he went to Bartimaeus's room and found the soldier uniform on the floor. Surveying the room, Bartimaeus had not taken anything except that which he brought with him from Jericho.

Joshua found Bartimaeus at the stable wearing the clothes that he wore when he returned to Jerusalem many months ago. He stood by as Bartimaeus led a horse from its stall and cross-tied it and proceeded to brush it. Joshua said, "I do not know what just happened between you and Hezekiah. He did not talk, but clearly, he was very upset. I cannot imagine what came between the two of you. It must be serious. I do not suppose that I can help, but I am a good listener."

Bartimaeus paid no attention and proceeded to pick the horse's hooves. Joshua watched, then he went to a stall and brought out another horse and began brushing it. Bartimaeus strapped on the saddle and pulled the bridle on. As he led the horse out, he stopped next to one of the stable hands and said, "I'm taking this horse. Tell them that they can deduct the price the next time they buy horses from my family." He mounted and turned back as Joshua swung up on his horse. He said, "What are you doing?"

Joshua responded, "I am going home too."

Bartimaeus rode out at a walk with the reins hanging loosely along the horse's neck. Joshua stayed behind Bartimaeus as they went through the street and out the gate. It was several miles before Joshua moved up beside his friend, and they continued in silence until they could see the walls of Jericho. Bartimaeus broke the silence. "I remember leaving Jericho after Jesus cured me. I went to Jerusalem with the expectation to thank the man, Jesus, that had restored my sight and to convince the man, Saul, who had come between me and Gamela, to allow me to renew our marriage. I did not accomplish either. The only thing that I have accomplished is to learn that the one man that I believed in and trusted all my life, that he had betrayed my father and cheated my mother out of her husband."

Joshua pushed his horse close to Bartimaeus and, without looking at his companion, said, "Bartimaeus, you are older than me, and I can only imagine what you have lived through. I respect you and thank you for all that you have done for me. I do not know what has happened between you and Hezekiah, and I do not need to. I do know that Hezekiah loves you as if you were his son—all of us saw that. That was accepted by most of us since you earned everything that you received from him. What you just said may well be true, but you left something out."

Neither man turned to look at the other. Then Joshua continued, "You did not mention how your life has changed in the last few months. You did not mention how you have changed. When I first met you, the only relationship that you had, the only relationship that you wanted, the only relationship that you cared about was with a horse. That was safe. You could trust them. They could not hurt you, not where it really mattered deep inside you. You tolerated the rest of us, but you would not let us in. What you did not mention, my friend, is the relationship that you now have with a roomful of people, probably hundreds of other people that would give their life for you, even if they did not know you."

They rode on in silence, then Joshua continued, "You said that you went to Jerusalem to thank the man that cured you and to learn about him. I think that you have thanked him many times in your heart and that you have come to know him. Because of you, I also came to know Jesus, a man I never saw or heard, much less touched me. And there are others that feel the same as I do. You have made a difference to many people. That is what you did not mention."

Bartimaeus stopped his horse and turned to face Joshua. "I do not know if you are right about others. I do not see it. But you are wrong about my relationship with others. I have a great relationship, and I love my mother, and my sister Susanna, and…" He stopped, and they both locked eyes for only a moment. What Bartimaeus could not say, Joshua was aware. He had known from the moment that they walked out of Monica's house. He and Bartimaeus both loved the same woman, Monica.

Bartimaeus smiled at his friend. "It is time to get home. Do you think that you can ride a horse at other than a walk without falling off?"

Joshua spurred his horse to catch Bartimaeus and yelled after him, "Probably not. You taught me all that I know."

They pulled up when they got to the west gate at Jericho and turned north. They rode in silence, and each felt comfort in having the other beside him. When they arrived at the road that led to Joshua's home, they stopped. Bartimaeus said, "Enjoy your time with your family. I would like to meet them."

Joshua responded, "Please visit us. I want them to know you too." They reached out and took each other's hand. "I thank God for you, and I will pray for you."

The sun was setting, and the summer heat was beginning to break as Bartimaeus rode to his home. He stopped at the stable and pulled the saddle as Ezra entered. Ezra was surprised and pleased to see him. Bartimaeus said that he would visit with him and the family tomorrow. When he asked about his mother, Ezra simply responded that she was getting old. Bartimaeus paused for a minute as if deciding which house he should go to first. Then he strode off at a rapid walk to Gamela's home.

When he walked in, Gamela had a large bowl of grain on her lap that she was sorting, and the children were together playing a game. Mariam immediately got up and ran to hug her father. Saul David looked over at his mother before going to his father and hugged him. Mariam started in on a string of questions and statements that never stopped to let her father answer. His son stepped aside for his sister, and Saul David's gaze went from his mother to his father measuring each of their reactions to the other.

Gamela rose and put the bowl aside then walked over and put her hand on the two children. "It is time to get ready for bed. Your father is tired, and he needs to have something to eat then to relax. He will be in to say good night to you shortly."

They watched as the children disappeared then turning to Bartimaeus she said, "I did not expect you. But I never knew when you would be home." She stopped then added, "Or if you would come home."

He stepped closer and reached down and took her hands. "I quit the guard."

There was no response. He really did not expect one. She squeezed his hands. "Why?"

"A lot has happened since I left here the last time. A friend just reminded me of that. I have a lot to tell you. That is why I came home."

She squeezed his hands again. "Bartimaeus, I have missed you. I am glad that you are home." She stepped closer, and he pulled her to him and put his arms around her. She looked up into his face, and he softly kissed her cheek. She turned her head and laid it on his chest. He bent over, and she tipped her head back. He kissed her again.

They sat up almost until sunrise; Bartimaeus telling his story with Gamela asking questions when she did not understand and commenting as she felt the need. Gamela remained silent and she had slowly nodded her head when he again told of his frustration and anger when he discovered that the man that had cured him,

Jesus, had been put to death by the Jewish leaders and Roman rulers, and she had placed her hand on his when he recalled how Saul had rejected him when he had reached out to reconcile with him and that nothing had been resolved with Saul.

Bartimaeus's tone changed when he began telling Gamela of finding Thomas and being introduced to Matthew but shortly after that the apostles had returned to Galilee. When they returned to Jerusalem, he had been introduced to Jesus's followers and they had welcomed him. He turned to look at her and he spoke excitedly as he told her the stories of Peter and John and of the other apostles and the troubles that they had with Caiaphas and the Jewish leaders. She was very interested in what he told her of the preaching by Peter and the stories that he told of Jesus from those that knew him, and she often had questions to help her understand the teachings of Jesus and what they meant. She was very interested to hear of the many people that had come to believe in Jesus and had been baptized by the apostles. He told her of Nicodemus and finally what Chuza told him of his father.

She had moved very close to him as he told the stories and had tucked her legs underneath her on the cushions and leaned her head on his shoulder. As he told her what he had learned from Chuza, she sat up and looked intently during that telling. He stopped at that point until she demanded, "What did you do?"

Then he told her about his confrontation with Hezekiah and how he had wanted to kill him. At the end, he told her of Joshua and that he had accompanied him back to Jericho, but he did not tell her all of what they had talked about and what Joshua had said. He was still sorting that out himself.

At one point, as Bartimaeus took a break and Gamela needed to process all that she was told, he had asked about his mother. She said that Ariel had been sick and had not fully recovered. She needed rest, and her age was showing more every day. She added that seeing him was the medicine that she most needed.

They fell into bed as the light from the sun was creeping up over the horizon across the river valley. They did not get much sleep as they heard the children but managed to stay in bed a bit longer.

They gave up when they heard calling at the door and Ezra's wife's calling to them. The children let her in, and they heard her say that Ariel was anxious to see her son.

After dressing, they walked together to Ezra's house where a table of food was waiting for them. After greeting his mother and the family, he sat down realizing that it had been a long time since he had eaten. Bartimaeus, with Gamela's assistance when he forgot to mention a fact that was most important, relayed much of what he had told Gamela to Ariel and Ezra's family. They too voiced vehement concern over the telling of Jesus's death and were equally intrigued over Jesus's rising from the dead and ascent to heaven. They had a few questions in that regard but essentially resigned themselves to the facts, as Bartimaeus related, with expectations of learning more later. He avoided the discussion of Saul completely. He expected to tell Ariel of that when they were alone.

He ended by telling them of Joshua and his remarkable achievement in learning to ride well and his rapid grasp of tending to horses. He told them that Joshua could be a fine horseman given the opportunity. He expected Joshua to come for a visit, and he was anxious for him to learn more about the care and breeding of horses. Ezra said that he would be glad to welcome him and that he could use help with the horses.

Bartimaeus avoided telling what he learned from Chuza and his confrontation with Hezekiah until after the children were excused and sent to do chores. Ariel was sitting beside him, and as the story unfolded, he held her hand and spoke directly to her. She remained silent through the telling. When finished, she leaned into him, and he held her close to him. No one spoke, each trying to come to grips with the tragedy. There was only one more item to tell, and that was that he was no longer a soldier. With that, Ariel had simply said, "You are staying home," to which he added, "Yes, *Ima*, I am staying home."

For the next several weeks, Bartimaeus enjoyed the simplicity of being with family and tending to the horses. Joshua became a frequent visitor. At first, it was every day, then he missed a few days, and more recently he was seldom at the stable. One day when Joshua was at the stable, he called Bartimaeus aside and told him that he had been seeing Monica. In an uneasy and stumbling fashion, he said that there was a strong affection between the two of them, but that she was not willing to let herself show the affection that he believed that she had for him. He added that that was puzzling to him, and he wondered if Bartimaeus, knowing Monica well and being like a brother to her, could help him.

Bartimaeus, well aware of what was occupying his time, feigned surprise at what Joshua said and congratulated him but then strongly added, "Monica will never give her heart to you!"

To that, Joshua indignantly responded, "Well, why not?"

Bartimaeus smiled recognizing that Joshua had taken the bait. With a shrug of his shoulders and in a factual tone, he said, "Because she does not like the clothes that you wear."

To that, Joshua shot back angrily, "What is wrong with my clothes?"

Bartimaeus's demeanor went from teasing to serious. "You do not understand. She will never give herself to another soldier. Her husband, my brother, was a soldier. I was a soldier. She was the one that took care of me when I was blind. My father was a soldier, and she saw what that did to my mother and to our family. She has endured too much to take that chance again."

Without hesitation, Joshua said, "Then I will quit. I will ride over to the guard house in Jericho tomorrow and give them my sword and uniform and tell them to send a message to Jerusalem."

"You cannot just quit!"

"Why not? You did!"

As they walked back to the stable, Joshua had one more question. "Do you think that Ezra would want to hire me to help him with the horses?"

"My friend, Ezra will be delighted. Let us go tell him."

After they talked to Ezra, Joshua left to return to his home. He wanted to tell his family of his decision to leave the guard. Although Joshua did not speak further of Monica, Bartimaeus was sure that Monica was soon to learn of Joshua's decision to leave the guard. He watched Joshua ride out, then he walked into the pasture and crossed a small irrigation ditch and sat under the old apricot tree along the bank of the ditch. He threw a stone into the brown water and watched the ripples flow downstream and soon disappear. He recalled as a child playing in the dirt in the cool shade of that tree with Barariel, and he thought of the times that they were there with Susanna and Ariel to pick apricots, and he smiled recalling a basket of that fruit on the table in summer when the days were hot and the cool fruit was sweet and refreshing to eat. He drew in a deep breath as he recalled when he and Gamela and Barariel had taken Monica there for the first time. That was shortly after they were married. Barariel had died before they could do that again. Monica never returned to that tree. He tossed another stone in the water. As the ripples disappeared, he was at peace that Monica had many good memories of his brother just as he did. As he walked away, he thanked God for the many blessings for those that he loved and could no longer be with. And he prayed that Joshua and Monica will make many treasured memories together.

Bartimaeus had at long last found his peace. His days were busy tending and training horses. The mature horses were trained to negotiate obstacles that they could encounter in battle. Bartimaeus enjoyed teaching a horse to have confidence and to trust that the rider would not ask the horse to do anything that it was not able to do.

When Bartimaeus returned home to Jericho, it had been the middle of summer. The days were now getting shorter, and he once more enjoyed the comfort of a light blanket on the bed at night with Gamela. Ariel was growing weaker. For the most part, she stayed at Ezra's house, and the families now ate all their meals there to be with her. Susanna often came to visit, and when she did, she would spend the night. When Susanna visited, she always brought special food with her from the markets of Jericho, and the women would gather at Ezra's house to prepare the meals, and they would invite Ariel to join in. It was a time of quiet contentment and joy. The homes were filled with laughter and love.

After the meals, the families would gather, and either Bartimaeus or Joshua would remember something that they heard either Peter or

John or one of the other apostles tell of Jesus, and they would share that with the families. Often one of the others would relate something that they recalled from the prophets or the book of wisdom that they related to what they had just heard about Jesus. All wished that they could travel to Jerusalem to meet the apostles and his followers to learn more about Jesus. At those times, there often was the question as to how the apostles would be able to spread the good news of Jesus to others and not just to those in Jerusalem. There was no answer to that question, but all agreed that God would surely send his messengers into the world as he had done with the prophets of old. They prayed that a disciple of Jesus would come to Jericho.

One day during those discussions, Ariel asked about baptism. She said that she remembered several years ago when a prophet named John was baptizing people on the other side of the Jordan River not far from Jericho, and that many people from Jericho went to listen to John and to be baptized by him and that even people from Jerusalem and Galilee had gone to him to be baptized. Bartimaeus added that he heard Matthew say that Jesus himself had been baptized by John there, and that is where some of the apostles from Galilee had begun to follow Jesus. Ariel said that she wished that she had gone to listen to John and to be baptized, and that she hoped that one of the apostles would come to Jericho so that she could be baptized. She ended by saying that with all that had happened to Bartimaeus and his cure by Jesus that she was glad that he had been baptized.

A few days later Susanna was once more with the family, but on that day, Ariel could not join them and stayed in bed. That evening Bartimaeus and Susanna stayed with Ariel, and Ariel once more talked about baptism. Susanna asked her mother if she would like to be baptized, and her mother nodded. Susanna turned to Bartimaeus, but not a word was needed. He said, "Let me call Gamela and the family." When they came together, Gamela had a pitcher of water. With Susanna and Gamela holding Ariel's head, Bartimaeus poured water on her and asked God the Father, his Son, Jesus, and the Holy Spirit of God to bless her. That night, in her sleep, with her family at her side, she joined her husband, Timaeus, and her son, Barariel, and all of God's children in paradise.

Part 4

Damascus

20

STEPHEN AND SAUL

Caiaphas and Annas and many in the Sanhedrin had mistakenly thought that the execution of Jesus would secure the continuation of their power and autocratic rule of the Jewish people. They had exercised their power for no purpose other than to demonstrate their dominance in all its hideous faces. Within days of that despicable act of crucifixion, their pompous gloating was punctured by the disappearance of Jesus's body and word of his resurrection from the dead. They countered this with lies that the followers of Jesus had stolen his body. Soon after, they were able to celebrate their ill-conceived attempt of deception when the apostles departed Jerusalem and returned to Galilee. The Jewish leader's worldly machinations to deny the people the good news that had been delivered by Jesus were buoyed up when the apostles were no longer publicly reminding the people of what Jesus had said and done. Then, with the conviction that Jesus, the Son of God, had come to deliver all into eternal glory with God the Father and strengthened by the Holy Spirit, the apostles had returned to Jerusalem. The apostles, teaching in the temple and ministering to the people, were now a far greater threat than the man that the apostles followed and that the Jewish leaders had condemned to death, Jesus of Nazareth, the Son of God.

In the few months since the crucifixion of Jesus and the return of the apostles to Jerusalem, a conflict ignited by the Sanhedrin and hierarchy of the temple against the growing community of believers in Jesus as the Christ and Son of God. An odious conflict that was rooted in the hearts of men that were so deafened by their own ego that they could not hear the voice of God. For some time, the priestly aristocracy of the temple had been confiscated by the Sadducee that did not believe in an afterlife. The Saducean faction of the Sanhedrin had achieved political power by bargaining behind closed doors with Herod and with the occupying Roman authorities. Much of the priesthood was fattened on the revenues of the temple. They were materialistic and corrupt. Worse, they were without faith, and they only paid opportunistic lip service to their God. To them, the teachings of the Nazarene and the preaching in his name by a small band of Galilean fishermen proclaiming the brotherhood of all, alms giving to the poor and the downtrodden, and worse, everlasting life for all must be stamped out.

The apostles, regardless of their arrests and beatings, continued in their open proclamation of Jesus as the fulfillment of the Jewish Law and as the living Son of God that had brought the promise of eternal life. To many, this was a teaching, a way of life that was a threat to the Sadducee power and privilege.

What Jesus had begun, he left his apostles and Christian followers to carry out. Within months of the apostles' return to Jerusalem from Galilee, where they had spent the last days with their Lord and Master and had been with him as he ascended into heaven, there were thousands in Jerusalem and travelers to the city that listened to the apostles. Many came to believe in Jesus as the Son of God and were baptized. But the apostles were burdened with an overwhelming onslaught. Not only were they to continue to teach and to bring new followers into the community of believers, but they also faced the complications of a diverse following of people from different lands and social distinctions.

This growing community of believers, although a welcome response to Jesus's instruction to preach to all, had become too great a burden for the small band of apostles. To assist them in this growing responsibility, they appointed men, called deacons, to assist them in their duties while many women took on the role of caregivers to all, especially the needy. One of these newly appointed deacons was a young man named Stephen. He began teaching and preaching at the Synagogue of Libertines where freed slaves and former Roman prisoners worshipped. Not all in that synagogue welcomed Stephen and his teachings, and those plotted with the Sanhedrin against Stephen.

It was not long before false testimony and charges were brought against Stephen. He was arrested by the temple guards and brought to a mock trial before the Sanhedrin. At the trial, after listening to the false testimony of blasphemy, Stephen had spoken with zeal and eloquence starting with testimony from the patriarchs and the prophets. He ended his personal testimony talking directly to the judges calling them stiff-necked and uncircumcised of heart, with ears that persist in resisting God as their fathers had done and as they did to that day. Stephen had no doubt as to his fate.

With accord, the judges screamed at him, "Stone him. Stone him to death," and they pushed him out into the waiting clutches of the prearranged mob.

Stoning was a legal form of Jewish Law, and its rules had to be observed. To see that the stoning was according to the letter of the Law, Caiaphas appointed, as the temple's chief observer, Saul of Tarsus, who was Gamaliel's brightest pupil and fervent adherent to all the Mosaic Laws. Such stoning must take place outside of the city walls. The mob shuttled Stephen, with the witnesses and Saul following, through the Sheep Gate near the temple to the lip of a small hill and an excavated pit with stones of the prescribed size in readiness for such executions.

Once at the stoning ground, the witnesses placed their hands on Stephen's head, then the guards stripped him of his cloak and tunic. He stood naked for his execution. The witnesses took off their own cloaks and laid them at the feet of Saul. With the witnesses casting the first stones, all quickly joined in shouting, "Stone the blasphemer!"

Through the din of the melee, Stephen could be heard to say, "Jesus, forgive them. Jesus, receive me." As he was bleeding on the ground, the young man looked into the eyes of Saul and died.

21

PAUL OF TARSUS

The first fifteen years of Saul's life was in Tarsus where he acquired three indelible traits: zealous passion for his Jewish faith and Mosaic Law, affection and fidelity to his family, and skill as a tentmaker. Prior to Stephen's stoning, he would not have conceived that he, a born and bred strict Jew, a zealot of his faith, and a scholar of Mosaic Law and adherent to its execution, would permit himself any critical retrospect in the stoning and death of the young follower of Jesus, Stephen. But in that self-inflicted conflict, he clung tenaciously to his Pharisee teaching and belief that Stephen, preaching in the name of the Nazarene, was a blasphemer and, according to the Law, must pay the ultimate price of his life. His sole comfort in that conclusion was that he must save others from paying that terrible price for such a misguided decision. The way to secure that solace was to remove those that had already fallen into that abyss by removing them from the public eye. Those errant, poorly educated Jews must be gathered up and have this deviant teaching driven from them, if necessary, by their death. For this, he had the support of Caiaphas, the Sanhedrin, the blind eye of Herod, and the tacit endorsement of Rome.

By now, as the ever-watchful guardian of the Law, Saul had come to believe that Bartimaeus, the husband of his sister, Gamela, had betrayed his place as the rightful protector of the family including its faithful observance of their God and the Mosaic Law. Saul was convinced that Bartimaeus had slid further down the slippery slope of damnation, and it was up to him to protect Gamela and her family from that tragedy. Saul took it upon himself to be the champion of the Jewish faith and to exterminate the errant followers of the Nazarene. In this, he devised a plan which Caiaphas readily endorsed. Saul would scour the synagogues to the north, in Galilee, the ancestral home of Jesus and his followers, and bind those that he sought and bring them back to Jerusalem to be dealt with as the Law required.

Caiaphas had equipped Saul with mounted guards and foot soldiers and had given him a packet of letters addressed to all of the synagogues of the north authorizing Saul in his pursuit. Saul's journey north took him through Jericho, and on the way, he stopped to visit Gamela. Before leaving Jerusalem, Saul had reports from the temple guards about the apostles of the Nazarene and had learned that some of Herod's guard, including Bartimaeus, were now seen among the followers. This had further incited his conviction that his brother-in-law was a public sinner and not worthy to be married to his sister.

When Saul and his entourage arrived in Jericho, he left the others to rest while he took a detour to Gamela's home. He came up the road past the stable, not pausing to leave his horse or to greet those there. He went directly to Gamela's house, and tying his horse, he proceeded in where he was greeted by Gamela and the children. Bartimaeus and Joshua were in the arena training horses and did not see Saul arrive.

After the welcoming and some refreshments, Saul grew serious and began to address Gamela. "I know that Bartimaeus left Jerusalem some time ago. Is he here?"

"Yes, he is here. Why do you ask? Do you know that he left Herod's guard?"

"Yes, and his being a soldier for Herod is no longer my concern, but I am glad that he is no longer serving that serpent."

Gamela stared at her brother anticipating what was to come. She turned to the children. "Please leave your uncle and I alone to talk. Mariam, see how you can help at the other house. Saul David, go to the stable and help Ezra. If you see your father, do not tell him that Saul is here. I will find your father and tell him myself."

Turning back to her brother, she said, "It is good to have Bartimaeus home. The children enjoy having their father back. I love him. He is at peace with himself and others. He has found some wonderful friends in Jerusalem and has been telling us about them. He has changed. What do you know of him?"

"Oh, yes. I know that he is spending a lot of time with those cursed followers of the Nazarene, and I believe that he has joined that outlawed sect and was baptized in that name. He has chosen the wrong road, and I need to protect you and the children so that you are not lost as well."

She bristled, "Bartimaeus is not lost. Of what I have seen of him lately, very much the contrary. Bartimaeus, my husband, has suffered much since his blindness, and I was wrong, very wrong in the way I reacted. I am sorry for that. I am sorry that I let your words influence me and to cause me to lose faith in the man that I love. I have seen the change in him, and yes, I am glad that he quit Herod's guard, but not for your reason. Not because that made him a sinner!" She stood and crossed her arms to her chest. Taking a few steps closer to her brother, she exclaimed, "And his blindness was not because he was a sinner! Not because he did not love me! Not because he was unfaithful! I know that now. I know that I should never have doubted him. I should never have listened to you."

In the ensuing silence, he rose. She reached out her arms toward him, then she added softly, "I know that you love me, and I love you. But you are wrong. I think that you are wrong in what you believe to be from God. I think that you are wrong about your God, my God. My God does not punish sinners. My God does not cast out sinners. If he did, we all would be blind. No, Saul, you look for God with that big wonderful head of yours. You need to look for him with your heart. If you listen with your heart, you will hear him."

She walked to him and put her hands on his shoulders. "Bartimaeus was cured by Jesus not because he was or was not a sinner. Jesus told him that he would see when he was blind, and

Bartimaeus got his sight back, but now I know that my husband really does see with the eyes of love. And I love him for that."

Saul took her hands. He said, "I do not know if you are right or wrong in what you just told me. I will think about what you said. Now I must leave. Tell the children goodbye for me. I will visit you again when I return to Jerusalem. And when I return, I will talk to Bartimaeus. I promise."

Saul's journey over the next several weeks took him through Samaria and Galilee where he learned that many, hearing of his mission, had fled to Damascus. He decided that he must pursue them to Damascus. As he was in sight of Damascus, suddenly his body was struck numb. In fright, he pulled back harshly on the reins, and the horse, to protect itself, reared and fell backward knocking Saul violently to the ground. He lay motionless on the hard ground from the violent impact to his head. He did not move; he could not move. How long he laid there motionless, he could not tell. In that foggy mist of consciousness, he heard a voice, not in his imagination, a voice clear and loud to his ears: *Saul, Saul, why do you persecute me?*

On the ground, not sure if he could move, not daring to try, he called out, "Who are you?"

In clear answer, louder than before, came the reply: *I am Jesus of Nazareth whom you persecute and wish to destroy. You cannot.*

Helpless and stunned, he searched his rattled mind for an answer. Finding no rational answer among his repertoire of existence, he simply responded, "Lord, what do you want me to do?"

The voice gave certain answer: *Go into the city, and there you will be told what you are to do.*

Soldiers tended to him and tried to raise him. They heard him speak, but no one other than Saul heard the voice talking to him. While speaking, Saul had laid there motionless, face covered with dirt from the trail, his eyes open but unfocused. Then, two men took him by the arms and, with a strong pull, raised him to his feet. He stood with arms outstretched pawing the air. Finally, he touched and then took hold of one of the men that had raised him, but his eyes did not look at the man. "He is blind," said one of the men. Saul cared little for what was said. Rather, he pondered what the voice that he had heard meant and what he was about to do.

The captain of the guard sent the mounted men onto Damascus with instructions to find suitable accommodations and a doctor to stand ready if needed. Those on foot stayed with Saul and helped him on his way. Saul remained silent until they came to the gate of Damascus. Saul then instructed the captain to send the remaining men to join the others. When they were alone, Saul instructed the captain that once they were inside the city, he was to ask where they might find a follower of Jesus. The captain objected and noted that he could be in danger if his identity was discovered. Saul insisted, and the captain agreed without understanding Saul's intent other than to possibly want to infiltrate that community. With blind Saul at his arm, the captain was led to the house of a man named Judas. Upon arriving, Saul begged the captain to withdraw. Shortly Judas opened the door, and Saul, in honesty, told him who he was and the mystery of what had just happened to him. Judas, casting his fate to the same Lord that Saul claimed to have heard, bade Saul to enter. For three days, blind Saul lay in bed and could be heard whispering.

Understanding the potential danger that Saul was in, the captain posted guards outside of Judas's house and monitored all who came and went. In Saul's incoherent state, he managed to mutter a message to Judas that neither the captain nor any of the men that accompanied him were to enter the house. Judas did manage to prevail upon Saul to allow doctors to see him and to treat his blindness and other injuries. What attention that he received had no effect on his eyes; he remained blind.

On the evening of Saul's arrival, Judas went out and met with the leaders of the followers of the Christ and told them of the unexpected guest at his house and what Saul had said to him. They questioned him as to the possibility that this was a ruse, but Judas assured them that Saul was truly blind and had been injured. Also, that he continually whispered. Much of the time those whispers seemed to be prayer, but other times he seemed to be talking to someone. It was agreed that Judas was to keep Saul at his house and to carefully watch him. They also agreed to immediately send a messenger to Jerusalem to inform Peter and hopefully receive back instructions as to what was to be done with Saul.

On the third day, a follower of Jesus the Christ that lived in Damascus named Ananias came to Judas's house where he was greeted and entered. He told Judas that he had heard from others of the strange story of Saul. Later, while at prayer, Ananias had heard a voice telling him to go to the house of Judas and to place his hands on Saul's eyes. Entering the room where Saul lay in bed, Ananias said to him, "Brother Saul, I am here because I heard the voice of our Lord, Jesus the Christ, to come to you." Saul reached one arm out toward Ananias who took that hand and said to him, "I was told that I was to place my hands on your eyes." Saul squeezed Ananias's hand then lowered his arm to his side.

Ananias placed his hands over Saul's eyes. With that simple act of obedience, God's will for Saul was set in motion. As Ananias withdrew his hands, he watched as the cloudy film on Saul's eyes faded, and Saul squinted to bring his eyes to focus. He turned and looked at Ananias. Those in the room placed their hands on Saul and gave thanks to God the Father, to his Son Jesus, and to the Spirit that breathes God's life into them.

For Saul, a man of passionate conviction and tireless dedication, he could not contain his desire to learn more of the man, Jesus, that he had previously swore to eradicate from the memory of his followers. Judas and Ananias and others came to Saul and told him all that they knew of Jesus. Saul, in hearing, would often jump to his feet and, pacing the room, would explain how the prophets of old foretold of that very thing. For Saul, not only had the sight of his eyes been restored, but the blindness of his life was lifted, and his heart soared. The more he heard, the more he learned, the greater was his fervor to share that with others. He wanted to burst through the door into the street proclaiming what he now knew, what he now believed, what he wanted to share with all.

When he heard Jesus's teaching that they were to go out and baptize all in the name of the Father, and the Son, and the Holy Spirit, he stated unequivocally, "Baptize me." When they poured the water of baptism over him, he proclaimed, "Saul is dead to me. That man no longer exists. I am now Paul, a servant of the Lord, Jesus the Christ."

Immediately, he begged to go to the synagogue. He strode boldly out the door with Judas and Ananias and others struggling to keep up. Those men still standing guard at the house fell in and cheered him on, not understanding what the new man, Paul, had in mind. On his part, Paul paid no attention to the men that had traveled many days with him on the previous endeavor. He was on a new mission, and there was no looking back. Those men were soon to hear this new man, as he hurried to the synagogue. Once in the synagogue, the learned Pharisee immediately began to explain the scriptures and how those words had been fulfilled in Jesus the Nazarene, now Jesus the Christ, the Son of God. He answered challenges by the rabbis, and he strengthened those that sought to learn more. Startled and confused, the captain of the guard sent men with the fastest horses to Jerusalem. Caiaphas must be told of what has happened to his champion. The captain also revised the orders for the others. They were no longer to be posted as guards for Saul. Now they were to be vigilant as to the comings and goings of this changed man and all others at this house. They were to always know where Saul was, who he was with, and what he was doing. Other messages would be sent to Caiaphas as they had more to report of this man that now called himself Paul.

22

MESSENGERS ARRIVE IN JERUSALEM

When Saul left Jerusalem, Caiaphas could not have expected to receive accounts from messengers of the startling events that were transpiring in Damascus. Nor was Caiaphas prepared for the report that Saul was not pursuing and arresting the followers of Jesus but was in fact preaching in the synagogue of Damascus that Jesus was the fulfillment of the prophets and of the Law. For Caiaphas, once convinced of the tale, the verdict was clear. The previously ardent defender of Mosaic Law must pay the price that he extracted of others. Saul, now calling himself Paul, must die. Further, he must die in Damascus and not be allowed to return to Jerusalem where he might try to spread this malicious heresy and blasphemy among others. Under Caiaphas's direction, orders were sent with temple guards and hired assassins to Damascus for the purpose of killing the traitor, Saul.

While Caiaphas was ultimately convinced of Saul's transgression, Peter was not willing to believe the account that the zealous Pharisee and guardian of the Law had capitulated his long-held beliefs and had adopted what he not so long ago had vowed to destroy. What Peter needed was a firsthand account of the man, now claiming the name of Paul, that had come to believe in Jesus of Nazareth not only as the fulfillment of the Law but as the Son of God, and that Jesus was sent to bring the truth and the way and the eternal life to mankind.

After Peter received the message from Damascus and the report of all that had happened to and by the man now calling himself Paul, Peter summoned the apostles to determine what was to be done. The decision was made that someone be sent to Damascus to investigate and to possibly meet with Saul to assess the veracity of what was being reported. That person would need to travel quickly and to be a reliable witness to determine the truth. Mostly, that person may be called upon to encounter Saul with those inherent risks. Thomas offered that Bartimaeus may be the person to send since he knew Saul better than anyone and could best travel and defend himself if needed. Peter agreed. Who better to send to investigate and even to interrogate Saul than his brother-in-law, Bartimaeus, a man that himself had been a victim of Saul's vindictive, religious posturing? Since Bartimaeus was in Jericho, someone would need to relay that request to him. Thomas added that there were friends of Bartimaeus in the guard that possibly could leave quickly and deliver a message to Bartimaeus. The apostles agreed that sending Bartimaeus to Damascus was the best source of information. Thomas immediately left for the guard barracks to solicit the help of one of Bartimaeus's friends in the guard while Peter composed a letter to Bartimaeus requesting his help.

Shortly, Thomas returned and told Peter that one of Bartimaeus's friends could leave immediately to carry a message to him. When Peter had finished writing a letter to Bartimaeus with instructions, Thomas took it to the guard stable where a soldier was waiting to depart immediately for Jericho with the message for Bartimaeus.

Within a few hours, the messenger arrived at Bartimaeus's home. The messenger stopped at the stable and left the well-used horse to be cooled and tended to. He was told that Bartimaeus was in his home for which he hastened. On entering Bartimaeus's house, he announced that he had an urgent message from Peter and handed him the letter.

Bartimaeus called for Gamela to join him and sent Saul David to bring Joshua to the house. He invited the messenger to sit and rest as he read the letter in case there were questions or a message to send back to Peter. By the time that Joshua arrived, he had read Peter's letter. He then proceeded to read it aloud for all. Peter's letter told the facts, as best they were known, about Saul's condition and him proclaiming to be a follower of Jesus and his preaching in the synagogue. The letter related that Saul had a fall from his horse as he approached Damascus and was struck blind. Immediately after, and for some time, Saul heard voices, presumably from Jesus. He was taken to the house of Judas where he was cared for, and shortly after, his blindness was cured. Immediately, after being cured, Saul began preaching of Jesus in the synagogue. Because of this, he was under surveillance by the temple guards that had accompanied him, but so far, there had been no attempt to stop his activities by either those that came with him or anyone from the synagogue. The letter stated that Saul now called himself Paul. It ended with Peter's request for Bartimaeus to ride to Damascus to determine the truth and to report back to Peter in Jerusalem. Bartimaeus asked if there was anything else that the messenger knew that was important. The messenger related the fact that not too long ago that Saul had been a witness to the stoning of Stephen and that there was question as to whether the reports of Saul could be trusted and that anyone going to Damascus would do so at serious risk.

Bartimaeus looked up as he finished reading the hastily composed and, at best, uncertain understanding of the facts. His attention was immediately drawn to Gamela who, looking directly at Bartimaeus with consternation in her voice, said, "You cannot go! It is too dangerous! This may be a trap for anyone, and if so, you would be at the greatest risk in dealing with Saul. The journey alone is too dangerous! You have risked too much already with your life. We need you here."

Gamela had barely finished speaking when Joshua stood up and interjected, "I will go to Damascus! You have done enough! You should stay here with your family! I can leave immediately."

Bartimaeus held his hand up to his friend. "Joshua, I appreciate your offer. That is very kind." Turning to Gamela, he said, "And I agree with you that we do not know what we will find in Damascus or what has happened, if anything, with your brother. And, yes, the journey will be long and dangerous. But let us think about this. The journey has risk, but I have traveled that road before with the guard, and I know safe places to rest and where to be more cautious. As far as meeting with Saul, no one knows him better than me, and who best to judge what he tells us?" Standing up, he added, "We cannot leave this unanswered. I must go to Damascus and find out the truth for Peter. I will leave early tomorrow."

Joshua and the messenger rose. The messenger said, "I will return to Jerusalem today and advise Peter."

Joshua said, "Let us go to the stable. I will give you a fresh horse for your return trip. I can exchange those the next time that we go to Jerusalem." With that, the two men departed leaving Bartimaeus and Gamela alone.

Bartimaeus went to her and helped her to her feet. He stepped close and put his arms about her. He said, "I know that this is difficult for you. We have so much enjoyed our time together. The last thing that I want is to leave you and the children. But this is something that must be done, and I am the best one to do it. We will talk more, but let me go to the stable and talk to Ezra and Joshua. I need to have their help in getting ready to leave tomorrow." He dropped his hands to hold hers and kissed her tenderly.

Bartimaeus walked to the stable thinking of what he would need on the journey. At the stable, he asked Ezra and Joshua to pick two good horses that were fit for a hard four day journey to Damascus without much rest along the way. Also, that the two horses were to be companions that would travel together during the journey because he did not want to lead one of the horses.

Gamela was standing alone outside of her home when Bartimaeus left the stable. As he headed her way, she walked toward him. They met and locked arms as they walked home. She said, "Bartimaeus, I am worried for you. It is a long trip to Damascus, especially alone. And what has happened to my brother? It is difficult for me to understand that he not only would stand by when a young man was stoned to death for his belief but that he played a part and endorsed his death! This is all very frightening! Now we are told that Saul had a fall from a horse and was struck blind."

They stopped walking and turned to each other. Taking his hands and squeezing them, she said, "That is what happened to you! What does this mean? Jesus cured your blindness. Then Saul was struck blind trying to destroy any memory of Jesus."

"Gamela, I wish that I knew what this means or had an explanation for you. I do not. There is so much about Jesus that is a mystery. And so much more about his followers that is an ongoing mystery. Just like with me, I cannot explain what I believe or why. I just do what I feel I am called to do. It is something inside, not just in my mind. I really did not know this Jesus of Nazareth, but I know his friends and I have seen what they are and what they do, and because of them, I have come to believe. I never saw the living Jesus, but I have come to believe in him."

"I have seen you change. The children and I talked about it when you were gone. We talked to your mother about it before she died. We have talked to Ezra and his family. We have all seen it in you. Because of you, we have come to believe too. We want to learn more. Joshua has answered many of our questions. He loves you. You know that, don't you?"

He nodded agreement but did not feel the need to answer. They continued to their home. Later they returned to Ezra's for dinner where Joshua joined them. At dinner they talked about Bartimaeus's travel to Damascus and possibilities of what he might find with Saul and how he could best deal with various situations that could occur. Bartimaeus then turned their attention to the possibility of danger from Caiaphas. That Caiaphas might well plant seeds of insurrection by the followers of Jesus with Herod to solicit his support. Joshua added that he had noticed some discontent among Herod's guard toward him and other soldiers that had become followers of Jesus. He felt a growing rift and even some aggressive behavior by some. Bartimaeus had the same feelings, and he was concerned that Caiaphas's overt actions along with even the slightest support by Herod could lead to violence not only in Jerusalem but elsewhere. Bartimaeus noted that he was concerned that any actions that he might take in Damascus could result in attention being drawn toward him. He himself was not concerned for his safely, but since any travel by others to and from Damascus required their passing through Jericho that that would place the homes of Gamela and Ezra under possible scrutiny and surveillance. He told them that while he was away in Damascus that he would like the family to go to Jerusalem. Joshua volunteered to take them and that he could drive a cart carrying Gamela and Mariam with Saul David riding a horse. The community of followers in Jerusalem would care for them, and Joshua would return to Jericho the next day. Gamela added that she was anxious to meet Jesus's apostles and that she would like to visit Jerusalem. With that resolved, they parted to prepare for their journeys starting early the next morning.

In the morning, Gamela and Joshua insisted that Bartimaeus leave first since he had a long journey ahead of him. When Bartimaeus mounted his horse, he noticed that there was a light pack of food and other necessities on the second horse and that a broad sword was strapped to the pack. When Joshua noticed that Bartimaeus had seen the sword, he said, "You may have left your sword in Jerusalem, but now you may find you need this one."

Bartimaeus looked back at his friend. "I could not use it the last time when I had good cause. Why would I use it when I do not?" Then he waved to all, and without looking back, he set off on the road to Damascus.

Joshua and Gamela finished loading the cart with what they would need. Saul David mounted a horse. They said goodbye to Ezra and the family as they took the road in the opposite direction toward Jerusalem.

When they had only gone a short distance, Joshua said, "I want to stop in Jericho to tell Monica where I am going and when I will be back. I also want to ask her to marry me when I return."

Gamela took him by the arm and said with a warm smile, "Can I come with you? I want to be with the two of you when she says yes." With that, Joshua drove the horse on at a trot.

23

Paul's Escape from Damascus

Bartimaeus turned north and picked up an easy trot toward Damascus. He was pleased with the horses that Ezra had selected for him. They were both geldings, about six years old, well trained, and companions to each other. Most importantly, they were sturdy and sound and of light conformation which would be important on the long and rugged journey. Both horses had been on pasture with light duty and were fresh and readily kept a brisk pace. That was important for Bartimaeus to take his mind off where he was going and what he was to accomplish, and, worse, what and who he was leaving behind. He feared as he rode away that the terrible haunting within him from the past would set him questioning what he was doing and the myriad of doubts that would plague him. The anxieties of the last few years were always lurking to snare him, and he knew that they were false emotions that preyed on his mind, especially the fear of the unknown. He also knew that being on a horse was a haven to keep his emotions and fears from paralyzing him.

As he brought the horse back to a walk, he focused on what was ahead of him rather than what was behind. There was no way that he could anticipate what he would find with Saul, nor what, if anything, his reactions would be. If the reports from Damascus were true, the Saul that he knew would not equate to the Paul that he was being sent to encounter and to measure.

He had made this journey other times on assignments for Herod. Those had taken six days, but those were with the company of several other members of the guard and without spare horses. Now, his plan was to travel about fifty miles the first day to Beth-Shean. Traveling along the river, he would have water and a few rest stops allowing the horses to graze along the riverbank.

On the second day, he would cross the Jordan River then travel up the east bank to the Sea of Galilee. He would find lodging there along with good stabling for the horses. That would be the easy and most pleasant part of the journey. He particularly looked forward to traveling the road that Jesus had traveled with his apostles between Galilee and Jerusalem. From the start of the journey, he was seeing the road and the land in a completely different light. He would imagine traveling with Jesus and the apostles and the stories that he heard about Jesus, his teachings, and his miracles along that road.

The evening of the second day, he took time to ride to the Sea of Galilee, also called the Sea of Tiberius, where he imagined Jesus calling Peter and Andrew from their boats to follow him. He watched as a bearded man pushed off a boat with younger men onboard. He talked with the man who said that it was his boat and those on it were his sons. Bartimaeus pictured Peter, then called Simon, pushing off his boat with his sons onboard as he left with his brother, Andrew, to follow Jesus. He wondered if Peter missed that life, and surely, he missed his sons and wife as he himself did. With that, he thought of all that they had left behind, what they cherished, including loved ones, in following Jesus. He knew that Jesus had not called him as Jesus had called Peter and the others. With that thought, he repeated Jesus's words to him, *"Oh, yes, you will see again,"* and after saying that, he acknowledged to himself, *"Yes, Jesus really has called me."*

The third and fourth days were the most difficult. Not only did he have more than fifty miles to cover, but he would also climb more than two thousand feet to Damascus. The road would be narrow and rocky with no water except at wells and little feed for the horses. It was now the heat of summer, and he did not look forward to that part of the journey.

As he neared Damascus, he thought about Saul falling from his horse and hitting his head and going blind. He shook his head at the irony; Saul had staunchly maintained that Bartimaeus's blindness was due to sin! He wondered how Saul was considering his own fate, especially since Saul was committed to rid the followers of Jesus from the Jewish people. Thinking of Saul changing his name to Paul, he shrugged and said to himself, *"He is still Saul to me!"*

He entered the south gate of Damascus on the afternoon of the fourth day and asked about the best stable for the horses which they had earned. He would need them, maybe soon, for his return to Jericho. By now, Gamela and the children would be in Jerusalem and would have met Peter and the apostles and would be well cared for by them. He also knew in his heart that they would be anxious to learn of Jesus after all that he had told them, and that they would embrace all that they learned. He thought that maybe they would be baptized before he could join them. That troubled him at first, but he came to peace with the realization that they would be anxious to join him in that new way of being. He mused at the idea of a new way of life. Certainly, he had been on a new way since Jesus found him at the gate of Jericho. That seemed so long ago, but it was only a little more than two years.

The messenger from Damascus said that Saul was at the home of a man named Judas on the street that is called Straight. He inquired of that street at the stable and was given directions. After a short walk and inquiry as to the home of Judas, he found himself outside the house where he expected to find his personal nemesis. Before knocking on the door, he said a prayer, *"Jesus of Nazareth, Son of God, give me the strength to do your will."* When the door opened, he announced himself, "I was sent here by Peter in Jerusalem to see the man called Saul. I am Bartimaeus. I am married to his sister, Gamela."

The man carefully eyed him and looked over his shoulder into the street. He saw those that he knew stood guard over the house and sought to capture Saul. Those same guards seemed to be just as curious about the stranger that had just arrived at the door. The man that answered the door said, "Please wait here," and he closed the door.

Bartimaeus turned and surveyed the street. His training allowed him to easily spot those that were watching the house, and for a moment, he regretted not having the sword that Joshua sent, but he had left it with other gear at the stable.

In a few minutes, the door opened, and the man said, "Please forgive me. We must be careful who we allow in. We understand that Paul's life is in danger. I am Judas. Paul says that he knows you. He was surprised to hear that you have come. He seems very troubled to receive you. That is not what I would expect from a man whose brother-in-law had traveled many miles to see him, especially under these circumstances. But he said to let you in."

Bartimaeus entered, and Judas bolted the door. As Judas led him through the house, Bartimaeus replied, "We have not seen each other for a while, and we are not particularly close."

Judas looked at him while nodding his head in an understanding way. "Sometimes family members do not see each other as they truly are."

"Yes, that is true." As if to change the topic and in an apologetic tone, he added, "Peter sent me."

"Oh, yes. That would explain why you are here."

Saul was standing at the far end of the small room when Judas stepped in followed by Bartimaeus. Judas proceeded to the center of the room, but Bartimaeus stayed at the doorway. Saul stood at a small table that contained pen, ink, and writing material. Behind him was a small backless chair that appeared to have been pushed back as Saul stood up. There was another similar chair, a cot, and a lampstand in the room. Judas turned and looked at Bartimaeus expecting him to speak. Seeing no response, he turned back to Saul.

The silence was broken by Saul. "Why are you here?"

"Peter sent me," was the quick reply.

Both looked as to weigh the other's words and what other meaning there may be. Finding none, Saul spoke again. "I had heard that you were no longer a soldier for Herod, and I see that you do not carry his sword."

"I no longer have use of a sword." Bartimaeus added, "You never carried a sword. You let others carry one for you."

The silence was broken as Judas stepped back and, holding his hands out to both men, said, "I will leave the two of you alone for a few minutes. I will go prepare some water so that our guest can wash himself. I am sure that he is very tired. Please excuse me."

Bartimaeus took a step into the room as Judas walked out. Saul looked down at the material on the table and, without raising his head, said, "What has Peter heard?"

"Messengers from Damascus said that you have been talking in the synagogue about Jesus. You are saying that Jesus is the fulfillment of the Law. That he is the Son of God."

"Yes, that is true."

"We have also heard that on the way to Damascus to arrest those that had fled from you in Galilee that you had a fall from your horse and struck your head. You were blinded. Your men led you here to the house of Judas to be cared for. Another man was sent to see about you. You told him that you were hearing voices. Jesus was speaking to you. That man cured you, and after that, you are now telling others in the synagogue about Jesus.

"Yes, Bartimaeus, that is all true. I was blind for three days. I heard voices. I heard God talk to me. It was Jesus telling me why he came as he did. That he was the fulfillment of the Law. I laid here for three days listening to him. All that I knew from our prophets, from our scripture had come true in him. I believe. Then Ananias came, and I was cured."

"Peter sent me to see you. To talk to you. To learn whether we can believe what is reported or whether this is a trick. I do not know whether to believe you or not, Saul."

"I am no longer the Saul that you knew"—bringing his hands to his breast in a pleading gesture—"I wish that you would call me Paul."

Bartimaeus bristled and stepped foreward, his voice rose, "If wishes were horses, beggars would ride… Paul!"

The two men stood facing each other. Bartimaeus could feel the hurt, the anger well up inside of him, and he glared at Paul. Paul showed no emotion, certainly no animosity or judgment toward his accuser.

Bartimaeus continued, "So you were blind for three days! Three days! Then cured. Now we are to believe you! Good people have been punished because of you. People have been killed. Jesus was killed by people that you followed. Why should I believe you? Why should we trust you?"

"Bartimaeus, I thought of you while I was blind. I was afraid that I might never see again. I thought of how I had treated you. How I had judged you. I thought of the pain that I caused you and my sister. I am sorry. I am sorry for you and for Gamela. I am sorry for the death of that young man, Stephen. I remember his words. I remember how he looked to heaven as his blood spilled onto the ground. Yes, I am sorry for not believing in Jesus. I am sorry for his death. I am sorry that I did not believe you. Jesus cured me. I ask you to trust me. I know that you should not, but will you?"

"Paul, you ask much of me. I forgave you before I came. Gamela and I forgave you. That is over. I can believe that Jesus cured you. He cured me. I do not know why for either of us. Jesus said that I would see, and I came to understand what he meant. I needed to be blind so that I could truly see. I suppose that you also needed to be blind so that you could believe, that both of us would see and believe in Jesus. It really does not matter that I believe you. What matters is what Jesus intends you to see. What is it that God has for you to do? Just as I was sitting at the gate of Jericho when Jesus called me, to change me, maybe so too you have been called. Maybe there is something that you are to do that no one else could do. I do not know, Paul, that is for you to find out. You ask me to trust you. I am not sure that I am ready for that, but I have learned to trust my God, to trust in his Son, Jesus. Will you?"

Bartimaeus's demand for an answer stunned both men. For Bartimaeus, where he stood, what he had just said to his greatest adversary and the cause of his most intense suffering, this was finally proof to him that he trusted the God that he now knew.

For Paul, to him, there was never a question of trusting God. The question that Paul was unsure of answering was did he deserve trust from his God.

The silence was broken when Bartimaeus spoke, this time with hands open and outstretched toward Paul. In a tone no longer a demand but a plea. "Will you?"

Paul looked down at the table before him. He reached out and gathered the scrolls together. He picked up one and held it out to Bartimaeus. "I am trying to write what I know in my heart, what Jesus has told me. But I cannot. The words will not come to me. I am like a child babbling. Yes, I can see but I cannot see the words of Jesus clearly. I see dimly, like I am looking into a mirror. I believe that Jesus has something for me to do but I am not ready. Like an athlete, I am not prepared for the race. I need time to train; time to ready myself to run the race for Jesus Christ." He dropped the scroll to the table.

Bartimaeus stepped to the table opposite Paul. He picked up the scroll that Paul had discarded. He held it but did not open it. He extended it toward Paul. "Jesus told me that I would see, and I did. But, like you, I did not see clearly until my friends taught me to truly see. Unlike you, I only heard a few words from Jesus. Jesus has been speaking to you, maybe he still is. For you, I hope so."

Paul extended an arm over the table with open hand toward Bartimaeus and the scroll. Without losing eye contact, Bartimaeus placed the scroll back in Paul's hand.

"Paul, I don't know what Jesus has for me to do. I hope that I am doing whatever it is. You don't know what Jesus has for you to do, but I am sure that he will tell you and strengthen you so that you can succeed. May we both do whatever Jesus asks of us."

Bartimaeus released the scroll to Paul as Judas entered the room. Judas stepped forward and looking first intently at Paul then at Bartimaeus, "Will you stay for dinner?"

Paul, still focused on Bartimaeus responded, "Yes, he is staying. I need him."

"Good. Come, I have water for you to wash, then let us visit and eat. I would like to hear what is happening in Jerusalem."

The three men shared dinner together while Bartimaeus answered questions from the other two. Judas was interested in what was happening with the apostles and the many followers of Jesus. Paul wanted to know more about the life of Jesus and what Bartimaeus had learned from the apostles, especially what Jesus had taught them and the crowds that had followed him.

Judas sensed that the tenseness between the two men had subsided, and he invited Bartimaeus to stay in his house, and Bartimaeus agreed.

When dinner was over, Bartimaeus excused himself to return to the stable. He wanted to gather the few items that he had brought with him and to check on the horses. Although that was the reason that he gave, he really wanted to learn more about the men that were outside watching the house and what danger they may present to Paul or to others. When he left the house, he noticed the men standing in the shadows outside Judas's house, and he knew that one followed him to the stable.

When he arrived in Damascus, he had gone directly to a stable that was recommended as the best. At the stable, he had spoken to a bearded man named Noah and had given him instructions that the horses were to be there for several days and that they were to be well cared for. Noah had assured him that he and his three sons would see to the needs of such fine horses. When Bartimaeus returned to the stable that evening, he saw that the horses had been washed and brushed and were in clean stalls with fresh feed. Noah was not in sight, but a young boy hurried to him.

Coming directly to Bartimaeus, the boy eagerly said, "Those are beautiful horses. I have never seen anything like them. Where did you get them?"

"My family raises those horses in Jericho. They have been bred from stallions and mares that came from Egypt. There is nothing like them here. They can travel long distances in the desert. They are very intelligent and easy to train. I am glad that you like them. My name is Bartimaeus. What is yours?"

"I am Joseph, and I help my father. I have two older brothers, and they also work here."

"When I arrived, I talked to a man named Noah. Is he here?"

"He is my father. He is not here now. He left me to watch the horses."

"Joseph, it is good to meet you. I am glad that you recognize fine horses."

He gathered the few items that he had brought with him, and this time that included the sword that Joshua sent. As he was leaving, he noticed large baskets in the stable that were used to haul hay for the horses. Being in no hurry to return to Judas's house and being much at ease in the stable, he turned to Joseph. "I see that these baskets have hay in them. The streets are very narrow. How do they deliver these baskets?"

Joseph, enjoying the attention, said, "Let me show you." Taking Bartimaeus by the hand, Joseph took him out the back of the stable that opened to the outer city wall. There previously had been a gate there, but that had been closed off, probably many years ago. Joseph took him to the wall where two thick ropes hung down.

With a smile, he said, "The baskets are filled from a wagon on the other side of the wall. Then they are lifted to the top of the wall with ropes. My brothers on top of the wall then move the baskets over to this side, and the baskets are lowered down. We send the empty baskets up in the same way. My father and my brothers do this for the owner. I will be able to help when I am bigger. The baskets are very heavy."

"That is very interesting. Thank you for showing this to me. I will be back tomorrow. Make sure that my horses are well cared for and have fresh water."

"We will take good care of them. They are beautiful. We do not usually have such fine horses here. I hope that they are here a long time."

Bartimaeus handed Joseph a small coin knowing that this would assure that the horses continued to be well cared for. Joseph, opening his hand and looking at the coin, with a big smile added, "Thank you. I will take good care of your horses myself."

Bartimaeus placed his hand on Joseph's head as he turned to leave the stable. Once outside, he returned the way that he came, and he knew that the man followed him once again.

Judas was on the roof waiting for Bartimaeus to return and had the door open to welcome him. He led his guest down a hall past

Paul's room. The door to Paul's room was closed, but the light from the lamp could be seen under the door. Judas said, "Paul is writing. He stays up late every night writing. I do not know what he has to write about."

Bartimaeus responded, "I do not know either, but there is much of this new man that I do not know."

Judas showed him to his room. "I hope that whatever has gone on between the two of you is over. He seems very sincere and anxious to tell others about Jesus. The men outside always follow him. So far, they have not bothered him. But I fear for him."

"Yes, I can see that. Thank you for letting me stay here. I believe that Paul is a different man, and our problems of old are no more. Good night." Bartimaeus said nothing about being followed that night or of his feeling of danger from the men outside.

After three nights of traveling, Bartimaeus was grateful for a comfortable bed, and he was soon asleep. He woke early, dressed, and left his room. He passed Paul's room, and once again he saw the lamp in his room was lit. Judas was already up, and Bartimaeus joined him. He said, "Thank you for allowing me the comfort of your home. I did not know what to expect when I got here. As I think that you realize, I have known Saul—excuse me, Paul, as he wants to be called—for many years."

"How do you know Paul?"

Bartimaeus told the story of him and Paul and ended with, "I was cured of my blindness by Jesus as he was going through Jericho on his way to Jerusalem."

Judas asked, "So you knew Jesus?"

"No. I never saw Jesus. It took a little while for my vision to return after he cured me and by then he had walked away on his journey to Jerusalem. I wanted to follow him, but I visited my family in Jericho before I left. When I got to Jerusalem, Jesus had already been crucified and had risen from the dead. As you can imagine, the fact that I was cured of my blindness by Jesus did not make things better between me and Paul. I, like many others in Jerusalem, became a believer in Jesus through the words of Peter and John and the other apostles. Messengers from Damascus arrived to tell Peter what had happen to Paul, but Peter did not know whether to believe the account or if this was a trick. As you now know, Peter sent me to investigate."

"And what now of you and your wife?" Judas asked.

"After learning of Jesus's ways, I did come to see as Jesus told me that I would. I came to peace with Paul's judgement of me, and eventually, Gamela saw that I was changed, not only from my blindness but inside of me. I had no control over Paul or his judgment of me. Nor could I change Gamela. Eventually, I told her about Jesus and his followers. I believe that she too was ready for a change. When I left Jericho to come to Damascus, she and the children were going to Jerusalem to meet Peter and the others. I am anxious to join her. It will be a whole new beginning for us. She will be glad and very surprised when I tell her of her brother. I am not sure that she will believe what I tell her. I am not sure I believe it myself."

The two spent time learning of each other and how they had come to believe in Jesus. Judas said, "Many people in Damascus have come to believe. They hear stories from the people that come here fleeing from Galilee, but Paul's preaching has convinced many. He speaks simply but with authority. His knowledge of the scriptures and of the prophets is very useful. He explains to the people that Jesus was the fulfillment of all that God has told his people, from Abraham through Moses and even to John the Baptizer. The people want to hear more from him."

"So he is preaching in the synagogue? How long has that been?"

"Since right after he was cured. He demanded to go to the synagogue."

"What about the men that are watching the house outside?"

"The first day, they all ran up to him. That was when they learned that he could see again. They wanted to talk to him. They were asking him about what they were going to do. Were they going to start to arrest the followers of Jesus? Paul would not answer them. He ignored them. He simply walked to the synagogue with the guards following him. Of course, once Paul was in the synagogue and he started talking to the priests and the people, the guards did not know what to think. Some were angry at what he said. Others were convinced that it was a trick to bring into the open those that they were to arrest. This went on for several days. Eventually some of them rode off. I suppose that they went to Jerusalem to tell Caiaphas."

"And now, what are the guards outside your door doing?"

"They have not done anything yet. They just follow him each day to the synagogue. They sit there and listen. Then they follow us back here."

"Do you go with him?"

"Yes, I like to hear him speak. He has much to tell."

"And what of the others in the synagogue?"

"More are coming all the time. All that fled from Galilee are there. They believe what he says. They want to hear from him. By now, they trust him. It is very strange. He tells them what he has done in the past. He tells them that he was wrong. That Jesus himself tells him what he is to say."

"When were messengers from the synagogue sent to Jerusalem to tell Peter what was happening?"

"It took several days of Paul preaching in the synagogue for his men to suspect that he had changed. But Paul never talked to them or tried to explain what he was doing. They were free to listen to him in the synagogue. The last few days some of them have been very angry and challenging what he says. He does not get angry. He thanks them. Can you imagine! He answers them with authority from the scriptures. When we saw some of his men ride off, we knew what they were going to do. The next day, we sent our messenger to Peter."

"That means that Caiaphas received word from his messengers about a day before Peter. Peter sent a messenger to me to ask me to go to Damascus the day that he received the message from Damascus. I was able to travel a day or two quicker than the others. That means that we can expect a response from Caiaphas here in Damascus any day. We need to be watchful. Caiaphas may send a message to arrest Paul, or even worse."

As Bartimaeus finished speaking, Paul walked in. "I do not intend to be watchful of anything that Caiaphas or any of the others could do to me. I believe that what God has done for me in these past days was done so that what I have learned is shared with others. I will not be quiet. I will dedicate my life to spreading the word of Jesus. I want to do that not only with the Jews. I am a citizen of Rome. I want peoples from all over the empire to know of Jesus. That, I firmly believe, is the plan that God has for me. This is just the start of my training. I have a race to run, and I will train to be a champion."

Judas responded, "Well said, Paul. You speak like a champion already."

"Only for Jesus. All else is nothing. But let us not talk among ourselves. I must return to the synagogue."

"If you do not mind, Paul. You may be able to live without food, but I have had little to eat for many days, and I believe that I smell warm bread from Judas's oven."

Judas added, "Yes, my friends. Let us eat well before we set off for the day. I am told that even Jesus liked a good meal. And he liked sharing it with others."

There was no more conversation while they ate. It was clear that Paul was anxious to return to the synagogue, and the other two realized that any attempt to delay this man of intense purpose was futile. Paul was the first to stand and, without word, hastened from the room. Bartimaeus and Judas shrugged their shoulders, took a last few bites of bread, and followed him. Bartimaeus went to his room and gathered his cloak. He looked at the sword on the chair, then turned and exited down the hall leaving the sword where it lay.

Paul was already at the door when Bartimaeus arrived with Judas close behind with a servant. The servant unbolted the door and swung it open. Paul took a step toward the opening, but Bartimaeus quickly stepped through the door in front of him. His attention, trained to guard important people in his care, immediately went to the men standing outside. He noticed that there were more than yesterday, and worse, some of the men were wearing the uniform of the temple guards. He knew then that those to do the bidding of Caiaphas had arrived from Jerusalem.

Paul stepped out and was closely followed by Judas. Bartimaeus saw that those guarding the house were advancing toward them. As he was watching those men approach, Paul stepped around him toward the street and the advancing men. Bartimaeus called out, "Paul, stop." But Paul kept moving forward. Bartimaeus rushed to Paul and, from behind, grabbed an arm. Paul pulled his arm back. Bartimaeus more forcefully reached out, this time forcing himself in front. By now, Judas had recognized the peril and had joined Bartimaeus in trying to restrain Paul. The two men were able to slow Paul enough for the servant to grab the back of Paul's cloak and drag him back to the doorway. With one last shove from Bartimaeus, Paul was back in the house. The servant was pushing the door closed, but Bartimaeus stood in the way. The first guard to arrive put his hand on the door as if to push it open, but Bartimaeus stepped between him and the door. The two men locked eyes. The guard's hand went to the sword at his side. Bartimaeus's stare never wandered from the other man. The guard had a choice to make: draw his sword and attempt to use it against this man that dared to confront him or to back away. The guard was good at playing the role of dominance against old men and women at the temple, but here was a man that clearly was not intimidated nor showed fear. He removed his hand from his sword and let his focus drop away. Then he turned to the others and signaled with his hand to stop. The servant pulled the door open as Bartimaeus slipped in and slammed it shut.

Paul was still facing the door. Judas put his arm on his shoulder and said, "I do not believe that you will be going to the synagogue anymore." The three men walked down the hall. Paul turned into his room but left the door open.

Judas said, "Let us go into the courtyard. We must talk about what we are to do."

The courtyard behind the house was a large area, fully enclosed by a wall made of rock and clay bricks. It stood higher than a man's head and provided a degree of privacy and security. Inside the wall was a variety of fruit and olive trees. At one side of the house was a gate that opened to the street. Judas beckoned him to sit in the shade of a large grape arbor.

"Bartimaeus, this is very bad. Paul is now a prisoner in my house, and it is not just Paul. It is I and my family that also are prisoners. What are we to do?"

"You are right, Judas. We managed to hold them off this time, but I would not want to try that again. I did not make a friend of the man that is probably their leader. The next time he will have other men with him, and there is nothing that any of us can do to stop them from taking Paul. And we cannot ask the local people to help. That would make matters worse and possibly cause injury."

"Peter has sent you on a very dangerous mission."

"Judas, as much unlike Paul and I are to each other, in many ways, there is something very unusual that has brought us together." He stopped and looked away.

Judas waited for Bartimaeus to look back. "What is that, my friend?"

"We were both struck blind, and Jesus cured us both. I never had a chance to know Jesus. I came to know Jesus through others. Paul chose not to know Jesus, but through him, others will know and believe in Jesus. Why? I do not understand Jesus's ways."

"Neither do I." Paul walked from behind the grape arbor. "I surely do not." Paul sat and stretched out his hands toward Bartimaeus. "From what you told me, you cried out to Jesus that day in Jericho. You cried out to him to have mercy on you. Have you not realized that he was the one to call out to you first? He was calling to you before you knew it. He called out to you when you were struck blind. If it had not been for that, maybe you would never have known him or wanted to follow him. You have been blessed."

Paul took a few steps away from the others and turned his back to them. "I was born in Tarsus of the tribe of Benjamin. Both my father and mother were Jews. I am a pure Jew. I was circumcised when a week old. I learned to read scripture. I know all of the scrolls from memory. I came to Jerusalem so that I could learn more, so that I could worship in the temple. But every time that I entered the temple, I became angry. Yes, angry! I wanted to tear it down and rebuild it myself. I was angry that Herod the Great had built that temple. I wanted to worship in the temple of Solomon. I believe that we should tear down that temple that is a sacrilege to our God. True Jews should build another temple. True Jews who obey all the Laws." Paul stepped away then turned to face them. "I became a Pharisee. I studied harder than any of the others. I knew all the Laws. I obeyed each one. I was righteous in all that I believed and all that I did. Anyone that broke even one Law was cursed and a sinner. The Law had made me a prisoner."

Stretching his hands out and looking one to the other, he continued, "I longed in my heart to have been a son of Abraham, to have been with Moses on Mount Sinai when he received the commandments from God, to have crossed the Jordan River alongside Joshua, and to see the walls of Jericho collapse before the chosen people. What right did this Nazarene have to claim to be what I could not? Why did the people listen to him when I had so much more that I could tell them? By what power was he able to cure people when I was the one that God should have claimed to do his will? Bartimaeus, when you told me that you had been cured by Jesus, it was like spitting in my face. I was angry. That blasphemer was the one that cured you, but I should have been the one to do that for my sister. God was laughing at me, and I struck back not against you but against my God. When I heard of Jesus, what he said and what he did, I hated him. Not because he broke the Law. No, I hated that he was free and I was chained to the Law. Where he was light and love—I did not know it then, but I do now—I was darkness and fear."

He turned and stepped away from them. "I did not call out for Jesus's mercy as you did, Bartimaeus. But mercy was his gift to me. Jesus freed me. It is no longer through the Law that I am right with God. I am only right with God through faith in God's Son, Jesus the Christ."

He turned back but kept his distance and spoke as if an embarrassment. "My life till now has been wasted. All is a loss. That is all behind me. It is forgotten to me. All I want now is to know the Christ, to become like him in this life, to experience his resurrection. Through faith, to be like him in death and raised to life with him."

In the stillness that followed, Bartimaeus watched two small birds as they flitted from vine to vine then flew off together. He rose and stood before Paul. "You said that Jesus called to me before I to him. You may be right. I do not know. I do know that he has called you. I know that you will find what he has called you to do, to be, and many will prosper because of it."

He walked to Paul, and with his hand on Paul's back, he brought Paul to sit with them.

Judas broke the silence. "We must find a way for Paul to escape. But how?"

Bartimaeus nodded in agreement. "He cannot exit through the door, nor do I want to try to sneak him out over these walls. We do not know how many men that they have or who is their friend and informer. Somehow we must sneak him out unseen."

Judas asked, "Could we disguise him and get him past the guards?"

"No. By now they know who is in the house. That is too great a risk if he is discovered. Let us leave it for now. We have much to think about, and I do my best thinking on a horse. I want to see what we are up against. They will not bother me. I am going to the stable, and this time I will carry my sword. Maybe seeing that it is Herod's sword that I carry that they will not want to bother me."

When Bartimaeus left the house, he had his cloak pulled back so that the hilt of his sword was in plain view. At first, a few of the men moved toward him but stopped when their leader, the man that had come to the door, held his hand up to them. Two of the men followed him, but they did not try to conceal themselves.

He entered the stable, and as expected, the men stayed in the street. Joseph was there, and he was proud to show Bartimaeus how well-groomed the horses were and the condition of the stalls. Joseph added, "Two men came in yesterday after you left. They were looking around. My father came in, and they talked. My father got very angry and told them to leave."

Bartimaeus asked, "Do you know what they talked about?"

"They asked about a man that has been preaching in the temple."

Then, Noah entered the stable. He had heard the conversation, and he added, "I did not like what they were saying. And I did not like them looking at your horses."

"Thank you for watching after my horses." Noah nodded, then Bartimaeus continued, "Can you tell me who they were asking about?"

"You must know him. They said that you were staying at Judas's house with him."

"They were talking about a man named Paul."

"Yes, we know him. My sons and I have listened to him at the synagogue. We like what he tells us."

"Those men want to do him harm."

"We do not like trouble from Jerusalem. I wish that they would leave." As Noah was speaking, two young men joined the group, and Noah introduced them as his sons, Samuel and Benjamin.

Bartimaeus noticed that they were young but full-grown and well-muscled men. But what was most remarkable was that they were identical. Although Bartimaeus and his brother, Barariel, were twins, they were not identical twins. With a laugh to his voice, he said, "So you two are twins! I too have a twin brother, but people could tell us apart. He was bigger and stronger than me. But I cannot tell the two of you apart."

Samuel and Benjamin laughed and poked fun at each other. After a bit of teasing of Joseph by the two older brothers, Noah said, "Excuse us, but the hay wagon is on the other side of the wall, and we need to bring the hay in." Noah and his three sons walked to the rear of the stable where Joseph had shown Bartimaeus how the hay was brought in.

Bartimaeus walked to the stalls where his horses were, and he was checking their condition after the hard ride to Damascus when he noticed Samuel and Benjamin carrying in a basket that was filled with hay. They set it against a wall and went back for another. Bartimaeus went over and, taking hold of one of the handles, gave it a tug. With great effort, he was able to lift one side off the ground. He stepped away as he saw the two bring in another basket. Although clearly very heavy, they hauled them with little or no noticeable effort. This was a chore, often repeated, that had built strong arms and backs. He looked at the size of the baskets and their ruggedness. A man could hide in such a basket. Bartimaeus waited until there were no more baskets to fill. Then he called to Noah. He said, "You said that you would like those men from Jerusalem to leave Damascus. They will not leave until they have Paul in chains, or he escapes the city. Would you be willing to help him escape?"

"Yes, but I cannot take up arms against them with my sons. If it is something that I can do, I will."

"Let me tell you my idea." Looking at one of the big hay baskets on the floor of the stable, he asked, "When will you be sending the empty baskets over the wall?"

"We bring enough hay for two days. Then we send over the empty baskets, and they are filled from the wagon and sent back full. Why do you ask?"

"I have a plan to get Paul away from here."

"All right, tell me and I will help, if I can."

Bartimaeus moved closer and told Noah what he was proposing. With Noah's help with vital details, they concluded the plan, and Bartimaeus returned to the house. Upon entering, he asked Judas to join him in the courtyard and informed him, "I want to bring one of my horses here for a few days."

"Where would you keep it? We do not have facilities for a horse."

"No, but you have a large piece of courtyard and garden with a wall."

Judas protested, "But a horse would eat our garden. It would damage the trees. It would, well, you know, make a mess everywhere."

"I will do my best to tie it off in that corner. But, yes, I am sorry. It will be a mess."

"Why do you want to do that?"

"Let me tell you." Bartimaeus proceeded to tell Judas the plan for Paul's escape.

Later that day, Joseph knocked at the door of Judas's home. When Judas opened the door, the horse that Joseph was leading, startled by the opening of the door, took a sudden jerk back. Joseph tugged gently on the lead rope and quieted it. Judas stepped out and, pointing, told Joseph to take the horse to the side gate. Judas reentered the house and closed the door.

The guards outside watched as the boy led the horse to the gate. Judas opened the gate, and Joseph led the horse in. Soon, the gate reopened, and Joseph exited and stood there looking at the street. Shortly, Samuel and Benjamin came out of the side street carrying a very heavy basket filled with hay. The lid of the basket was slightly ajar, and hay could be seen within. As the brothers were in the middle of the street, feigning struggling with the load, they dropped the basket. The lid tumbled off, and some hay spilled out. By now, several of the guards had drawn near, and they came up to the basket and kicked the hay that had spilled in the street. With a shrug of the shoulders to each other, they returned to the shade that they had left.

The brothers once more lugged the basket through the gate being held open by Joseph. Within a few minutes, the gate opened, and the three brothers exited with the empty basket between Samuel and Benjamin. Joseph closed the gate behind them, and the three strode casually to the street from which they had emerged.

For the next two days, Paul was almost continually in his room, only coming out a time or two each day to eat. Judas spent most of the days in the courtyard keeping the horse out of the garden and away from the fruit trees. And Bartimaeus paced throughout the house hardly talking to anyone.

It was in the afternoon two days later that Samuel and Benjamin again came to the gate. Judas was there to open the gate, and he left it open. Soon, the brothers once more exited the gate with the basket once more between them. They swung the basket between them as they laughed and joked down the street returning to the stable the way that they had come. The guards were not stirred by the bucolic scene playing out before them.

Before the brothers had arrived, Bartimaeus had gone over the plan with Paul and Judas. After hearing the plan, Paul went to his room and returned with his arms filled with scrolls and writing materials. Bartimaeus, realizing Paul's intent, reacted, "Paul, there will be little enough room in the basket for you, much less for all that. Can you leave those with me or Judas?" Paul, without word, shook his head. Bartimaeus, realizing the futility, acquiesced. "All right. When you get to the stable, you can get out of the basket, but you must stay out of sight. I will meet you at the wall once it is dark."

Paul simply replied, "As you say, but I wish that I could return to Jerusalem."

Bartimaeus responded, "You cannot for now. You would be in danger, and that would add to the danger to Peter and the others. Someday you can return to Jerusalem. Gamela will be happy to have you join us."

When Samuel and Benjamin returned with a basket filled with hay, they entered through the gate and emptied it as before. This time, Paul climbed into the basket with his scrolls and writing materials, and the lid was secured. The brothers, with little effort, picked up the basket and, in the same manner as when they had previously left with an empty basket, walked into the street swinging the basket and departed for the stable. The guards, familiar with this scene, paid no heed to the brothers or the unsuspected contents of the basket.

A few hours later, the door to the house opened. Bartimaeus and Judas stepped out. Bartimaeus wore his cloak with the sword at his side, and he had a pack on his back. The two men talked in the doorway, and then they embraced. With a parting blessing from Judas, Bartimaeus walked to the street and turned toward the stable. Once more, two guards followed him.

At the stable, he talked to no one. He saddled the horse that remained at the stable. He mounted and walked the horse onto the street toward the gate of the city. Walking slowly, his followers easily kept him in sight. He exited the city through the gate, and he continued at a walk toward Jerusalem. Once out of the gate, but still within sight of the walls, he dismounted and checked the girth. Looking back up the road, he saw no one following him.

He remounted and rode until he was out of sight of the walls. Then he turned off the road and picked his way carefully back toward Damascus through the desert. It was dark when he arrived at the wall at the location where the hay is transferred to the stable. There was a rope hanging from the top of the wall. He dismounted and tugged on it. Soon, he saw one of the brothers on top of the wall. The rope was pulled up and tied to a basket. Then the basket was pushed off the top of the wall, and Samuel and Benjamin lowered it to the ground with the rope. Once on the ground, Bartimaeus lifted the lid, and Paul rose.

"I am glad to be out of that. I wonder how much pleasure it gave you to have me in a basket. You probably wished that you could have done that long ago." Both laughed.

Bartimaeus said, "Here is my cloak. Give me yours."

He handed the reins to Paul. "I do not know that I can trust you with a truly good horse. You ride like a sack of wheat! No wonder you came off your horse and went blind! Try to stay on until you are well away from Damascus. Stay in the desert and away from the city walls. You will come upon the road to the east and take it to your destination. I wish you well." Then with an embrace, he added, "My friend."

Paul thanked him and mounted the horse. He turned back and said, "This is only the start of my race. It is slow now. But I will train hard, and with Jesus the Christ with me, I will run it to the end. God be with you." And he, too, added, "My friend."

Bartimaeus watched until Paul was out of sight. Then, he once more tugged the rope and climbed into the basket with Samuel and Benjamin waiting on top of the wall. Noah and Joseph were on the other side to congratulate him when he climbed out.

24

BARTIMAEUS LEAVES DAMASCUS

Samuel and Benjamin easily raised the basket with Bartimaeus inside and then lowered him to the stable below where Noah and Joseph waited. They gave him a hand to climb out and greeted him with a slap of success on his back. Joseph showed his glee and said, "I knew that they could do it. They often put me over the wall in a basket to help the men load the hay from the wagons. Once they did not bring me back, and I had to walk around to the gate to get back in. Father was angry with them for doing that, and he told them that he would cuff them if they did that again."

Soon, Samuel and Benjamin came down from the wall and joined the others in the celebration. Together, they related the entire adventure, each adding colorful detail to the story. "Nobody saw us. We were quiet. We watched Paul ride away. He needs to stay away from the gates or he might be seen. That is a nice horse that he was riding. Are you going to want it back? Can we do it again sometime?"

Joseph added, "If the horse comes back, can I ride it? I will take good care of it for you!"

By then, Noah was shaking his head. "That is enough for now, boys. You all were very helpful. Now let me talk to Bartimaeus alone." The three walked off with Joseph pestering his two older brothers about playing a game with him.

Bartimaeus thanked Noah for his help and added, "Now, Paul must find a safe place. I probably will not know where he is until he feels that it is safe to return. Maybe someday he will come to stay with us in Jericho. That might be safe from Caiaphas. But knowing Paul, he will want to be in Jerusalem. I am sure that Caiaphas and many others in Jerusalem will not forget what Paul has done. They will want to hunt him down and put an end to him. He is a threat to them. I trust that eventually he will return to Jerusalem. I look forward to him joining his sister and me. We have much to make up for. You know how families can be!"

Noah nodded, and smiling, he said, "God willing, Bartimaeus, that he is safe and that he returns to you. I heard the two of you speaking. He kept repeating to you that he was sorry and was asking for your forgiveness. He also asked you to tell his sister—I understand that she is your wife—to forgive him. He had tears in his eyes."

Bartimaeus said, "Paul is no longer the man that I knew before I came to Damascus. With his blindness and with God's grace, he has seen the light. With God, there is always the light, if we are strong enough to see it, if we are strong enough to be it. I think that Paul is strong enough to be the light for others. I believe that he will carry that light to many." Bartimaeus stopped as if to ponder what he had just said, then he added, "Now, I need to get back to Judas's house without being recognized. Hopefully, those guarding the house believe that I have already left and that I am a visitor to Judas."

Noah called to his sons, "Joseph, bring a cloak from either Benjamin or Samuel and give it to Bartimaeus. He can wear it to return to Judas's house. That will help disguise him so that he will not be recognized."

The three sons joined them, and Joseph had a large cloak over his arm that he handed to Bartimaeus. Taking it, he said. "Ah, this is a nice big one. I will wrap up in it when I return to the house. I will ask Judas to return it to you. Tomorrow morning while it is still dark, I will put on Paul's cloak, and I will ride out from Judas's house. I hope that those guarding the house think that it is Paul trying to escape. They will try to stop me, but I think that I can get away. If they follow, I need to stay ahead of them."

Samuel and Benjamin commented together, "We have seen their horses. You should have no trouble staying well ahead of them with your horse."

Bartimaeus agreed and added, "That is true, but there are many ways for things to go wrong, and it is a long journey to Jericho. Once there and undiscovered, my pursuers will think that Paul was successful in returning to Jerusalem. I can relax then. In Jericho, I will rest, but I am anxious to return to Jerusalem myself. I have much to look forward to there. And now I must leave. I thank you for helping me and for being my friends."

Samuel and Benjamin grinned broadly and responded, almost as one, "Oh, that was great fun. We would like to see you surprise those others when you come out of the gate on that horse of yours. I do not think that they will have much chance catching you. They will eat your dust!"

He grabbed the two brothers by the shoulders. "I like your confidence, and I wish that you were coming with me. With you two along, I would not fear from anyone along the way. But I could not take you away from your father, and you have much to teach Joseph." Turning to Noah, he said, "Now I will put this cloak on and pull it up around my head. I need to get into Judas's house without being recognized. It is dark. There is no moon tonight, and that will help with my plans. Thank you, my friends. Shalom."

He embraced each of them one last time, then he strode through the stable, and with his head hung low into the wraps of the cloak, he exited into the dark street and walked quickly to Judas's house. When he turned onto the street called Straight, he carefully surveyed where the guards were. There were only two of them, both sitting together to keep an eye on the door and the side gate. Keeping his head down and his back to the guards, he hurried to the door and knocked soundly. Judas was waiting inside for him, and he opened the door. Bartimaeus stepped inside, and Judas immediately closed and bolted the door before the guards could respond. "Thank God that you made it safely back." He asked, "Has Paul escaped?"

"Yes, all went well. Thanks to God. I was not followed, and Paul got over the wall without anyone noticing. It is up to him now and to the protection of God."

"Do you know where he is going or what he will do?"

"He is not sure where he will go. He plans to stay in Syria and find a large city where he can disappear among the crowds. He is a tentmaker, and he can support himself. I suspect that he will try to contact followers of Jesus wherever he is. He is very anxious to share his knowledge and the messages that he receives from the Lord with others." They continued to walk through the hall in silence, then he added, "It is very peculiar that Jesus chose him. Why him? And why in that way? If there is anything that I have learned since Jesus touched me, is that his ways are not my ways. All that I can do is to listen for his call and then to trust him."

Judas added, "Both you and Paul are examples of the way that we are to trust our God. We Jews forget that it was the same with Abraham and Moses and Daniel and the prophets that put their trust in their God. I heard Paul say several times that he was not righteous by obeying the Law. He came to know and to believe that it was only through Jesus, and him crucified, that he was justified to God. That is now his desire, to teach others what he has come to know through the mercy of Jesus."

"After all of these years knowing Paul, I avoided him. Now, when I would like to be with him and learn from him, he is taken away from us. I do trust that he will return to Jerusalem someday. What God has planned for him, I do not know. Maybe it is something that only he can do. I hope that I can be there with him, something that he and Gamela and I can do together. Maybe something that my children can do with him. God willing." They came to his bedroom. "I will rest now. I will leave before the sun rises. The guards outside will recognize Paul's cloak, and we look enough alike in the dark that they should think that it is Paul trying to escape. I will ride quickly through the gate, and I will not stop until far away from Damascus. I suspect that they will attempt to follow me, but I should be able to stay well ahead of them."

Judas said, "I will be awake, and I will have breakfast for you, and food and water for the trip. We will not light any lamps. We do not want those outside to know that we are awake until that gate opens, and you ride out."

"Thank you, my friend. I should be away from your home soon, and you can return to your life."

Bartimaeus tried to rest, but he could not sleep. His mind was on the events that he had just been a part of and Paul's escape to freedom. But his thoughts were mostly about Gamela, and he was anxious to return to her and to tell her of her brother and how he has changed. She would want to hear everything that Paul had said. Regrettably, he knew that he would be, at best, a poor messenger. Paul spoke not only with wisdom, which he surely possessed, but more importantly with passion and unwavering conviction in what he now knew to be the word of God, the truth of God's Son, Jesus the Christ, and him sent to bring the truth of God's compassion and promise of everlasting life. Paul had said that God's message was not only for the Jewish people but, as Paul so strongly stated, was for all people. Gamela would agree that Paul can be very strong in what he believes.

No longer able to lie still, Bartimaeus rose from bed and strapped on his sandals. He went out of the room to find Judas waiting for him. Bartimaeus ate and drank heartily knowing that it may be a long time before he could eat or drink again. Neither he nor Judas spoke. All that was necessary had been said. Bartimaeus strapped on the sword not knowing if he would need it or even if he could use it. He gathered up Paul's cloak, and the two men walked in darkness to the courtyard.

Bartimaeus saddled the horse and pulled on the bridle. Judas gave him the pack of food and the skein filled with water. He strapped those to the saddle. All in ready, both men, knowing that there was nothing more to say, embraced, and Bartimaeus mounted. At the gate, with a last clasping of their hands, Judas opened the gate. Bartimaeus squeezed the horse, and they bolted into the street.

As expected, the guards on duty sprang to their feet with the clamor of the horses' hooves breaking the silence of the morning.

They ran out to intercept him, but they were powerless to resist the speeding horse. They yelled after him, and he scanned ahead to see if that alerted others down the street, but he saw no action. As he rode past a dark side street, he heard a shout, and a horse and rider flew out in pursuit. He was confident that he could outrun whoever was following him, but he also did not want to risk undue fatigue to the horse or possible injury in such a flight. Ahead of him, the street opened into a market with a row of low booths in the middle. He slowed and allowed the pursuer to pull closer behind. As they entered the market, he suddenly pulled up on his horse and veered off to the left leaving the pursuer to take the passageway to the right of the booths. Immediately, he squeezed his horse to keep pace with the other rider who was now in the lead racing toward the far end of the market.

At the end of the booths, the market took a right turn before exiting to the street. That would be an opportunity for Bartimaeus to dispose of his adversary. The booths being low allowed Bartimaeus to see that the other horse was cantering on a left lead. He also knew that his horse would, at his cue, execute a flying change to a right lead as the market turned to the right. As the riders passed the booths and entered the right turn, the other horse remained on a left lead and, not being well balanced, swung wide to the left. Bartimaeus, once clear of the booths and into the right turn, immediately put the horse into a right lead. He easily pulled alongside the other rider whose horse was struggling through the turn on the wrong lead. Bartimaeus pushed his horse hard to the right against the side of the other horse further unbalancing it. He quickly reached down and grabbed the other man's stirrup strap. With a strong tug upward and to the back, the other man was unseated and tumbled off the horse onto the ground.

Bartimaeus did not need to look back to know that the rider would not continue in pursuit of him. The horse, free of its rider, ran on ahead then slowed to a trot. Bartimaeus pulled up alongside and took ahold of the dangling reins. He led the horse through the streets, and once out of the gate, he released it. He continued at an easy canter to put space between him and any pursuers that might follow. So far, all had gone according to plan. What lay ahead of him was a long ride with little rest until he crossed the Jordan River. There he would rest before continuing on to Jericho. It would be a hard ride, but at the end was Jericho where he could rest before traveling again to Jerusalem to be with Gamela and Saul David and Mariam and his friends. He felt comfort with that thought, and he prayed, *Jesus of Nazareth, Son of God, thank you for the blessings of my family.*

25

THE WAY OF BLOOD

After leaving Damascus, Bartimaeus held the horse to a steady canter and then had alternating periods of canter and trot to allow the horse to recover. By midmorning he had traveled many miles, and he dismounted and walked the horse, which, by then, he needed as much as the horse. There was no sign of anyone following him, nor did he expect anyone that may have followed to keep pace with him. He was confident that no one would overtake him. He removed Paul's cloak and discarded it well off the road under some rocks. If others were to overtake him, which was unlikely, it was Paul that they were after, not him. Even so, he did not want to run the risk of an ugly encounter with temple guards who may recognize him as having been with Paul in Damascus. He remounted and kept up a rapid pace but allowed more periods of dismounting and walking the horse.

It was midafternoon when Bartimaeus arrived at the turnoff to the Sea of Galilee, and he remembered spending the night there on the way to Damascus less than a week ago. Since leaving Damascus that morning, he had covered about fifty miles of hard riding. He dismounted and assessed the horse's condition. Although the horse showed signs of the hard ride, he decided that it was fit to push on to the Jordan River. He would rest after crossing the river. With a good rest for the horse, and barring any difficulties, he would make it to his home in Jericho by the end of the following day. That would be challenging, but he believed that the horse was up to it. Key to that plan was finding a place to rest. He knew a horse breeder in that area, and after crossing the river, he turned off the main road and went there. The owner graciously received the weary traveler and had the sweat washed from the horse and turned it out into green pasture along the river. Bartimaeus told him that he was returning to Jericho from family business in Damascus and that he was anxious to get home.

Bartimaeus was offered and accepted the gracious hospitality from the host, and he appreciated the extra attention that was given to him and his horse being that his family was well known to the man as breeders of fine horses. The exceptional treatment that he received would be well rewarded in any future dealings between the two families. Bartimaeus told the man that he would leave in the morning. He accepted the comfort of the cot on the roof of the house, and wrapped in a heavy wool blanket for warmth from the cool desert night air, he was quickly asleep.

When he woke, the sun's rays were barely breaking over the horizon. He went to the parapet wall and looked out into the pasture. There was enough light to see that the horse was grazing. He was greeted in the house with food and supplies for the remaining journey to Jericho. He thanked his host, saddled the horse, and walked to the road. He would not need to push as hard that day. If all went well, he expected to make it home that night.

The sun was setting as he came within sight of the walls of Jericho. The horse still moved with a steady trot as Bartimaeus turned off the main road toward his home. He stopped at the stable, and Ezra and the family came out to greet him. They talked briefly, and all agreed that what he needed most was a bath and meal, in that order.

He asked about Joshua and Monica and was told with smiling faces, "Oh, yes, the newlyweds are doing well. They will be happy to have you back. And they are not alone. One of your friends is here."

He asked, "Who is that?"

"Hezekiah arrived the other day. He did not talk much to us. But I have seen him and Joshua together talking."

He turned toward his house. "I did not expect to see him here. I was told that he left the guard. That happened shortly after the last time that we were together in Jerusalem." He walked toward his house as he said, "What brings him here?"

Joshua, Monica, and Hezekiah were sitting at a table when he entered the house. Joshua immediately rushed to greet him with an embrace. Hezekiah rose and remained standing alongside the table. Monica stayed seated, but she wore a warm, welcoming smile for him. Joshua said, "You must be exhausted and hungry. You look worn-out."

"Joshua, it is good to be home. I do not want to do that again, not ever." He turned to the table. "Monica, it has been a long time since I saw you sitting at my table. It is good, and I could not be happier for you and this lucky man. I think that he is too lucky! I do not know that he deserves you! But I am happy for both of you."

He turned his head toward Hezekiah, and the joy in everyone's eyes turned a more serious note. Bartimaeus turned to face him. "It has been a long time since you sat at our table. What is it that brought you here from Jerusalem?" With that, Joshua motioned for Bartimaeus and Hezekiah to sit, but Bartimaeus did not move and held his hand up to Joshua.

Likewise, Hezekiah remained standing and responded, "Bartimaeus, I can only imagine your surprise at my being here. I will not test your patience and hospitality. After I tell you why I am here, I will leave."

Joshua took a step toward Bartimaeus. "He has told us everything. He told us how your father died. We do not expect you to forget that, and you may not forgive him. I do not know that I could. But I know that he cares for you. You were like a son to him, maybe you still are. He comes as your friend. You need to listen to him."

Bartimaeus responded matter-of-factly without emotion, "I have been asked by others lately to listen to them. I am getting better at it."

Monica rose. "We have all, at one time or another, done something that we now regret. Maybe we did it out of fear or weakness or desperation"—she dropped her head, then almost whispered—"or out of love." She looked toward Hezekiah, then continued, "But we go on as best we can. I know that this man cares for you and loves you, as we do. Please give him that." Turning back to Bartimaeus, she stretched her hand toward the table. "Please sit with us."

He looked upon the beautiful, young woman that had cared for him when no one else would. The love that he had for her was still deep within him, which he knew would never leave. He wanted to go to her and embrace her, but he knew that he no longer needed that nor did she. From across the room, she reached out her hand to him. He stepped forward as she turned to Joshua and extended her other hand to him. Joshua came to her. She took his hand and gently pulled him to her. Joshua put his arm around her and, reaching out his other hand toward Bartimaeus, said, "Come, my friend, join us."

Monica looked back toward Bartimaeus who came forward and grasped each of the hands that waited for him. The three walked to the table with Monica between the two of them. Bartimaeus looked across the table and, motioning to Hezekiah, said, "Please sit. You are welcome at our table."

Hezekiah began, "As you know, Caiaphas is a shrewd old fox, and he is well informed of all that happens. As soon as he received word of Saul in Damascus, he immediately set about to discredit and to destroy him. He was informed that you are related to Saul. He also learned through friends with Herod's guard that a messenger was dispatched to you from Peter. By now Caiaphas must know that you were in Damascus with Saul. I do not know what else has happened in Damascus. You certainly know that better than anyone." He stopped talking, and all looked toward Bartimaeus who nodded but said nothing. Hezekiah continued, "Caiaphas not only knows about your relationship with Saul, and he does not care if you are friends or enemies. He also knows of your ties with Peter and the followers of Jesus. On both counts, you are an enemy to Caiaphas. Although I am no longer with Herod's guard, I am well informed by many in Jerusalem. I was recently informed that Caiaphas wants to have you brought to him, or maybe worse. We have seen what is happening throughout Judea and Galilee. Caiaphas clearly has plans to destroy any following of Jesus. Not only you but many of your friends are in danger."

Bartimaeus leaned forward and spoke. "What of Gamela and the children? They are in Jerusalem."

"I sent a message to Peter, and he is aware of the dangers to him and others from Caiaphas. I suspect that there is also danger from Herod. Jesus was successful in uniting those two adversaries that are now working together for no good. I understand that your friends are aware of the dangers and that they will do the best that they can to protect your family. I came here to warn you. Joshua confirmed that you had gone to Damascus to see if what was reported about Saul is true. What can you tell us of that?"

Bartimaeus told them all that had happened. He told them how Saul, now wanting to be called Paul, had escaped Damascus and presumably was in refuge from Caiaphas. He ended with how he had escaped being disguised as Paul. He expected that the temple guards that were in Damascus were returning to Jerusalem, possibly only a short distance behind him. He added, "Those following me are probably not too anxious to get to Jerusalem. Caiaphas will not be happy to hear that they let Paul escape. Maybe by now they have surmised that it was not Paul that fled on the horse. They may need to confess that they do not know where Paul is, but it would be unlikely for Paul to return to Jerusalem at this time."

Bartimaeus stopped, and all remained quiet. Monica rose and brought food to the table. She said, "You must be hungry. Let us eat. Then you need to rest."

Turning to Monica, he said, "The food looks delicious. I hope that you will save some for me. But what I would like most is to bathe and put on some clean cloths." Turning to Hezekiah, he said, "I hope that you will stay the night. There is much that I want to talk to you and Joshua about, and, of course, to my dear sister, Monica."

All nodded agreement as he rose to leave. When he returned, they were still at the table, but the food and dishes had been removed. Monica rose when she saw him and proceeded to fill a plate with food and a basket of bread. Joshua filled a cup with wine and replenished the others.

Monica put the food before Bartimaeus and said, "You look much more relaxed now."

Joshua added, "And we greatly appreciate your bath, believe me! I checked on your horse. What have you done to the poor animal? He is exhausted. We turned him out to pasture. We think it best that he keeps moving. He will not be put to any work for a week."

"Thank you, Joshua. I would have been very angry if any of the soldiers returned a horse in the manner that I brought this one back. He is a fine mount. We must keep him."

Bartimaeus turned to Hezekiah. "So what are we to do? I do not think it wise to stay here. There are too few of us for protection, and I do not want to endanger Ezra's family. Besides, I need to report to Peter and the others on what happened in Damascus with Paul."

Hezekiah responded, "I think it best that we go to Jerusalem. The sooner the better."

Joshua added, "Monica and I will join you. We want to be with you and Gamela, and you might need me."

"And I need to be with Gamela. Thank you, Joshua and Monica. We need both of you. We are family."

Hezekiah interjected, "I suggest that we leave early tomorrow. Let's not be on the road at night. That road is dangerous with robbers and outlaws." They agreed and discussed how they would travel and what they would take.

Joshua said, "It may be best for you to trim that beard so that you are not mistaken for Paul if we meet the guards from Damascus tomorrow."

"Better yet," added Monica, "please shave it off. You look better that way."

"Are you saying that I am getting old?"

"No, but I do not want you to look old either!"

"Then, I will ask Ezra's wife to shave me. I need to tell her and Ezra what has happened and that we are going to Jerusalem."

The next morning the four of them walked to the stable. Each had a sack with clothes and items that they would need in Jerusalem. Joshua carried two sacks. The larger one contained clothes for Gamela that Monica had packed knowing that her friend would be wanting some fresh clothing for an extended stay in Jerusalem.

When they arrived at the stable, there were two horses saddled and a third hitched to the cart. Joshua helped Monica into the cart then walked to the other side. Bartimaeus met him and took him by the arm. "Would you mind riding a horse? I really do not have the heart for it today. Besides, I will enjoy talking to Monica. I could use a gentle presence today." Without waiting for a response from Joshua, Bartimaeus climbed into the cart and sat next to Monica. He looked toward her, but she was smiling and waving to Joshua, then she turned to Bartimaeus and said, "Thank you for riding with me. I will always welcome you at my side."

With that, the four waved goodbye and started down the road toward Jericho and Jerusalem. When they rounded the bend at Jericho and turned up the road to Jerusalem, Bartimaeus said, "It has been almost three years since you walked with me to the gate and I sat by the wall." She did not respond or turn to look at him. Bartimaeus continued, "A lot has happened to both of us since Jesus cured me. I wonder if Bar-El is still there begging every day. I thought about him many times. Sometimes the uncertainty of what had become of him would haunt me. Since that day at the gate, I often wanted to come back and find him. I do not know what I would say, and that bothered me even more."

She turned to him. "I remember those nights when I could hear you tossing in bed. Then you would get out of bed and pace the room. It was as if you had a demon inside you, but there was nothing that I could do to release you from its grip."

"That demon was worse than the blindness. It is gone now. When I feel it coming back, I pray as I did that day at the gate, 'Jesus of Nazareth, Son of God, have mercy on me.'"

Monica looked at him and said, "You were blessed by Jesus. You did not know it then, but we know it now. If you had not been struck blind, you would not have been at the gate crying out to Jesus to have mercy on you. Then you tried to find Jesus and thank him, and that brought you to his apostles. You have learned so much from them. And you brought others to know Jesus and to follow him.

Hezekiah told us that he and Rachel are listening to the apostles and that they have been baptized. They love you. They always have. Hezekiah told the apostles how Herod the Great had ordered the babies in Bethlehem to be killed because of his fear of a new king being born to the Jews. Jesus's mother, Mary, wept when she heard that. She said that her husband, Joseph, had a message from an angel to take her and the baby to Egypt so that Herod could not harm them. When Herod the Great died, they returned from Egypt. They went to Nazareth to be away from Herod's son, the Antipas, and from the Romans. Hezekiah told us of his role in the killing of the babies and that he was the one that had your father killed so that the people would not hear of the atrocity that Herod had performed. Hezekiah has suffered greatly for that mistake. He would give his life to take that back. He would give his life to protect you as he has done in coming to warn you. He loves you."

"I know that he loves me. I have forgiven him. I will tell him and thank him for all that he and Rachel did for me and Barariel. Those were glorious times when my brother and I went to Jerusalem to join the guard with him. He cared for us as if we were his sons. I cannot forget that."

She smiled at him. "Telling him that you love him will make him very happy."

Bartimaeus returned the smile. "I will tell him. Paul talked about making mistakes and about asking for forgiveness. He told me that he knows that he made a mistake in what he told Gamela about me and that he is sorry. Gamela will be glad when I tell her. Our worst mistakes are with those that we love and cherish the most. I love you because my brother loved you, but in my hurt and hunger for love, I made a mistake. My mistake was the belief that sharing that love with you for the moment would secure that love for all time. Rather, it kept me from your love until now."

Monica reached out and touched him. "Bartimaeus, I too have loved you. Your love for me is what sustained me when Barariel died. I was desperate in my loneliness without him. You sustained me and gave me hope that love was not lost. With you, I was able to share what we had both lost. In you, I had a purpose for the love that had nowhere else to go. By you, my love stayed alive. Because of you, I have Joshua, and I could not be more in love. Thank you, I will always love you and cherish you." She leaned over and kissed him softly on his cheek. It was warm and sweet and good. As she leaned back, she reached out her hand and wiped her tear from his cheek then wiped the wetness from the corner of his eye with her finger. They looked at each other as their smiles turned to childlike joy as they relished in the presence of the other.

They rode on in silence, each with their own memories. Finally, Monica spoke. "Joshua tells me stories that he has heard from the apostles and others. He said that one of the apostles was a tax collector before Jesus called him and that he is good with keeping records. He is writing the stories that are being told."

"Yes. That is Matthew. There is another younger fellow, named Mark, that likes to talk to Jesus's mother, Mary, and he asks her questions about Jesus. He is watching Matthew, and I think that he also wants to write what he is learning from Mary and others. That will be good. Others will want to know what Jesus said and did. You will enjoy listening to them. They not only tell stories, but they tell us what they mean."

She responded, "Tell me what you have heard. What have you learned from Jesus's apostles?"

Bartimaeus nodded, then he smiled and said, "Matthew is a good storyteller. We all like to listen to him. He said that once when they were traveling with Jesus in Galilee that they came upon a shady place at the base of a hill. It was in the spring, and the hill was in bloom with wildflowers from the winter rain, and the air was fresh and filled with the scent of the flowers. Jesus told them to rest, and they sat in the shade of the trees amid the flowers. All was quiet except for the humming of the bees. When Jesus spoke, he said to rest their minds and to listen with their hearts since he had much of importance to tell them. He said that blessed are they that are simple in spirit for they are not held by possessions and are free. And blessed are they when they feel pain for they shall also find joy in their time. And blessed are they when they are kind and merciful to others for God will reward them with his mercy. And blessed are the pure for in their pureness they will be one with God. And blessed are they that strive for peace for they will turn the battlefields to a garden to feed God's children." He stopped and looked at Monica. "Matthew had more to tell, but I cannot remember all of what he said. I am sure that he will tell that again and much better than I can."

"Bartimaeus, what you just told me makes me feel good. I can understand why so many are drawn to Jesus. Joshua has told me much of what he has learned, and I listened to him and Hezekiah talk about Jesus and what they have learned from the apostles. I am anxious to meet them and to learn more. It will be good for Joshua and me to be together with you and Gamela in Jerusalem. There is so much for all of us to learn and to share with each other. I have never felt a greater sense of joy and peace as I do now. Thank you, Bartimaeus. I love you."

Bartimaeus reached his hand to her, and she took it. He said, "I heard John say that Jesus told them that they are even to love their enemies. John said that when Judas, the betrayer of Jesus, greeted Jesus that night in the garden, that Jesus called him friend. Jesus knew what Judas was about to do, and he still called him friend. I cannot understand how he could do that! How are we supposed to call someone friend when we know that they intend to do us evil? That is not the way that I have lived my life."

She shook her head and replied, "No, Bartimaeus, that is not the way any of us have lived our lives. But I know you. I know the goodness that is you. You just returned from Damascus where you went because your friends asked you to find out what Paul was doing. You went to meet with a person that had done great harm to you and to those that you love. You went knowing that you might be killed, maybe even killed by the man that you were there to meet. You not only met with him, but you may have saved his life. You may not have done that because you loved Paul, but you did it because you have love inside you. You are love. We all see that, and we love you for what you are."

Bartimaeus shrugged his shoulders and said, "I have heard that when the guards came to arrest Jesus in the garden that Peter cut off the ear of one of the servants. If I had been there and Jesus was my friend, I would have used my sword for more than cutting off an ear!"

"Bartimaeus, no, I do not believe that you would."

"Maybe not, but I would do whatever is necessary to protect the ones that I love, to protect you."

She squeezed his hand. "Yes, I know that you would."

It had been several hours since they departed from their home. Joshua and Hezekiah had ridden ahead, and they were waiting where the road was lined with large boulders with a narrow passage through the boulders that opened into an oasis on the other side. As Bartimaeus joined the two, he recalled the last time that he had been to that oasis. It was the morning of the day that he left Monica to go to Jerusalem to find Jesus. He thought back on how, after leaving Gamela, he had ridden past Jericho on his way to Jerusalem. But then he turned around and went to Monica. He had needed to see her, to be with her one more time. He had not intended to stay, but he had. He wondered if she, too, was recalling that night. He turned to look at her. She did not notice. She was smiling and waving to Joshua.

As Bartimaeus pulled up to the others, Joshua called out, "Bartimaeus, let us stop at this oasis. The horses can have a drink, and we can rest in the shade of the trees. We will be in Jerusalem soon enough."

Monica replied, "Joshua, that was good of you to think of me. I am not used to these long rides as you are." Once there, Joshua helped Monica from the cart as Bartimaeus swung out and began stretching his legs. Hezekiah led the two saddle horses to the water while Bartimaeus unhooked the other horse from the cart. After the horses drank, they were led to a grassy patch to graze.

Joshua and Monica, arm in arm, joined the other two. As they drew close, Joshua said, "I was telling Monica one of Jesus's stories that we heard from Matthew. It is the one about the traveler on this very road from Jericho to Jerusalem. The man was robbed and beaten and left to die by the side of the road. Jesus said that a temple priest and a Pharisee both passed by the man without helping him. Then a Samaritan found him and cared for him. Jesus told that story to answer the question of who is my neighbor. He said that we are to love our neighbor as we love ourselves."

Monica shook her head and added, "I do not know how anyone could pass by a person that is hurt without stopping to help. Why would they do that?"

Hezekiah, speaking directly to her, said, "Monica, I have heard only a little of what Jesus said and what he did. I still do not understand why he died the way he did. But I have come to believe that he was sent by God and that he is the Son of God. I also believe that he rose from the dead and that he promised us that we too will rise from our death. I know that Jesus cared for others. He cured many people, even those he did not know, like Bartimaeus. Maybe all that he said and all that he did, even his death, was to show us how much God cares for us, and that we, like the Samaritan, are supposed to care for each other. Even to love each other. To call each other neighbor and friend."

Hezekiah was interrupted as three men on horses came through the narrow passage. They rode past the oasis and halted at the cart where they dismounted. One took the reins while the other two approached the wary four. Joshua had stepped in front of Monica when he saw them coming their way. Hezekiah recognized one of the men and shouted, "Maximus, I hardly recognized you without your uniform. What brings you here?"

Maximus replied, "We are hunting. I am told that there are lions here that have been preying on sheep. Maybe"—he jerked the spear in the air—"we can hoist one on our spears."

Bartimaeus spoke, "I have never been much for hunting, but I would not want to hunt lions with a spear. But, as I recall, you preferred a spear rather than a sword."

The two men locked eyes, and Hezekiah raised his hand to Bartimaeus in an attempt to quell the long simmering animosity between the two men. Maximus kept his menacing stare fixed on Bartimaeus and advanced until he stood face-to-face with the man that, in his mind, had always stood in his way. He spun the spear in his hand and jammed it into the ground at his side.

"I will not need a spear to do my hunting today." He dropped his gaze to Bartimaeus's belt then looked briefly at Hezekiah and Joshua. Returning to look at Bartimaeus, he spoke in a guttural tone, "I see that neither you nor Joshua carry a sword." Turning back to Hezekiah, he said, "But I see that you still carry the sword from when you had the favor of Herod. It is good that you left his service. Herod sees you as old and weak. I now have your position. Herod would have given it to me even if you would have stayed after your friend here insulted you. You should have had him killed. I would have. I now serve the wishes of Herod, and I will carry out his desires better than you ever could. I will not disappoint him."

Hezekiah, sensing the threat, stepped toward Bartimaeus. Keeping his attention on Hezekiah, Maximus said, "It is not lions that I am after, and it is not by chance that we came upon you today. I know why you left Jerusalem the other day and that you went to Jericho to warn your friend."

Maximus glanced toward Bartimaeus, and tension flared stronger, both men with eyes firmly locked on the other. Looking back to Hezekiah, he said, "You of all people should know better than to make enemies, especially an enemy of Herod. It does not matter to me what you said to Herod after you and your friend here had your little disagreement, nor do I care. I was glad to see you two part company. And I was certainly pleased to have you both leave the guard."

Hezekiah responded, "Yes, I know that Herod made you the captain of the guard. Something that you always thought that you could do better than me. I am sure that Herod will be pleased with your service. On my part, I am glad to no longer be serving the desires of either Herod the Great or his son."

Maximus continued, his voice rising, "Now that you no longer serve the king's needs, you may foolishly think that you can tell others what you know about him. That would be troubling to Herod, and Herod wishes to avoid what would cause him trouble."

Bartimaeus, as a soldier, had long ago learned to read signs of danger not only in the way that a person spoke but more importantly the signs that are subtly transmitted. He sensed the danger that Maximus presented; not to him but to Hezekiah. In an instant of awareness, he knew that Maximus intended to kill Hezekiah. Just as quickly, he understood that Maximus could not leave any of them to tell what had happened. With that reality of danger, as a soldier, his hand instinctively went to his belt to find a sword but realized that it was in the cart. For a moment, he regretted his decision to no longer carry a sword, but in following Jesus, he no longer could.

In that same instant, Maximus drew his sword. Bartimaeus, having no recourse but to shield his friends from danger, lurched between Maximus and Hezekiah and grabbed the arm about to wield the sword down on his friend. They fought, Maximus being the larger, stronger man could not win out over the more determined adversary. In this struggle over life and death, neither weakened nor gave ground. Face was pressed to face, legs tangled, and both men fell to the ground still intertwined. Bartimaeus fell on Maximus, the impact with the ground sent the sword flying out of Maximus's grip. With his hand free and momentarily out of the grip of Bartimaeus, Maximus reached behind him and withdrew the dagger. He brought it up to thrust it into the other man, but Bartimaeus once more clutched the hand with the weapon. The two men struggled, each trying to gain advantage over the other. Maximus was successful in rolling to the top of Bartimaeus, and his hand disappeared between the two men. With a last measure of energy, Bartimaeus arched his back, and with all of his strength, he pushed the other man over and, with arms and legs tangled together, landed on top. For a moment there was animal fear in the eyes of the pinned man, then with a savage cry, the dagger hand broke free of Bartimaeus's grip and disappeared between the two bodies. As quickly as the battle started, all was still. The eyes of both men were closed. Neither breathed as if both dead. Slowly Maximus's eyes opened. With a shove, he pushed the body of the other off him. Blood gushed from the wound of Bartimaeus who laid lifeless on the ground.

Maximus gathered his sword and rose. As he took his feet, Monica dropped to Bartimaeus's side, bent over his body; one hand over the wound with blood spilling between her fingers, her other hand clutching her own heart. Hezekiah, kneeling, joined her on the other side of his friend's body. He pulled the dagger out and pushed his hand firmly on the wound to stop the outpour of life from his friend's chest. Monica placed her hand upon Hezekiah's, the dagger lying on the lifeless chest.

Maximus moved to stand at Bartimaeus's head with his back to Monica. He looked down on Hezekiah. He raised the sword with intention of killing the kneeling man. As the sword went back for the fatal blow, Monica grabbed the dagger from Bartimaeus's chest and drove it deeply into the leg of the man that had delivered her searing grief. With no expression other than deep sadness, she sank the dagger to the hilt in the man's leg. With a bellow of pain, Maximus, with sword still held high, turned from Hezekiah toward Monica. She remained where she knelt beside Bartimaeus. Maximus looked down upon her and the bloody body of Bartimaeus on the ground beside her.

As Maximus's arm was about to come forward to deliver a death blow to Monica, with a jerk of his body, he was motionless. With his arm clutching the weapon above his head, he suddenly threw his head to the sky and raised his left arm to cover his eyes. His right arm fell to his side, and he dropped the sword. His eyes now closed, his mouth open, he stood as if receiving an unfathomable command. Finally, in a voice of terror, he screamed, "What? Who are you? Stay away from me!" He stepped backward. With both hands now shielding his face, he stumbled backward and tripped on a rock. He fell to the ground with his head impaled on a sharp rock. He lay motionless, blood streaming onto the ground.

Joshua was the first to move. He picked up the sword. With it hanging at his side, he looked down at Monica with her face buried in the still chest of Bartimaeus. Hezekiah remained kneeling but no longer pressed on the now lifeless body. He rose and went to Maximus who laid where he had fallen. Joshua turned his attention to the man that had accompanied Maximus. Without taking his eyes from Joshua, the man said, "I was paid to help kill a man. Two men are dead. There is nothing more for me here." He turned and walked to join the other man. They mounted and left as they had entered.

Joshua raised the sword in his hand, and without looking at it, he flung it into the water of the oasis. He knelt beside Monica and comforted her with his embrace. Monica was the first to rise. In silence, the two men loaded Bartimaeus's body into the cart. Then they watched as Monica climbed in and placed his head in her lap. They stood there not wanting to disturb that precious but grief-filled scene before them. Together, as if having the same thought, they turned as one and looked at the other man's body as if to ask, what are they to do with him? But their attention was drawn back to Monica as she lowered her head to Bartimaeus as if to kiss him one last time, but rather than bring her lips to him, she turned her head and held her ear close to him. When she lifted her head, she quizzically looked upon him, and with a smile, she tenderly kissed him on the cheek. Slowly and deliberately, she raised her head. In what seemed an eternity of silence, she spoke while turning her attention to the body of Maximus lying on the ground where it fell. "He said to put him in the cart too." With tears once more streaming from her eyes but now with a gleam of joy-filled surprise to her voice, she said, "He is alive. They both are."

26

THREE YEARS LATER—PAUL RETURNS TO JERUSALEM

It had been more than three years since Paul rode out of the gated walls of Jerusalem on his personal quest to eradicate the followers of Jesus, the man who had dared to blaspheme his God. Now, as he approached Jerusalem from Jericho, he intently watched the horizon for when he would once more see those gray stone walls looming before him, and behind those walls the temple. When he first saw the wall rise up before him, he stepped out of the caravan. He dropped his pack and fell to his knees. He trembled with the thought that he would no longer see the temple or the city or the Jewish people as he had before. He bowed his head and prayed, *Jesus the Christ, son of God, the God of Abraham, the God of Isaac, the God of Moses, and of my God. Hear my prayer and forgive me, your lowly servant. I left your city in my vanity to destroy those that you had gathered to yourself, those that you had brought into the light of your salvation. In my willful pride, I had rejected your light and had stayed in the darkness. I had clung to learning rather than accepting the truth. I had rejected love in favor of man's rules. In your mercy, you had compassion on me, and like a sheep lost in the wilderness, you lifted me from my darkness and bore me into your light. I am the least to be called to follow you. I am unworthy to serve you. But with your grace, my Lord, I will reenter your city a new man, born again to serve you and to bear your name to all people. Have mercy on me, Lord Jesus. Let me serve you in truth and in faith. So be it, amen.*

Paul rose and in stillness continued to gaze at the wall in the distance. He knew that nothing would be the same. Now, every street, every pool, every beggar would be a reminder of Jesus and the painful regret that was his in not following Jesus then. He stepped back into the long line of slow-moving camels and ox-drawn carts and those trudging tiredly along in the caravan. But he was not tired; he was filled with the energy of a well-trained athlete. He was anxious to return to Jerusalem. Now, he wanted to see the city with different eyes. It was the loss of sight on the road to Damascus and the call by Jesus that opened more than his eyes. He no longer saw with merely his eyes, and his thoughts were no longer conditioned on what he had been taught by other men. He now saw with the eyes of faith, he thought with the inspiration of love, and he moved with the surety of hope.

When the caravan arrived at the city, he did not enter with the others but rather continued on the rocky road outside the wall. He passed by the Golden Gate that would have taken him directly to the temple, but he knew that he did not yet want to go to the temple. That was no longer his focus for learning of his God. He would return to the temple but only because that was where Jesus had taught the people. In a short while, he came to the trail to the Garden of Gethsemane. He stopped and thought of Jesus there the night that he had been arrested and taken as a lawbreaker to be falsely tried and crucified. Again, he knew that now was not the time to visit that sacred site. Only a few minutes further, he came to where he had witnessed the young man, Stephen, being stoned to death. He prayed in his heart, as he had every day since Damascus, for forgiveness from God for what he now knew to be a self-righteous and loveless act. He had vowed to never judge another person more harshly than he judged himself.

Paul's steps were lighter as he walked along the road thinking of Jesus walking that same way. He paused once more where the road turned north to Samaria and to Galilee, and his thoughts were of Jesus traveling that same road back and forth as he visited Jerusalem.

His heart pounded with regret that he had not been one to join Jesus along that way. With that he stopped. Memory of Bartimaeus flooded his mind. He recalled Bartimaeus visiting him in Jerusalem and telling him that his sight had been restored by Jesus. He prayed, *Oh, why did I not believe what he told me? How could my heart be so hardened that when hearing the good news from the man married to my dear sister that I rejected what he told me? Why was I so lost in what I wanted to believe rather than to see the truth before me? My Lord, thank you for striking me blind so that I could see. Jesus, forgive me. Bartimaeus, forgive me. Gamela, my gentle sister, forgive me.*

He was nearly blinded by his tears as he entered the Fish Gate, and his eyes fell on Golgotha in the distance. In all the time that he had lived in Jerusalem, he could not remember ever having been to that dreadful hill. That was where sinners were taken to pay the full measure for their disregard of God's commands. That was not where a follower of God's law would be. That was not where he ever expected to be. Now, he stood looking up at that site with consternation that God's chosen people, people with his shared beliefs, could mistakenly and horrifically put to death the fulfillment of God's promises through the prophets that he had so carefully studied.

He trembled with a heart bursting with sadness for Jesus the Christ, the God made man, which he, of his own volition, had denied even when confronted with the truth that he so desperately sought. Paul had come to believe in Jesus as the fulfillment of God's promise. Jesus, as the Son of God, having been sent by God, had been the stumbling block for Paul. Paul had not believed that God would so love his people that he would humble himself to live as a man and to die as a man but also to rise in glory so that all people could also rise in glory.

Starting with his blindness as he approached Damascus and his hearing the voice of Jesus in Judas's house to his escape from Damascus and living three years in Syria, Paul had come to more than believe in Jesus the Christ sent by God the Father. He had also come to believe that all men were to know and believe in Jesus. Looking up at Golgotha, he confirmed the purpose for which he had come out of refuge and returned to Jerusalem. That purpose was to find the apostles of Jesus and to ask them if he could tell others of Jesus so that they too could see and believe as he did. He did not expect to be accepted as equal with those that had been with Jesus from the beginning in Galilee, but he wished to receive the blessing of the apostles so that he could take the good news of Jesus the Christ to people throughout the Roman Empire.

That day, standing on the trail to Golgotha, Paul's thoughts were not on his past; rather, they were on his savior, Jesus. He wanted to create in his very being the scene of Jesus walking that trail from the city and to him being brutally nailed to the cross and hanging there to die. He did not know if he would ever return to that holy place, and he wanted to know it deep inside himself so that he could tell others of it. To tell others of Jesus, of his death and his rising in glory, was all that Paul wanted.

Paul stood there on the brow of that rocky hill looking across at Golgotha until his shadow on the ground before him faded with the setting of the sun. When he finally moved, he solemnly walked to where the cross had been set in the ground. He knelt and lowered his head until it touched that sacred ground, and he wept. It was dark before he rose and entered the city of Jerusalem.

It had been more than a week since Paul had left his refuge in Syria to return to Jerusalem. He had joined a caravan in Syria, and after several days, he arrived in Damascus. There, he kept himself wrapped in his cloak as he entered the synagogue where he had once told the people about Jesus. The followers of Jesus, now calling themselves Christians, no longer met in the synagogue out of fear of the Jewish leaders, and Paul did not attempt to join them for fear of being recognized which could cause trouble not only for him but also for others. After leaving the synagogue, he stood watch over Judas's house and waited for him to exit. Then, he followed Judas, and when Judas was alone, he quietly approached him. Judas was gladdened to see the return of the man that he had witnessed being called by Jesus. Judas told him that there was no longer a threat from the Sanhedrin to him in Damascus if he did not call attention to his presence. Judas invited Paul to stay with him, and while there, a few of the Christians visited him and wished him Godspeed on the journey before him.

Paul, in his fashion, used those gatherings to share his newfound belief in Jesus and how Jesus had been foretold by the prophets of old.

Soon after entering Judas's house, and with great excitement, Paul had asked Judas what, if anything, that he knew of the man that saved him, Bartimaeus, and his sister, Gamela. Judas, with careful detail, told Paul the story of the attempted assassination of Hezekiah by Maximus and the heroic act by Bartimaeus to save the life of Hezekiah before being fatally stabbed by Maximus. Then Monica striking Maximus with the dagger to save Hezekiah and Maximus's subsequent fall and head injury that killed him. Of course, the most amazing part of the story was the account by the witnesses—Joshua, Monica, and Hezekiah—that Bartimaeus was, in fact, dead due to the wound delivered by Maximus, and that Maximus likewise was dead on the ground where he fell. He then added that Monica is most fervent in her claim that she held Bartimaeus's dead body in the cart before he spoke, and when Bartimaeus did speak, it was to save the life of the man that had killed him. Paul, wanting to dispel any misinterpretation of what he heard, asked, "So Bartimaeus was dead, and then after being placed in the cart, and with Monica holding his head in her lap, he spoke to her?"

Judas answered with a hearty laugh, "Yes, and not only that, Maximus, who likewise lay dead on the ground, returned to life when he was laid beside Bartimaeus in the cart!"

Paul pondered this then added, "Why did Maximus want to kill Hezekiah?" To this, Judas told the story of Bartimaeus's father, Timaeus, witness of the death of the baby boys of Bethlehem in an attempt by Herod the Great to kill the baby Jesus. Then, with Timaeus learning that it was Herod who ordered the atrocity, Herod had Hezekiah silence Timaeus by arranging his death as he returned home to Jericho. Upon hearing that, Paul stood and walked to a window. When he turned back, he said, "It was God's goodness to send his son as a baby to share humanity with us and to show God's love for us. Herod the Great attempted to thwart God's plan but failed. But that set off a chain of events that played its role in my salvation and my rescue by Bartimaeus, the son of Timaeus. Jesus, on that day in Jericho when he called Bartimaeus to him, did more than return sight to a blind man."

Paul walked to Judas and, with a look of wonderment on his face, said, "I do not know what road Jesus has for me, but this convinces me that there is a road that I am to take, and with the blessing of God, I will run to its end."

The next day, a visitor that had recently been to Jerusalem knew of Bartimaeus and Gamela, and he informed Paul that they were living in Jerusalem with Hezekiah and his wife, Rachel. Paul smiled contentedly and nodded his head when told that all in that house were Christians and active in the community of believers in Jerusalem.

After those few days in Damascus, Paul had again joined a caravan of travelers and merchants to Jerusalem. The caravan had stopped when it reached Jericho. Paul had entered the city through the same gate that Jesus had passed on his way to Jerusalem, and inside the gate he had shared what little he had with the beggars. Then he had recalled Bartimaeus sitting there and of him being cured by Jesus. With that thought on his mind, he had prayed a psalm asking for forgiveness from God and forgiveness from Bartimaeus for the evil that he had committed against the man that had saved him.

After a few days in Jericho, Paul had joined another caravan to Jerusalem. Paul stayed to himself those many hours as he walked that road called the Way of Blood. He recalled the last time that he was on that road that led him to Damascus and to his saving call by Jesus. When the caravan arrived at the oasis, it turned in for a rest and to replenish water jugs. At the oasis, he had gone off by himself with thoughts of the times that Jesus had traveled that road. First, as a child leaving Egypt and going to Nazareth with his parents to live and to grow to be a man. Then as a youth to visit the temple for the Jewish feast days with his parents. But the thought that kept returning was of the times that Jesus the man had traveled that road going to Jerusalem or returning to Galilee. He especially pondered deep in his heart the last journey that Jesus made along that road and what Jesus knew awaited him in Jerusalem.

Now, back in Jerusalem as he walked away from Golgotha and entered the city, he purposely avoided the Essene district where he had lived and the temple mound where he might be recognized by priests and Jewish leaders. He found a small inn along a dark alley and took a room. The next morning, he was up early and took his pack with him in the event that he could not return. In Damascus, he had learned of the perils that Christians faced in Jerusalem, and he knew that he must be cautious and not call attention to himself or other Christians, but he also intended to meet Peter and the apostles to tell them of his desire to spread the good news of Jesus not only among those in Judea but also to those in other lands. On the way to Jerusalem, he knew that the first person that he needed to find was Bartimaeus. He and Gamela were to be found at the house of Hezekiah, and he knew of that house. They would best know how to contact the apostles, especially the one that he knew to be their leader, the man called Peter.

Paul walked the streets of Jerusalem with new eyes. Although he had been in the temple on numerous occasions in the past, not only in observance of Jewish holy days but also in private prayer reciting the psalms and praises of his God. As he entered the temple, he recalled Jesus casting the merchants and money changers out. He remembered how outraged he was then to hear that the troublesome Nazarene had arrogantly acted in opposition to the priestly condensations of the matters of the temple. On this day, he sadly shook his head as he witnessed the exorbitant business practices in the temple and he wished that he too, like Jesus, could act with righteous zeal for the house of God. Mostly, he fondly pictured Jesus teaching in the temple and the people absorbed with his words of a loving, caring God, a God that Jesus spoke of with humble pride and authority as a Son.

Paul stopped at the marketplace where Jesus had written on the ground when some Pharisees had brought a woman taken in adultery to him. How self-righteous he had thought of Jesus when he was told of that incident. Now, he wished that he could find the woman to beg her forgiveness and to ask what Jesus's words of comfort and healing had been for her.

BARTIMAEUS, THE BLIND BEGGAR OF JERICHO

Paul walked from there to the Pool of Siloam where Jesus had cured a blind man. He recalled his outrage that the man had been cured on the Sabbath in opposition to the Law, and that no man should be in opposition to God. He sat against the wall near the pool and pulled the cloak over his head. He stared at the clear reflections in the water. The air was calm, and he could see an image of the people and the buildings in that smooth, gleaming surface. Suddenly, a gust of wind with dirt and debris swirling about struck the water and distorted the images. He pulled the cloak over his face to protect his eyes from the dirt that impaled him. As quickly as it hit, the gust was gone. He pulled the cloak back, the water calmed, and the images once more appeared. With that, he recalled the blind man being cured by Jesus at this pond. In wonder, he said to himself, *The wind was not in opposition to the pond, and the pond took no offense at the wind. Why had I taken offense to Jesus's cure of that man?* And he was flooded with thoughts of the blind man, of Bartimaeus, of Stephen, and of his call by Jesus asking why he persecuted him.

With those thoughts, he jumped to his feet and pulled the cloak away from his head and dropped it to the ground. He stood there hoping to be discovered and taken to the Sanhedrin. Oh, to have the blessing to speak to those that had condemned Jesus and to tell them of their wrong and that Jesus would forgive them just as Jesus had forgiven him. He longed to speak of the love of their God and of his Son, Jesus. With that resolve, he set off for Hezekiah's house to find Bartimaeus and Gamela and ask them to take him to Peter. Paul had much to tell Peter and to convince him to be allowed to spread the message of Jesus. Like the wind bursting in his soul, he wanted to shake the world and, like the pond, be a reflection of an ever-loving God.

Hezekiah and Rachel warmly greeted Paul when he arrived and sent for Bartimaeus and Gamela. When they entered the room, Paul, with his eyes fixed on his sister, thought that she looked as beautiful as the last time that he saw her in Jericho on his way to Galilee. He unknowingly cocked his head in surprise as she rushed to him and threw her arms around him. Bartimaeus quickly joined her, and the three locked arms and exchanged warm embraces and kisses of welcome. They were in a timeless embrace of three souls longing to speak but not needing to, each knowing in their heart what the other was feeling deep in their soul. This was not as he had expected. Of all the regrets that he had endured these past three years, one of the most disturbing to him was the acknowledgment of the pain that he had inflicted on his sister. Second to that was the shame that he felt knowing that the man that had saved his life in Damascus had unduly suffered on his account. When he departed from Syria, he longed not only to meet with Peter and the apostles of Jesus but also to make amends with Gamela and Bartimaeus for the needless pain that he had caused them. With this unexpected and gracious reception, nothing more was needed from him. He was forgiven and loved by those most dear to him.

Bartimaeus, leaning back and squeezing Paul's shoulders, said, "Paul, it is good to see you again. We have been worried about you and where you were." Then with a laugh added, "I do not suppose that you brought my horse back with you!" And with that, a relaxed sense of peace filled everyone in the room.

When Gamela finally lifted her head from her brother's chest, she stretched her hands out to clutch his. He said, "I have prayed for this day. My worst fear when I was in Syria was that I would never see you again, that I would not be able to ask for your forgiveness."

"Paul, how easy it is for me to call you that, but I have said your name so often in my prayers that I no longer think of you as that person named Saul. There is no one that I could want to see more than you. Bartimaeus and I had forgiven you when we forgave each other many years ago. I am happy to see you. Now, you must tell us everything. Bartimaeus has told of his travels to Damascus and of your escape, but we know nothing of you for the past three years."

"Gamela, my dear sister, I have much to tell you of what has become of me since I was struck blind by the hand of God until now. God the Father, through the mercy of his Son, Jesus the Christ, and by the power of God's Holy Spirit, has blessed me. I have been taken by the hand and led out of the wilderness. I do not know why, but I believe that God has set me on a course of his choosing to do his will, and there is nothing and no power that can keep me from staying that course."

The three sat together for several hours each telling the others about what had transpired since they last met. Gamela had just finished telling Paul about the children, and that Saul David had changed his name to Paul David, when Rachel returned and asked Paul to stay for dinner. Paul immediately declined, but Gamela, with Rachel's support, would not accept anything other than his acquiescence. Paul finally agreed when Gamela told him that Paul David and Mariam would be disappointed if they could not see him when they returned from helping to serve a group of Christians that gathered every day.

At dinner, Hezekiah insisted that Paul stay with them and that there was no safer place in Jerusalem for him. That evening it was decided that Paul David would take Paul to Peter and the apostles the next day. Paul David often carried messages for Peter and was seen accompanying others throughout the city, and his accompanying Paul would not cause any undue attention.

The next day, Paul was the first to rise, and he was sitting in the outer courtyard when Gamela joined him. She sat beside him. Paul spoke first. "I was thinking of when we were children in Tarsus before our parents died."

Gamela responded, "I do not remember that time. I was too young. I only remember living with our uncle, and I remember that you were the one that cared for me. Those should be happy memories. They are not sad, but my only memory of those times is of you. Then I came with you to Jerusalem. I quickly made friends here, but they were nothing more than friends. We had no family. You were busy at the temple studying, but you always took care of me, and we loved each other. It was not until I found Bartimaeus and we married that I found complete joy. First, we lived in Jerusalem with Hezekiah and Rachel and their three young daughters. I finally learned what it was to be family. Then we moved to Jericho to join Bartimaeus's family. Ariel was the mother that I never had. Then Barariel married Monica, and she became my sister. Those were glorious, happy days in Jericho surrounded by those that I loved and that loved me. Of course, that happiness was fractured when Barariel was killed. He and Monica had not been married long when that tragedy hit. That was hard for all of us, especially for Ariel but also for Bartimaeus."

Gamela paused, and Paul interjected, "Then Bartimaeus was blinded. I am sorry that rather than caring for you in your pain, I added to it. I was wrong. Terribly wrong. I will do anything to make that up to you. I hope that I can."

Gamela took his hand. "Having you back with me…with us, is all that I ask, all that I need."

Paul said, "Tell me what the children are doing. I understand that they spend time with the apostles."

"Yes, Paul David is with the apostles and some of the Christians. He has made a friend of a young man from Cyprus named Barnabas. The two of them are good for each other. Paul David left early this morning to tell Barnabas that you have returned to Jerusalem. He wants to tell him how his father helped you escape from Damascus."

"Bartimaeus did more than help me escape. I never would have been able to leave Judas's house. I would have been killed trying if it were not for him."

"Paul David will introduce you to Barnabas. I am sure that you will like him. He reminds me of you when you were young."

Laughing, Paul added, "I am not sure that is a good thing. I trust that I can help him avoid my mistakes."

They looked up and saw Mariam standing at the doorway. She said, "And I want to introduce you to the women. Jesus's mother, Mary, is my friend. She tells us stories about Jesus as a boy. She lives with the apostle named John, but she joins us each evening."

Gamela stood and reached her hand down to Paul. "Let us join Hezekiah and Rachel. Paul David said that he would come back after he tells Peter that you are here. I told him to ask if Peter was available to meet with you and, if so, where and when."

Paul stood and hugged Gamela. Mariam ran over, and Paul put his arm around her too. Then turning to Mariam, he said, "I very much want to get to know you. You remind me of your mother when she was young. I hope that I can be with you from now on." The three walked together into the house.

It was noon when Paul David returned and told them that Peter was available to meet with Paul and that he would take him to Peter. He said that it would be best if Gamela were to follow them but to stay behind in case there was anyone that recognized Paul. Mariam said that she wanted to go with her mother. Hezekiah said that he would send a servant along with Gamela so that the servant could return and alert him if there were any problems along the way. He said that he still had friends in the guard and with many influential Christians in the city, if needed.

Paul David then escorted Paul to meet Peter. When they entered the room at the inn, there were four men sitting at a table: Peter, the apostle Thomas, James, and Bartimaeus. James was not one of the original apostles of Jesus but was a righteous man from Jerusalem that was an early believer after the resurrection of Jesus. James, being a Judean rather than a Galilean, was influential among the early Christians in Jerusalem, and Peter had come to rely on James for decisions that could affect the community of believers in Jerusalem. Shortly, Gamela and Mariam joined them. Peter welcomed them and invited them to sit at the table.

Peter spoke first. "I understand from Bartimaeus that Paul is the name by which you want to be known. We have never met, but I have long known of you. I, of course, know your sister, Gamela, and her husband, Bartimaeus, who was one of us from the beginning here in Jerusalem, and he is the man that returned Thomas to us after the death of Jesus. I asked him to join us since he knows you the best of any of us and is a witness to you in Damascus."

Peter stopped and extended his arm toward Thomas who then spoke. "Welcome, Paul, it seems that we both owe much to our dear friend, Bartimaeus, although I understand that Bartimaeus's rescue of you was much more exciting than his rescue of me."

Peter continued, "I have also asked James to join us. He said that he often saw you in the temple and knew of you as a learned Pharisee. I will rely on both Thomas and James as what we are to make of your return to Jerusalem. I hope that you understand that you have serious enemies in the Sanhedrin. Some of the older members of the Sanhedrin, such as Nicodemus and others that joined us, have since left the Sanhedrin, but the remaining Jewish leaders are our enemies. Now Herod has been won over by the Jews, and he may not leave us alone. It is dangerous here in Jerusalem for you and for all of us. But we have grown in numbers, not only in Jerusalem but throughout Judea and Galilee and surrounding lands. Enough of that for now. Please tell us about yourself. We have reports from Damascus and from Bartimaeus. We need to hear from you."

Paul related all that had happened to him in coming to know and to believe in Jesus as the Son of God. Starting with the stoning of Stephen, he told of his travel to Damascus and his being blinded, then hearing Jesus speak to him and Jesus asking why he persecuted him. He told of his coming to believe while in Damascus and then of the three years in exile and how during that time he had resolved to himself that he would spread the word of Jesus throughout the Roman Empire. He ended with a plea, although most unworthy to be called a disciple of Jesus, to be allowed to go to other lands, away from Jerusalem and Judea to tell others of Jesus. When Paul finished, Peter said that he needed to speak with the others about what they had just heard.

With that, Paul, along with Gamela, Paul David, and Mariam, left the room. When they came out, Joshua and Monica were waiting for them with their two children, a small boy named Bartimaeus and a baby girl named Gamela. It was not long before Thomas opened the door and motioned Paul to enter, but he asked the others to remain outside.

When the door opened again, Paul walked out and joined his sister. He said, "They told me that now was not the time to join them. They said that I should not stay in Jerusalem. That would likely put all the Christians in greater danger. And that it was not the time to allow me to go out speaking in their name about Jesus to others."

Paul started to walk away. After a few steps, Gamela hurriedly followed him and, taking him by the arm, asked, "What are you going to do?"

"I had decided that if I could not join them now in doing what Jesus has called me to do, then I would return to Tarsus and wait."

"Tarsus." Bartimaeus looked to Gamela and the others for affirmation. "I have a friend that is from Tarsus. He told me the other day that he wants to return home to tell his family and others what he has learned of Jesus. He would be a good companion to you, and hopefully you can keep each other out of trouble."

"What is his name?"

"Maximus. He has your zest for life. And between the two of you, there will not be a quiet or a peaceful moment for anyone on sea or on land."

"And Bartimaeus and Gamela, what of you?"

"Our work is here in Jerusalem or wherever Peter and the others need us. Jesus's last instruction to his friends was to go to the ends of the world and to teach others of him. Thomas is looking to do that. Maybe Gamela and I will join him."

Paul turned toward Paul David and Mariam and asked, "And what of you two?"

Paul David, without hesitation, said, "I have friends here in Jerusalem, and we want to stay and help here. Maybe later we will go elsewhere."

Mariam, looking first to her mother and father, then to Paul, said, "Can I go with Paul? I want to see Tarsus, and I want to help him there. Can I?"

Paul opened his arms, and she rushed to him.

Epilogue

Although we know very little of Bartimaeus except that he was cured of blindness by Jesus at the gate of Jericho, there is much that is known of Paul the apostle as contained in the Acts of the Apostles in the New Testament of the Bible. The accounts of Paul at the stoning of Stephen and his conversion and escape from Damascus are taken from the Acts of the Apostles with embellishments added into this fictional story of Bartimaeus. This story ends with Paul planning to return to the city of his birth, Tarsus in Cilicia, present-day Turkey. Paul spent thirteen years in Tarsus before returning to Jerusalem. When Paul returned to Jerusalem from Tarsus, he was welcomed by the apostles and the Christian community, but he did not stay long and soon departed on his goal of preaching the good news of Jesus to Jews and pagans alike throughout much of the Roman Empire. Paul spent the next fourteen years on three journeys of preaching. At the end of Paul's third journey, he returned to Jerusalem against the advice of many that the Jews still intended to kill him. Paul arrived in Jerusalem with Luke, the evangelist and author of the Acts of the Apostles. Within a week of his arrival, Paul was recognized in the temple, and a mob dragged him from the temple and would have killed him except that, due to the riot, he was arrested by a Roman tribune and taken by soldiers to the Antonia Fortress. While imprisoned at the fortress, more than forty Jews took a vow not to eat or drink until they had killed Paul. Their plan was to have the Sanhedrin request that Paul be taken to them from the fortress to examine him more closely. The conspirators planned to ambush and kill Paul en route through the city. As recorded by Luke in the Acts (23:16), "But the son of Paul's sister heard of the ambush they were laying and made his way into the fortress and told Paul." The Roman tribune, learning of the conspiracy, had Paul transferred to Caesarea and ultimately to Rome where Paul, as a Roman citizen, was tried and eventually beheaded. In this story, "the son of Paul's sister [Gamela]" is Paul David, the son of Bartimaeus.

The Gospels of Matthew and Luke tell of the cure of the blind beggar at the gate of Jericho, and Mark names the beggar Bartimaeus, the son of Timaeus. In this fictionized telling of that gospel account, Timaeus is the witness to the slaughter of the innocents of Bethlehem by Herod the Great, and Bartimaeus saves Paul from the assassins in Damascus. I hope that you enjoy my tale. So be it!

ABOUT THE AUTHOR

The author of *Bartimaeus, the Blind Beggar of Jericho* incorporated his Franciscan spirituality, his experience as a horse trainer and competitor, and his familiarity with the Middle East in weaving this story of a follower of Jesus and early companion to the apostles. He has a bachelor's degree from Saint Louis University in St. Louis, Missouri; master's and doctorate degrees from Colorado State University in Ft. Collins, Colorado; and has studied at the Franciscan Institute of Saint Bonaventure University in Olean, New York. He was a member of the graduate faculty at New Mexico State University in Las Cruces, New Mexico. He has more than seventy technical publications in trade journals, conference proceedings, professional manuals, technical reports, and has recently published a book of Franciscan spirituality, *Peace and Good, Franciscan Meditations of the Gospels*.

He has assisted with and conducted more than one hundred pilgrimages and service retreats for more than twenty-five years to the Franciscan mission in Guaymas, Sonora, Mexico. He makes presentations and conducts retreats in Franciscan spirituality in Colorado,

Arizona, and New Mexico. He conducts podcasts of Franciscan spirituality titled *Meditations of Peace and Good* which are available through his website, georgesabol.com. He is a member of the Casa Franciscana Outreach board of directors for the mission in Mexico.

He is a horseman by intent and a builder and woodworker from birth. He has been married for more than fifty years to his life-mate and fellow journeyer, Joyce. Together, they have two marvelous sons, Daniel and Michael. Dan and his wife, Christina, have blessed them with six grandchildren; Miguel, Angelica, David, Meredith, Samuel, and Benjamin. He is blessed to be a child of God for which he gives thanks.

Printed in the USA
CPSIA information can be obtained
at www.ICGtesting.com
CBHW062146171024
16002CB00031B/167